Invisible Ink

TERRY GRIGGS

RAINCOAST BOOKS

Vancouver

Raincoast Books gratefully acknowledges the ongoing support of the Canada Council for the Arts, the British Columbia Arts Council and the Government of Canada through the Book Publishing Industry Development Program (BPIDP).

Edited by Elizabeth McLean.
Cover and interior artwork by Cynthia Nugent.
Cover and interior design by Teresa Bubela.

LIBRARY AND ARCHIVES CANADA CATALOGUING IN PUBLICATION

Griggs, Terry
       Invisible ink / Terry Griggs.
ISBN 10 1-55192-833-7
ISBN 13 978-1-55192-833-3
       I. Title.
PS8563.R5365I58 2006   jC813'.54   C2005-905460-3

LIBRARY OF CONGRESS CONTROL NUMBER: 2005932965

Raincoast Books   *In the United States:*
9050 Shaughnessy Street   Publishers Group West
Vancouver, British Columbia   1700 Fourth Street
Canada V6P 6E5   Berkeley, California
www.raincoast.com   94710

ANCIENT FOREST
FRIENDLY

Raincoast Books is committed to protecting the environment and to the responsible use of natural resources. We are working with suppliers and printers to phase out our use of paper produced from ancient forests. This book is printed with vegetable-based inks on 100% ancient-forest-free paper (40% post-consumer recycled), processed chlorine- and acid-free. For further information, visit our website at www.raincoast.com/publishing.

Printed in Canada by Webcom.

10 9 8 7 6 5 4 3 2 1

PRAISE FOR CAT'S EYE CORNER

Cat's Eye Corner was shortlisted for a Mr. Christie Book Award and the Red Cedar Award, and it was a Canadian Children's Book Centre "Our Choice" selection.

———

"A clever, nervy and likable young hero, Olivier is joined in this witty, fast-paced and humorous adventure by an inventive cast of characters ... At turns creepy, chilly and silly, Griggs' story celebrates language in a way your kids are sure to find infectious."
— *Today's Parent*

"Olivier considers Norton Juster's book *The Phantom Tollbooth* to be a friend, and clearly Griggs shares her young hero's affection for the classic and its clever use of phrase ... The parade of fabulously strange characters, from the leafy 'woodwosc' to the talking fountain pen, will remind readers of *The Wizard of Oz* series and Harry Potter, as well as *Tollbooth*, but the real spirit of the book lies in Griggs' delightful twists and turns of the language itself." — *Booklist*

"This is a cleverly written novel, and the wordplay alone makes it a joy to read. Olivier is a believable character, and his awareness of the adventure he is on and his obvious knowledge of other literary adventures is entertaining and adds a nice twist to the story. Fans of Eva Ibbotson and, yes, Harry Potter are sure to enjoy this quirky read." — *School Library Journal*

"Griggs writes with uncommon sparkle and wit ... *Cat's Eye Corner* is unpredictable but logically satisfying, full of adventures, puns and clever imagination." — *Toronto Star*

PRAISE FOR THE SILVER DOOR

The Silver Door was shortlisted for the Diamond Willow Award.

———

"Without missing a beat, this second installment continues with ten-year-old Olivier's experiences at the rather unusual home of his grandfather and step-step-stepgramma, Sylvia de Whosit of Whatsit … Olivier has already completed an exciting scavenger hunt and is now about to embark on another thrilling, albeit strange, adventure arising (literally) from the pages of an amazing book of facts given to him by his step-step-stepgramma. *Enquire Within Upon Everything*, the title of this weighty tome, not only contains information about anything one might want to know, but its entries pop right out of the book, which is exactly what ghostly Peely Wally does. The only problem is he can't seem to climb back in again … **Recommended**."

— *Canadian Materials*

"… a headlong descent into wild and woolly bully times and the battle of good versus evil, without giving up its classic kids' book love of nonsense and silliness … It's funny and fun."

— *London Free Press*

"Griggs introduced her hero, Olivier, in *Cat's Eye Corner*, and her appetite for no-brakes punning, madcap plots, and *deus ex machina* resolutions so unforeseen they're gleefully, confrontationally silly seems only to have increased." — *Georgia Straight*

For Tara

Table of Contents

One

S trange. That's what Olivier thought the moment he woke up. *Splish, splash?* In his dream these watery sounds made sense, for he'd been listening to waves lapping against a shore. It had been an extremely pleasant dream as he'd been swaying gently in a hammock that was slung between two trees on the very edge of a lake. Yet when he stirred and opened his eyes, he could still hear the waves lapping. Where *was* he? He blinked and gazed up at the ceiling, then let his gaze fall to the wardrobe, to the chair by the door … why, of course, he was in his room at Cat's Eye Corner where he was visiting for the summer, and where there seemed to be no end of strange happenings. But still. *Splish, splash.*

Olivier turned his head slightly so that he could see the open pen case nestled on the pillow beside his. He wondered if Murray, his barrel half-empty and churning with hunger, was making that splishy-splashy noise.

Murray was a fountain pen, but not just any fountain pen, as Olivier had discovered on his first incredible day at Cat's Eye Corner. He could talk! That is, he could *write*, which, with Olivier's help he would do at great length given the opportunity. Already, he and Murray had experienced some pretty zany adventures here, and something told Olivier that today was going to be no exception.

Too write! Murray would have agreed if he himself were awake, but he was utterly stilled, caught in one of those boring, frustrating dreams that go on and on like a run-on sentence. In this dream Murray was due — overdue! — at a lavish ceremony where he was to receive a prestigious writing award for his brilliant penmanship, but first he couldn't find his formal cap to wear, and then his acceptance speech went missing, and then, although he was beautifully polished and looking staggeringly handsome, he found that he'd broken out in a rash of icky fingerprints!

As Murray seemed to be sleeping soundly, Olivier turned his head the other way toward the dresser, and spotted the book resting on top of it that Sylvia, his step-step-stepgramma, had given him to keep him entertained while he was visiting. The book was called *Enquire Within Upon Everything*, and boy, was it ever entertaining. It was almost as unpredictable as the house itself, which was huge and full of numerous and *very* interesting rooms, some of which had a habit of shifting around and changing their identities and disappearing on adventures of their own. As Olivier stared at the book, he realized that it had to be the source of the sounds he'd been hearing. *Splish. Splash.*

He jumped out of bed and walked over to it, and then bent down to listen. Sure enough, it was making splashy, gurgling noises, as though it were a brook rather than a book. The funny thing about it was that sometimes *Enquire Within* was a normal book, packed with information like an encyclopaedia, and other times ... it was like no other book in the world. Tentatively he opened the front cover, then flipped through the first few pages. The words did seem to be unsettled, as if afloat on the paper, and some had come apart, their letters drifting to the corners and clumping up there like seaweed in meaningless heaps. He turned a few more pages, and then stopped cold. He had come to one that *was* liquid, as if the text had dissolved into a dark inky pool — a Murray-sized swimming pool — that was contained on the page, but barely. The surface of this pool was disturbed, slightly ruffled with small waves that splashed up against the margins.

Curious to know how deep it might be, Olivier dipped a finger in it to see. His finger sank in past his nail, his knuckle, and then his whole hand slipped in. With his other hand he rolled up the sleeve of his shirt (he'd been sleeping in his clothes again), and then dipped his arm in up to his elbow, a little farther, and then ... he gasped and yanked his arm back out, splattering beads of inky water on himself and the dresser. What he had felt down there was something, some*one*, another *hand* that had touched his own very lightly. No mistake, he hadn't imagined it, or touched anything else, weeds or rocks or whatever else there might be submerged in the bottom of a book. *Fingers* had brushed against his own.

He slammed the book shut, ran back to his bed and dove in, accidentally hitting the pen case as he did so. Murray shot out of the case, rolled off the pillow and, as he was about to tumble onto the floor, Olivier nabbed him. What a rude awakening! Murray was grumpy in the morning at the best of times, and Olivier wondered if he dared get out the notebook they conversed in. His pen friend would probably give him a few choice words. But then, he had to tell Murray what had happened, and so mumbling his apologies, he retrieved the notebook from his pocket and positioned Murray at the very top of the page.

Much to Olivier's surprise, Murray wrote, *My boy, thankyouthankyouthankyou! What a wretched dream! Naturally I deserved the award, about time I'd say, but I was never going to get it, was I? The taxi took me to the WRONG place, some convention for creative anachronists, ballpoints done up as quills, Knights of the Plume, if you can imagine and, say ... how on earth did you get a blue arm? And blue ... spots? You haven't been quaffing MY breakfast, have you? Dear me, I hope we haven't slept in.*

"Nah," Olivier said, about to explain to Murray that sleeping in was what you were supposed to do on the holidays. Then, *uh-oh*, he thought, *but not today*. How could he have forgotten? This was the day that Sylvia was holding her yard sale. They'd been preparing for it all week, sorting through all kinds of junk in the basement. Gramps had only married Sylvia recently (his third wife, which is why Olivier called her his step-step-stepgramma) and hadn't lived here long enough to accumulate much, but she had mountains of stuff, most of which was unusual, or goofy, or just plain weird. (This was not entirely unto-ward if you considered that Sylvia was a witch, or so Olivier suspected, which is another reason why he called her his step-step-stepgramma — he liked to keep a safe distance from her.)

"What's *this*?" he had asked her, holding up a peculiar object that he'd pulled out of a battered cardboard box in a dark corner of the basement.

Sylvia had pursed her lips and tapped her chin with her index finger, her long pointy nail as purple as her dress. "Goodness, I don't recall having one of those."

"One of *what*, though?" It seemed to be a tool of some sort, with a handle at one end like a brace, and a hammer device positioned to strike a metal knob at the other end.

"Why, it's a combination eyeball-whapper and dimple-maker, dear. The former function is most useful if your eyes bug out, and the dimple-making procedure is employed more for cosmetic purposes."

Olivier raised an eyebrow.

"Dimples? You know, they go nicely with ringlets and apple cheeks, the whole cutie-pie ball of wax. Would you care to try it? Not that you need it, you're quite handsome enough as it is."

"No, thanks." Olivier hastily deposited the device on an accumulating pile of objects that included a motorized Frisbee, three lightning rods, a box of non-melting snow-balls, a broken umbrella, a pair of grass skis, a package of stick-on pockets, an ugly orange lamp, a bucket of fossils, a pair of false teeth that clacked when you walked past them, a kaleidoscope, a pair of shoes with headlights on the toes, a jar of Sylvia's homemade ice jam (it had a skull and crossbones on the label) and a hammock exactly like the one in his dream.

That had been a couple of days ago, and this morning all those possessions of Sylvia's, plus hundreds of others, would be set out on long tables in the front yard of Cat's Eye Corner, ready to be snapped up by the avid bargain hunter.

Dad, the crystal inkwell, Murray wrote, more urgently now that he was fully awake. *What if it's gone? My heart is set on it!*

"And the *carpet*," added Olivier. He couldn't believe that Sylvia was getting rid of the Persian carpet from her sitting room. It *was* tatty and worn and a bit moth-eaten, but it was still beautiful and valuable — that seemed obvious, even to someone who didn't know anything about carpets. He had asked Sylvia if he could have it, but she had refused, saying it would be bad for his allergies — *fatal*, was the word she used — what with all that stardust ground into it, not to mention mounds of dander from the Poets (which is what she called her cats), plus it housed an ancient dynasty of fleas. She promised to buy a spiffy new one for his room instead, but Olivier was determined to have it.

Hurryhurry, Murray squeaked, as his words jammed into one another in his rush to get them onto the page. *There are voices outside, can't you hear them? We're late, the sale has already begun!*

"You're right, hang on, here we go." Olivier slid Murray into his usual place in his shirtfront pocket. He grabbed what money he had, some change and a ten dollar bill, from the bed's headboard cubbyhole and jammed it into his pants pocket along with the notebook. Then he tore out of his bedroom and down the stairs, the disturbing incident with that inky pool in his book temporarily forgotten. As he was running toward the front door, though, he ran right into a shortish, thinnish, oddish person who was wandering in the hall, and knocked him flat.

"Gosh, are you okay?" Olivier stopped to help this person up, noticing as he did so that the fellow was wearing a funny little coat that appeared to be made of potato peels all stitched together. As well, he had on green pants that were made of the small, overlapping leaves of Brussels sprouts and shoes that were completely covered in blue mould. He also had a bulging leather satchel slung over one shoulder.

"Don't step on my shoes," snarled the little guy. "Or I'll turn you into a piece of cheese."

"I wouldn't want that." Olivier had to smile. The garage sale must have drawn some real oddballs out of Sylvia's neighbourhood. The fellow barely came up to Olivier's chin, and he had plain, if somewhat pointy features, especially his ears. His hair was a dirty mustard colour, and worn in a slicked-back, old-fashioned style, combed up into waves on the top of his head. "I didn't mean to knock you down, sorry. But if you're all right, I have to get to the sale. I'm late and I promised to help."

"Well, I'm not all right, am I? See here, you've ruined my new jacket." The fellow bent down to pick up the tiny nub of a potato root that had been knocked off his coat in the collision.

"I wouldn't say it's *ruined*," contested Olivier. "I think it looks better without those root things growing out of it. Are those eyes?" He looked closer at the jacket — definitely potato peels.

"Mind your own business."

"I *do* have to mind my own business. Why don't you come outside with me and I'll buy you a glass of lemonade? You'll feel better then." Then maybe you won't be so grumpy, Olivier thought. No one should be wandering around in Sylvia's house anyway, talk about minding your own business.

The fellow crossed his arms and stood his ground, refusing to budge. Olivier didn't have time to waste, so simply shrugged and said, "If you change your mind ... " his words trailing off as he dashed out the front door.

Already there were lots of people crowding around the sale tables, some elbowing others to get a closer look at the items on display, others picking objects up, poking them, shaking them. A few customers were going back to their cars already, staggering under the weight of all the bargains they'd scored: a molten, metal blob that had once been a toaster, a marble statue of the man who invented donut holes, a business suit of armour and a carton of no-fail bowling balls — **A STRIKE EVERY TIME!!** claimed the ad on the side of the carton.

Sylvia, standing at the head of one table, was listening with evident amusement to a woman who was singing to her. This woman was clasping a vase in one hand, and with the other hand extended expressively, was warbling away in an operatic vein.

Gramps meanwhile was manning the refreshment table, busily setting out clean glasses and a couple of big frosty pitchers of lemonade. Olivier always loved to see his Gramps first thing and so ran over to his table for a morning hug.

"Mornin' Ollie." Gramps reached out to ruffle his hair. "By ginger, I was beginning to wonder where you were." Next came the hug — his gramps wore the softest, freshest-smelling shirts.

"Slept in, Gramps, wouldn't you know it. How's business?"

"Booming. Sold out of coffee already. Lots of this left." He indicated the pitchers. "Want some?"

"Maybe later, thanks. Oh, but there's this little guy with blue shoes. If he comes by, I said I'd buy him a lemonade."

"Friend of yours? On the house then, son."

"Actually, he's *in* the house, and he's no friend, I don't know who he is. Should I tell Sylvia?"

Gramps frowned, and glanced back briefly at the mansion. He rubbed his whiskery chin, looking thoughtful for a moment, then said, "I wouldn't worry. That old place can take care of itself. Sylvie could likely use a hand, though."

A *hand*. Olivier suddenly remembered his book, and the inky pool, and the fingers that had brushed against his own. He shuddered, then quickly dismissed the thought. "Sure thing. See you later, Gramps."

"I'll save ya a glass." Gramps began to pour himself a lemonade, filling it right to the brim. He then added, in a more serious tone than usual, "Ollie, by cracky, be careful, eh."

Olivier didn't think Gramps was worried about him breaking anything, or being cheated by one of the customers, so what was there to be careful about? If he weren't late already, he would have asked, but at the moment he wanted to stay on Sylvia's good side (Gramps only *had* good sides). "I will," he promised, as he hurried away.

"Did you have a restful sleep, young man?" Sylvia said, when he arrived at her table. "No time to wash? Did that precious pen of yours backfire on you?" She didn't wait for any answers (she usually knew them all anyway). "Do you recall that dusty old Ming vase we found in the cupboard downstairs? You'll never guess, it went for a song."

"But … *wasn't* it priceless?"

"Exactly so. How could I put a price on it in that case, hmm?"

He wasn't too sure about the logic of this, but Sylvia wasn't suffering cash-wise — the pockets of her apron were bulging with bills, not small denominations either. Even as they spoke, a man came up and begged her to take two hundred dollars for a tacky piece of chipped Blue Mountain pottery, a swan exactly like the kind Olivier's mother had received as a gift from Great-Aunt Lillian and that she'd accidentally broken soon after by using it as a hammer.

As Sylvia was counting the twenties and fifties, chuckling to herself, Olivier decided the time was ripe to broach the subject of the Persian carpet. He could see it out of the corner of his eye, rolled up and propped against an old swing set. A tall, aristocratic-looking woman, wearing a wide-brimmed hat and a feathery shawl, was fingering the fringes and peering closely at a corner of the carpet through a lorgnette. She was making him nervous, and even Murray seemed agitated — he'd heated up, as though he had a fever.

"I could have it cleaned," he blurted.

Sylvia snatched at one of the bills that had escaped her grasp before it floated to the ground, and said offhandedly, "Why, that would ruin it. Wash the magic right out. These modern chemicals, you know. Very powerful."

"Magic?"

"Did I say that? How silly of me. I meant *mildew*, naturally. Goodness, why I get those two words confused is a mystery to me."

Magic, Olivier thought, I *knew* it. He glanced anxiously over at the woman who was considering the carpet, but after giving it a thorough evaluation she lost interest and strode off. Whew! A close call.

"Dear, I tell you what. If you would be so kind as to assist that bearded gentleman at the far end of the table, the one wearing the top hat, my, he *is* an odd duck, isn't he? I can see he wants to buy the crystal inkwell, that worthless old thing. Ten cents should suffice. Go and fetch the cash, and then we'll discuss this matter of the carpet. I *know* for a fact that it won't be healthy for you, but if you're absolutely sure you want it …"

"Yes! *Yes*, I do." The *inkwell*, he thought, I've got to get that, too! "I'll be right back, don't sell my carpet, okay?"

Although it wasn't that far from one end of the table to the other, it just so happened that he didn't make it right back. When he hurried toward the top-hatted gentleman who was assessing Murray's inkwell, and who then fixed on him a most calculating look as he approached, it was the beginning of a whole series of incidents that only took Olivier further and further away from the yard sale and from Cat's Eye Corner altogether.

Splish, splash came the disturbingly familiar sound as the man began to shake the inkwell. *Strange,* indeed.

Two

"How can it be making that sound?" Olivier asked the top-hatted gentleman, looking him almost directly in the eye (his height was mostly invested in his hat). "It's too small, and there's no ink in it, and it's *cracked*," he added hastily. "You wouldn't want to buy it."

"Do tell. Who might you be?"

"Olivier, sir. I'm helping out here."

"A pleasure, Master Olivier." The man bowed slightly and the top of his hat flipped up like a lid, then dropped back down again. "My name is Blank. Professor C. Blank."

Blank, eh? The name certainly seemed to fit, for the man's skin was as white as paper and his features were nondescript, except for his eyebrows, which slanted toward the bridge of his nose like French accents. His beard was bushy enough to hide behind, and his longish black hair curled over his collar. He was dressed in black, too, and in very formal attire for a garage sale — a morning coat, dress pants and, not so formally, black sneakers.

"I detect no flaw," he said, holding the inkwell up for closer inspection. He gave it another shake. "Nor do I hear this sound to which you refer. Perchance it was that device over there you heard." So saying, he reached for a small staff that was leaning against the table and pointed it at an alarm clock on the other side. The same tall woman who had been considering the Persian carpet was bent over and examining this clock through her lorgnette, and at the same time grousing aloud, "What junk! Dreadful stuff. Dollars to donuts this thing doesn't work." She then pressed the button on the top of the alarm and a jet of water shot out of the clock and splashed her full in the face. "Ohh!" she gasped.

A water alarm. Olivier had filled it himself, and now had to bite his lip to keep from laughing as the woman stalked off, spluttering and flicking drops of water off her lorgnette.

Professor Blank watched impassively, although the top of his hat flipped up and down a couple of times as though it were amused.

"Neat hat."

"I agree. It is a personal air-conditioning system of my own devising. I am enormously clever. The price of the inkwell?"

"Too much."

"Try me."

"Um, one hundred dollars."

"Sold."

"No, wait, I forgot. It's already been spoken for."
Olivier mimed regret. "Sorry."

"You are mistaken, Master Olivier. I will have that pen
as well." He inclined his head toward Murray. "It is a com-
monplace instrument of little value, but I will take it off
your hands. Or *hand*, perhaps I should say. I observe that
it leaks."

(Leaks! Little value!! *&@!!∧$$*>?!!!)

Olivier clapped his ink-stained hand protectively
against his shirtfront pocket, but a bit too hard, uninten-
tionally giving Murray a smack as he did so.

(Ouch! Injury to insult!! Pattes de mouche!!)

"Look, Professor Blank, I'll go and check with my, um,
with Sylvia, this is her stuff. I could be wrong about it
being sold already. I better take it to show her." He reached
for the inkwell and plucked it out of the Professor's hand.
"Thanks. I'll get right back to you." Perchance!

"See that you do, young fellow." Annoyed, Blank's eye-
brows plunged deeper toward the bridge of his nose, but
he didn't try to snatch the inkwell back. "Please give her
my card." He flicked the hand that had been holding the
inkwell and a business card appeared between his fingers.

"Certainly," said Olivier. He accepted the card, and
stole a quick glance at it. It was completely blank! *Right*,
he thought, as he moved away. The Professor had already
turned his attention elsewhere and was picking through
the bucket of fossils, carefully scrutinizing each one.

Olivier headed back toward Sylvia with every inten-
tion of buying both the inkwell and the carpet and settling
the matter once and for all. He was stopped on the way,

however, by the same tall woman who had gotten the soaker from the alarm clock. She stepped out in front of him, and reaching a thin, oddly talon-like hand toward him, clutched his shoulder. As she bent down to speak to him, he saw that a drip of water trembled still on the tip of her nose. She whispered, "I *know* what he's looking for." She nodded significantly toward Professor Blank and the drip of water flew off in his direction.

"Really? That's good." Olivier squirmed out of her grip.

"It wears a coat of elemental brown," she whispered again, more urgently.

Swell, he thought, a nutbar. "Excuse me, but I have to — "

"The 'C' in his name stands for *Carnifex*. That's something worth remembering and, *dash* it, I just remembered, there's a call for you."

"A call?"

"Here." She picked up a large conch shell from the sale table and handed it to him. Sylvia must have put it out as a last-minute item, because it hadn't been on the reject pile they had accumulated together. He would have made some excuse and escaped from the tall woman's crackpot attentions, but he had encountered a shell very like this not long ago in a store called an odditorium. Surely this couldn't be the same one? Slipping the inkwell and business card in his pocket, he put the conch shell to his ear and listened. He heard the usual ocean sounds, then a crackly static noise, and then ... a voice. A voice that seemed to be coming from a great distance.

"Help! Olivier, can you hear, are you there? You've got to come. We're in rrrrrrr bzzzzzznnnnn." There was more static, and then the voice faded out entirely.

He stared hard at the shell — it *was* the same one, or the same kind — then put it to his ear again. This time all he could hear was a loud roaring sound, like that of a powerful wind rushing through treetops. He could even feel it, cool in his ear, shushing against it. Slowly, he put the conch back down. The voice had been faint, but he recognized it. It was that of his friend Fathom, who like his other new friends, Sylvan and Linnet, lived in a corner of Sylvia's estate that wasn't always accessible. He knew this because he'd hunted for them a few times in the forest behind Cat's Eye Corner, and hadn't been able to find them. And now they *needed* him! He looked around searchingly, trying to think of what to do. The tall woman was gone, so he couldn't ask her anything about what she might have heard, or for that matter, who she was and what she had meant about Professor Blank.

As he stood there, uncertain about what to do and trying to figure out the best course of action, a small hand shot out from under the white cloth that covered the sale table and grabbed his leg, an incident that was followed by a loud, hair-raising scream. He almost jumped out of his skin. *Eeeeeeeeeeeeeeeeeeeeeeee!* he heard again. Someone was testing out Sylvia's spray can of scaerosol — press the nozzle and it sprayed a long agonizing stream of scream — but he didn't know that. He was already feeling anxious about his friends, and then earlier there had been those creepy fingers that had brushed against his own in the book ... so when the hand grabbed him he leaped back in fright, jerking his leg away. But the hand held fast, tugging on his pant leg. A light gust of wind lifted the tablecloth, and Olivier saw then that it was only a kid, a girl of about five or six, who had crawled under the table and was crouched there like a little imp, grinning up at him.

"Hey," he said, not unkindly.

"Hey," she said, letting go of his pant leg. "Want to buy this?" She held up a small stone.

"Sure, why not. What are you asking for it?"

"Lots."

"Will this do?" Olivier dug out a dime and offered her that. She nodded eagerly and gave him the stone in exchange. "It's nice," he said, feigning admiration for what was really only an ordinary piece of gravel that she must have picked up off the driveway. He shoved it into his pocket, saying, "I have to go now, though. I'm in a hurry."

"Me, too." With that, she crawled out from under the table, and with the dime in her hand and the wind at her back, she *did* hurry. She practically flew over to Gramps' lemonade stand.

That's when Olivier noticed how very windy it had gotten. Moments ago there had hardly been a breath of air, but now everything seemed to be in motion — the long grass in the yard was swishing back and forth, the bushes and trees were shaking. People's clothes were flapping and billowing, and they were hanging onto their hats, or their hair — one man's toupée shot off his head and landed with a smack on the bald head of a baby who shrieked in terror. A couple of empty plastic bags scudded away, plump with air. The ugly orange lamp blew over, crashing onto the sale table. A deck of Russian playing cards rose up, were shuffled chaotically, then dealt out in all directions (there was going to be a serious game of 52 Pickup somewhere down the line). A Frisbee whizzed past Olivier's nose, and it wasn't even the motorized one.

Puzzled, he glanced down at the conch shell, which he'd set upright on the table. He put his hand in front of it and could feel a current of air gushing out, stronger and faster by the second — it was the source of the wind!

Everyone began to duck and shield their heads with their arms as more sale items began to fly off the table. People who had been walking quickly away were now running down the lane, some shouting in alarm. Sylvia was leaping up, snatching at the bills that were swirling out of her apron, while Gramps was trying his darndest to pour lemonade into a glass. A long arc of it flew out of the pitcher like a cloudy scarf tossed into the air. The little girl with the dime still clutched in her hand laughed to see it, and then began to cry miserably as her mother raced over and bustled her away.

"Olivier!" It was the tall woman again. She was by the front steps of the house waving and pointing at something behind him. "Watch out. *Run*."

He turned and saw Professor Blank heading toward him with that small staff of his raised menacingly. "Boy," he shouted, "stop right where you are." The wind didn't slow him down any. In fact, it didn't even seem to touch him, for his clothes were unruffled and his hat remained undisturbed on his head. He cut straight through it, a mad glint in his eye.

Olivier took off toward the house with the Professor after him and gaining ground. Unlike Blank, Olivier had to fight his way through the wind. It pushed him back toward his pursuer and roared in his ears. As he passed the tall woman, who was hanging onto one of the stone posts by the front steps, almost blown off her feet, he heard her say, "The *storm* door." The storm door? Wherever that was. All he wanted to do was get past the *front* door so he could slam it in Professor Blank's face and lock it. *If* he could make it in time — a big if — the guy was almost on him. And that's when the Poets came to his rescue.

A whole gang of them, including Emily and Anonymous (who were usually very shy and retiring cats), streamed out from the bushes near the front steps and attacked the Professor the very moment that his staff, raised high, was about to come down hard on Olivier's head. Eliot leaped onto his back and sank in his claws, Emily and Anonymous had him by the ankles, Wystan and Stevie, backs arched, were hissing and spitting, blocking his way, while Poe, who was only a kitten, was clamped fiercely onto one of his sneakers (a good thing, as Poe might have blown away). The man was so astonished that he dropped his staff and the lid of his hat began to flip wildly up and down. He grew even paler than he already was, shading into grey, and he opened his mouth to scream, but nothing, not even a peep, came out.

The Professor must have a cat phobia, Olivier thought, or a poet one, who knows, but he didn't wait around to find out. He struggled up the steps and pushed through the front door, then fought the wind to get it closed behind him. Panting, and still shaking from the close escape, he grabbed the lock to turn it, then hesitated. If he did that, then no one else would be able to take shelter from the wind — not the cats, not Gramps and Sylvia, not even the tall woman, who had warned him about Blank. He wasn't sure what to do. He could hide in the house until the coast was clear, although that seemed cowardly. It might be better to sneak out the back way and see if anyone needed help. The thought of the Professor raging around the yard and maybe hurting Gramps was too much.

Pretty amazing how upset and violent the guy had gotten about a crummy old inkwell. But then Olivier considered how upset Murray would have become, his ink boiling hot and searing their notebook, if he hadn't gotten his hands on it. He was glad he'd tricked the Professor, even though it had set him off like a firecracker. Touching his shirt front pocket (more gently this time), Olivier was about to get Murray out for a consultation, when someone began banging loudly on the front door. Blank! He dropped his hand and began to run down the hall, worrying about what had happened to the Poets — he shouldn't have left them outside with that maniac. That decided it — he *would* sneak out the back way and see what was happening. The Professor better not have harmed them. If he had, Sylvia would fry him in a pan and serve him for dinner!

As he ran, and ran, and ran, Olivier realized that the hallway had stretched somehow. It seemed much longer than it had been yesterday. The rooms looked the same, or at least the closed doors of the rooms he passed did. They were simply farther apart. A couple of weeks ago this might have troubled him, but he had gotten used to the strange habits of the house and how it acted up from time to time. He supposed that it was only having a stretch. What did trouble him, though, was that knocking sound. It was no longer behind him at the front door, but ahead of him. BANG ... BANG ... BANG. He listened closely as he ran. What if the Professor had gone around to the back of the house? No, this sound was different, probably the wind banging a loose shutter. It wasn't so much a knocking as a ... a ... BAM!

"Ow! Blast, it's you!! Fine, fine, you asked for it, what'll it be? Cheddar? *Cream* cheese? How about Swiss, full of holes, eh? Like your head. Is that what you want?"

"You again. Sorry," said Olivier. He had run into that same funny little man, the one with the coat made of potato peelings, and knocked him flat once more. He helped him up and dusted off his jacket, knocking off a few more roots.

"You're REALLY asking for it. Something smelly, then. Lindbergh? I *know*, gorgonzola, a drippy, runny one. That's you, can't stop running."

Olivier was staring at the little guy's jacket, while trying to stay clear of his mouldy shoes — he didn't want to get into more trouble. "Would you describe your coat as being, ah, 'elemental brown?'"

"No-o-o-o, it's more a bottom-of-the-bag shade. It *is* smart, isn't it?" The fellow gazed at his jacket with great fondness, and fussed with a cuff, which immediately dropped off.

"It's something else," said Olivier truthfully. He stooped to retrieve the cuff for him. "If you don't mind my asking, who are you?"

"I do mind." He'd forgotten about the cheese threats, at least. "But if you *have* to know, I'll tell you." He worked away as he spoke, trying to wrap the cuff around his wrist, to no avail. "I suppose you recognize me. I'm Alvis, the *King*. King of The Heap." He struck a proud and faintly ridiculous pose. The potato peeling fell to the floor again.

"Wow. A king?"

"Er, no ... not quite. *I'm* Alvis, the Broken-Crown Prince."

"Yeah?"

"That is, Alvis, the Mangy Magician." His proud pose was deflating with each declaration.

"Uh-huh."

"Okay, okay, I'm Alvis, the ... Doorstop."

"Did you say doorstop?"

"Don't sneer! It's challenging work. Not everyone can do it, smarty. Big shot."

"I'm not. It sounds very ... interesting. So, Alvis. What are you doing here?"

Alvis sighed, and shook his head. "Kids these days," he muttered. "I am here to stop the door, what else would I be doing?"

"What door?"

"The *storm* door. Can't you hear it banging? You don't want all kinds of creatures getting into your house, do you?

Werewolves, and whatnot. Ghouls, devil dogs, harpies, vacuum cleaner salesmen."

"What does this storm door open onto?" Olivier was getting excited. "Where does it lead?"

"To the Dark Woods, of course." He shook his head again, marvelling at Olivier's ignorance.

"Alvis," he said. "You *are* a prince. Let's go!"

Three

Olivier was expecting to encounter two doors, the outer one made of metal and glass like the storm door at his own house. When he walked to the end of the hall, then down some stairs, and then up some stairs, and around a corner or two, or three, what he did finally encounter was a single wooden door painted as blue as Alvis' shoes and sporting a classy crystal doorknob. The door was swinging open, but no longer banging noisily against the jamb. It was swaying back and forth, softly creaking, and letting a warm breeze drift into the house, the storm's violence already spent. This breeze reminded Olivier of Linnet and her windy familiars, and he half expected her to poke her head around the door. He *wished* she would. Since Fathom's call he'd had an uncomfortable, nervous feeling in the pit of his stomach. He couldn't imagine what was going on with his friends and what kind of fix they might be in.

He pushed through the door, with Alvis at his heels grumbling about rusty hinges and broken locks and people who didn't close doors properly, or turn off the lights, or throw out decent garbage … he had a fairly long list of complaints. Olivier ran down the back steps, then stopped abruptly. The Dark Woods stretched out before him all right, but it was *really* stretched out. The wind that had swept through it had done a shocking amount of damage. It must have been hurricane force. There were trees down everywhere, huge roots thrusting up into the air. Most of the ones left standing had branches ripped off, and these lay thick and twisted on the ground. Some trees were leaning against others, while a few were swaying slightly. It wouldn't take much more to bring them down. Besides all the torn leaves and branches, the wind had also littered the Woods with other debris, although nothing he recognized from Sylvia's yard sale. He spotted a golden helmet snagged on the topmost branch of an oak, and a red cape caught on another, lower down. Right at his feet lay a beehive, an empty picnic basket and a small shoe made of glass.

"A real plot twister," said Alvis, reaching down to pick up the shoe.

"Plot twister?"

"That's what I said, didn't I? Every forest has an understorey, every knobhead knows that, but this one only has stories, lots of 'em, and they'll be all mixed up now. There'll be *Little Red Riding Boots* and *The Three Little Hamlets,* and who knows what else. No more happy endings, either … only in the tragedies."

"You're joking, right?"

"Nope. See that pirate over there? Blown straight out of some blood-curdling yarn."

Olivier looked to where Alvis was pointing and saw a tubby man stuck fast in the crook of a sycamore tree. He was certainly dressed like a pirate, and had on the standard piratical accessories — bandana, earring, eye patch — and as he flailed his arms and legs, he was saying, "Yaar, yaar."

"Holy, we'd better help him down."

Alvis blanched. "Not on your life, kiddo. He's a desperate character. He'll make us walk the plank, cleave us in two, fire us out of a cannon."

"No, I won't," the pirate shouted. "I'm not at all desperate. Well, I *am*, but only because I'm stuck. Yaar."

"Don't listen," said Alvis.

"I'm really very sweet," pleaded the pirate. "Once you get to know me. I collect stamps. I gave my mummy a bottle of rum for her birthday, and it wasn't half empty, yo ho ho."

"Bad as they come," said Alvis. "Rotten to the core."

"Please, please, please. Pretty please with sugaaargh on it!"

Olivier wanted to believe the pirate, but he didn't want to be taken in. He had to find his friends, and plank-walking was definitely out at the moment. Murray would know what to do. He was a good judge of character (or characters, being a writer). Again Olivier reached for his pen pal to ask his advice, and again was interrupted. Someone, or several someones, was tromping though the woods, whacking branches out of the way, and shouting,

"Bertie, *Berrrtieee*, where are ya?"

"Up *here*, lads!"

"Yaar, Bertie."

"Yaar, lads."

"*More* of them, and armed to the teeth," hissed Alvis. "Let's scram."

More pirates *had* appeared, cutlasses raised, but mainly because they were using them to blaze a trail through the thicket of fallen branches. Five of them now gathered around the base of the sycamore tree, staring up at the unfortunate Bertie and scratching their swarthy, whiskered chins, or frowning and sucking their teeth. "That was some wind, eh Bertie?" one of them ventured.

"Lor, Cecil, never seen the like. One minute I'm in the crow's nest, and next I'm in a robin's nest."

"Haar, haar," the pirates all cracked up at this. "That's a good one, Bertie."

"Awww, lads." Bertie blushed.

"They don't seem so bad," whispered Olivier. "Hey, why are you doing that?"

Alvis was energetically whacking the glass shoe against a big lichen-covered rock. "It's not broken in, is it? You always ask dumb questions, as well as knocking people down?" Once the heel of the shoe had an ugly chip taken out of it, Alvis nodded, pleased with his work, and shoved it in his satchel, which, Olivier couldn't help but notice, was already stuffed full.

"You can't just take it. What if the owner comes looking for it?"

"Finders keepers," said Alvis smugly. He patted the bag,

then turned and trotted off into the Woods, climbing first over a massive tree trunk, then under an arch of tumbled branches. "Come *on*," he called back to Olivier. "Before they run you through."

It was clear that the pirates weren't about to run anyone through, because they themselves were presently too busy running to take cover. The tree that Bertie was stuck in had begun to sway dangerously.

"Oi, lads," he called. "Look out, here I come. Aaaaaaaaaarrrrrggghhh!"

Olivier cleared the spot fast, and not a moment too soon. As he darted into the Woods, the sycamore came down with a resounding crash, its branches snapping and flying off in all directions. He hoped Bertie hadn't been hurt in the fall, for he did seem like a decent sort. Olivier wondered if the pirates who came from stories were more like employees or actors. He was tempted to go back and check on him, but was certain that his buddies would take care of him. Besides, Alvis was getting too far ahead, deftly hopping over branches and scampering around obstructions. Not that Olivier particularly wanted to travel through the Woods with him — he wasn't the most desirable companion — but he had no idea how to find his friends, and Alvis just might.

Olivier plunged ahead into the forest before Alvis disappeared altogether. The colour of his clothes blended in a bit too well with the foliage, so Olivier tried to keep an eye on his shoes, which flitted up and down and away like a pair of blue butterflies.

"Hey, Alvis," he called, "wait up!"

Either Alvis didn't hear or he didn't care to, for he kept on, moving easily through the tangle, whereas Olivier had to pick his way, half running, half walking. The last thing he needed was to trip and fall or get poked in the eye with a jagged branch. One thing that helped were the dropped potato peelings that marked Alvis' route — they were scattered here and there on the choked path, one on a bed of moss, another crowning a toadstool, and another skewered on a twig. Alvis wasn't going to have much of a jacket left by the time they got to where they were going. Wherever that might be. It was entirely possible that the little guy was leading him further and further astray.

"ALVIS," he tried again. "Hold on a sec, eh! I have to talk to you."

Olivier didn't really expect him to stop, but he did. Alvis had leaped onto a downed tree trunk and was about to jump to the other side, when he paused, and stood very still.

About time, Olivier thought, running to catch up, and cracking a few branches noisily underfoot.

Alvis turned sharply, and with exaggerated gestures — he was screwing up his face and waving his arms — he made it clear that Olivier should *stop* and *be quiet*.

"What's up?" he was about to ask, when he saw a large grey wolf heading directly toward them. It was growling fearsomely, its long, sharp teeth exposed and its yellow eyes flashing with annoyance. What detracted from its frightening appearance, though, was the bonnet it was wearing, clumsily askew on its head, the ties undone and trailing loose. Alarmed, Olivier scrambled to get out of its way, although the wolf didn't even seem to notice him. It was preoccupied, and as it stormed past, Olivier thought he heard it grumble something about a new job and how he didn't like dwarves: *They were tough and you had to use yards of dental floss to get them out of your teeth, grrrrrr.* That's what it sounded like anyway.

"Typical celebrity," Alvis sniffed, once the creature was well out of the way. He hopped down from the tree trunk. "Good thing you didn't ask for his autograph, he might have bitten your head off."

"Yeah, wow. Things really are mixed up." *Who* might they run into next? "Look, Alvis, I hope you know where we are, because I've got to find … uh, what are you eating? You didn't pick that up off the ground, did you?"

"Yep, sure did. Tasty." Alvis' cheeks bulged like a chipmunk's. "Fly flavour," he said appreciatively, gobbling what looked like a bread crumb. "Yum. Essence of earthworm, notes of dead slug and a hint of bear droppings. You know how it is, eh, once you get started you can't eat just one." He ran ahead and found another bread crumb, and then another farther along, both of which he crammed into his mouth.

Olivier spotted one that Alvis had missed, one that was so filthy and disgusting that even a stream of ants were taking a detour around it. *Oh no*, he thought, not *that* story. The nasty stepmother, the kids lost in the woods, the witch … it definitely wasn't one of his favourites. That *oven*, he shuddered. Then again, he wouldn't mind checking out the gingerbread house, maybe snapping a chunk off the corner. What with sleeping in, and the yard sale, and the ferocious wind, it only occurred to him now that he hadn't eaten any breakfast. (For some reason, his adventures at Cat's Eye Corner never seemed to start after a hearty meal, or any meal.) That feeling in his stomach wasn't all anxiety. He was starving. Murray must be too!

"Say, you all right?" He lifted Murray out of his pocket along with the notebook, and positioned him to answer.

Perishing, Murray managed to eke out, his ink alarmingly faint. He wasn't kidding.

Olivier felt terrible. He should have made sure that his friend had a full barrel before setting out. "Hang in there, Murray. Save your strength. We'll go straight to Sylvan's place. He'll have ink, the very best."

Blaaaaaaa.

Enough dawdling, Olivier reproached himself. He slipped Murray and the notebook back into his pocket, determined to forge ahead to his destination, with or without Alvis. When he glanced around, he saw that it might indeed be without. Alvis was gone. He had moved along even faster than before, gobbling up those horrible bread crumbs, and now was nowhere to be seen. Olivier set out at a run, dodging and swerving around the treefall, certain he'd be able to catch up with him. As he ran, he kept watching the ground for potato peels, but didn't see a single one. Alvis must have headed in a different direction.

He tried not to panic, but it was scary without any company, and there were too many things to worry about. What if he was lost, and only running in circles? Or what would happen to Murray if he didn't get some ink into him soon? Or what if he encountered some monster or ghoul cut loose from a horror story and looking for something to do, or someone to eat?

Sensibly, he decided that there was nothing for it but to stay focused on the job at hand. He needed to stay alert and keep an eye out for anything familiar. He *had* been through these woods before, so surely there would be some landmark or sight he'd recognize. Or even a sound. Like water flowing, which might lead him to the river that Fathom lives in.

"Nevermore. Evermore. Liverwurst. *What*ever."

He stopped and looked up. There was a raven sitting on a branch not far above, staring down at him, her head cocked to one side.

Since Olivier especially liked crows and ravens, he was very happy to see this one. It might be able to help him out.

"Hi there," he said to the bird.

"Hello, quoth me. Greetings. G'day. Salutations."

"Um, you wouldn't happen to know Dr. Blink, would you? A Dr. Sylvan Blink? I'm trying to find his place, but I'm not sure which way to go."

"Blink? Blink? Blink! *Sure*."

"You *do*? That's great."

"Follow me. *Screee*. Tweedledum. Tweedledee."

With that, the raven flew a short way ahead and settled on another branch, waiting for Olivier to catch up.

"Name's Olivier," he said for good measure, not wanting to be confused with either of those silly twins. "Did a smallish person with pointy ears come through here, by any chance?"

"*Si*. Nope. *Nyet*. Maybe."

Aha, Olivier knew ravens were smart, although it wasn't a very helpful answer. He wondered if the bird was any good at riddles. "There's something I've always wanted to know," he said, as they continued to move through the Woods. This seemed a perfect opportunity to ask, "Why *is* a raven like a writing desk?"

"Riddle. Rattle. Rrraven Wrriting!"

"Right, rrright! I get it, *r*aven and *w*riting sound the same, first letters anyway." Olivier was no slouch himself in the smarts department. "I hadn't thought of that."

"Think. Thank. Thunk. *Screeee*."

The raven continued cheerfully on, and Olivier kept up a brisk pace following not far behind. The devastation didn't lessen any. If anything, it got worse, with more trees down and even more intriguing litter scattered on the ground or caught in the branches. He saw a musketeer's hat, a very large spotted egg, a hand mirror in an ornate golden frame, and an axe that was entirely green, from handle to head. These fascinating objects all seemed to glow with a soft radiance, and he was almost unbearably curious about them. How he wished he could stop and examine each one, but he simply had no time for that. He pressed on, following his guide, and eventually stepped out of the Dark Woods into a clearing that he recognized. It was the same clearing that he and Murray had arrived at not so long ago, and in it sat Sylvan Blink's cottage.

What was left of it.

Olivier let out a cry of dismay. The cottage was totally wrecked. The roof was gone, the chimney tumbled, two walls nothing but rubble, the windows smashed, the furniture tossed around the clearing, most of it broken.

"Nevermore," the raven croaked sadly as she circled the ruin, then settled on one of the walls that remained standing. She opened her beak to say something further, then snapped it shut.

Alvis was sitting near the wall on a lamed piano bench, its legs snapped off. He was munching on a lemon. When he saw Olivier, he waved, and nodding toward the wreckage said, "Nice place."

"Nice *mess*," said Olivier, hurrying over to the cottage to see what, if anything, was left inside. His first thought, naturally, was for Sylvan. What had happened to him? He could only hope that his friend had gotten himself away safely to some shelter before the gale swept through and destroyed his home.

"*Screee?*" The raven inclined her head toward a pile of debris in one corner of the cottage, where the kitchen used to be. There were boards, shards of dishes, a twisted curtain, a wok, a potato masher, and numerous other items all in a big, scrambled heap. If you listened very carefully, as the raven was doing, you could hear a faint sound emerging from it. Music.

"Radio?" The raven flew down and landed on the pile. "Amadeus? Ludwig? Bill?"

"It's Sylvan," exclaimed Olivier. He'd know that music anywhere. Instantly, he clambered over one of the shattered walls, headed straight for the pile and began to dig frantically.

Four

As Olivier tossed aside chunks of drywall, bricks and shingles, appliances and cookbooks and cutlery, the music grew louder. It was flute music, and the melody being played was complicated, and beautiful, and a bit sad.

"You're going to a lot of trouble just to turn up the sound," observed Alvis. He was leaning on one of the broken walls, watching Olivier work, while finishing up the last of the lemon — seeds, rind and all. "Not bad." He smacked his lips.

"You *could* help," said Olivier, dragging a heavy plank off the pile. "Where did you get that lemon, anyway?" There was a good chance he'd found it on the ground same as the bread crumbs, but Olivier had to wonder about that big bowl of lemons that he'd seen in the kitchen yesterday, all set for Gramps to make lemonade with. Would he have used them all? And what exactly had Alvis gotten up to while he was at large (or little, considering his size) in Cat's Eye Corner?

"Don't be so nosy," Alvis snapped, although he didn't threaten to turn Olivier into any dairy products. "You're ruining that heap of junk, you know." With that, he wandered away and picked up a damaged guitar, its strings sprung and its neck hanging loose. "Too perfect," he said.

"Never mind. No matter. Nohow," counselled the raven, as she scavenged several bright objects off the pile — a silver spoon, a napkin ring, a candlestick. "Decent! Decent!"

Olivier continued to work feverishly.

"Sylvan, can you hear me in there?" Why did he keep playing that darned flute? If Olivier could have crossed his fingers for luck, and still dig and drag away debris at the same time, he would have. He was worried that it might only be a radio or tape recorder he was listening to.

The music stopped. "Olivier?" was the muffled reply. "Is that you?"

"*Yes*. I'm almost through. Are you hurt?"

"No, I'm fine."

Sylvan, too, now began to clear away obstructions from the inside, and soon a hole appeared through which he stuck his head. "It is *you*," he said. "Fantastic. You saved me, Olivier. I was so wrapped up in my composition I didn't even hear you. Did you like it?"

Olivier had to laugh — same old Sylvan, although he wasn't *old* at all. Sometimes he was like an absent-minded professor, and a brilliant one at that, except he was only ten years of age. "I did," he said, as the hole widened and he helped pull his friend out the rest of the way.

"It sounded great. But maybe you should have tried to dig yourself out first, and saved the music for later."

"Couldn't do that, I might have forgotten it." Sylvan held the flute away from himself with one hand as he brushed himself off with the other. He was covered in plaster dust and flour, and with his silvery white hair, he looked like a ghost. "Fortunately, the kitchen table is sturdy. I know because I built it myself, used tree trunks for legs. When that wind started ripping the place apart, I took refuge under it. Figured I'd be safe, and it was good and roomy." He gazed around at the wreckage and let out a low whistle. "Place is trashed."

"Afraid so," said Olivier, sympathetically, although he knew that while Sylvan was assessing the damage, plans for a new and even better cottage were already taking shape in that very active mind of his.

"It's strange, though," said Sylvan. "That wasn't a natural wind. I thought at first it was Linnet playing some trick. I was working on my composition when this current of air came through the window and drifted around the room. It blew around and shuffled papers and lifted things up, as if it were searching for something. Then it circled around me, and the next thing you know it was trying to pull the flute out of my hands. It got stronger and stronger, and pulled harder and harder, but I wouldn't let go (good thing I do weight training). That's when it started wrecking everything, blasting around the cottage and smashing things like some sort of thug."

"That *is* strange. I wonder if Linnet is involved some-how — and Fathom, too. He called me for help, he was in some kind of trouble, that's why I'm here."

"We'd better find them, then. Let's go."

"Wait a sec, Sylvan," Olivier touched his shirtfront pocket. Murray felt unusually cold. "I've got to get my hands on some ink first. Murray's so weak he can barely write."

"Absolutely. I have a whole case in my study, all kinds of ink, some special vintages. I have a new Japanese lacquered pen, too, a real beauty. I'm sure Murray would love to meet her." Sylvan carefully set down his flute on a mangled music stand and began picking his way through the debris. "The study's this way, you didn't get a chance to see it last time … *no!*"

"Where is it?" Olivier was following directly behind, and as Sylvan stopped abruptly, he gazed over the younger boy's shoulder into the empty shell of a room.

"*Gone*. I can't believe it. My papers, books, music, paintings, desk, *everything*. The ink, too, and that lovely new pen."

"They might be outside. That wind scattered all kinds of things around."

"Possibly." Sylvan didn't sound too sure, or very happy, either. "It's sure a clean sweep. Suspiciously clean." He shook his head, frowning.

The raven flew over and landed near them on a crumbled chunk of the wall. "Think. Blink. Ink. Well!"

"Hello there," Sylvan said. "Say, you look familiar."

"She helped me find my way here," said Olivier. "What do you mean about the ink?" he asked the bird. "Did you see it outside?"

"Well. Well. Well!"

"Do you have a well, Sylvan? The wind may have dropped the case of ink down it. Tricky to retrieve, but not impossible."

"No, I get my water from an underground spring. I devised a system myself … never mind," he sighed, and gazed around again in dismay at his wrecked cottage. "Think Blink." He scratched his head. "Did you mean inkwell?" he asked the raven. "All of mine were in the case."

The raven glided down from the wall and landed near a pile of spilled coffee beans, having spotted something that was sticking out of it. "Well!"

"*I* have one, but it's useless," Olivier said, digging in his pocket and drawing out the inkwell he'd taken away from Professor Blank. "See? Empty." He gave it a shake to demonstrate. But again, it made that *splish splash* noise.

"Doesn't sound empty. Why don't you open it?"

Olivier grasped the silver hinged lid between his thumb and index finger and tried to lift it, but it wouldn't budge.

"Hasn't been opened for a long time, is my guess," said Sylvan. "That model dates from turn of the century, eighteenth century that is. It's a real oldie, diamond glass, and in great shape. What a rare find, Olivier. Try again."

Olivier did try, this time using his whole hand and a lot more elbow grease (as Gramps would say). The lid finally budged, making a tiny rasping sound as he flipped it open. "Success!" He peered inside. "Nothing. It's empty, like I said."

Sylvan looked in, too. "Just because we can't see it doesn't necessarily mean there isn't anything there.

Here, let me try putting Murray in."

Before Olivier could protest and tell his friend that they were wasting Murray's time, of which he might not have much left, Sylvan lifted him out of Olivier's pocket and submerged his nib in the inkwell.

Almost at once they heard a small noise that sounded very much like slurping. The boys looked at one another and smiled. "He's warming up some," Sylvan announced after a moment or two.

"Incredible. But what is it?"

"Invisible ink," Sylvan shrugged.

"Yes, of course. I wonder what it looks like on paper. Will we be able to see anything at all?"

Olivier got out the notebook and Sylvan positioned Murray to write. Murray was definitely feeling better, *much* better, because he danced across the page. He performed leaps and pirouettes and swirls, then speed skated back and forth doing figure eights and triple lutzes. He suddenly had so much energy and was writing with such enthusiasm and élan that Sylvan could barely hold onto him. And they didn't have a clue what he was saying.

"I wish I knew what kind of invisible ink this is," said Sylvan.

"There's more than one kind? I made some once with lemon juice."

"That's one of the simpler formulas. This is a more sophisticated one. I'd try out some experiments on it if I had something left to work with here."

"We'll just have to figure out what he's saying later. My guess is he's singing 'Roll Out the Barrel'."

"Could be," Sylvan laughed. "That ink must have been well aged. He's sure *got* a barrelful."

Kechuh, kechuh, kechuh. The raven meanwhile had pulled a white-handled object out of the pile of spilled coffee beans and, holding it in her beak, was giving it a lively shake, as though she were accompanying Murray. The thing did resemble a small maraca — *kechuh, kechuh, kechuh.*

"A rattle?" said Sylvan. "What's that doing here? I never had a *rattle* when I was a baby, I had harpsichords and dulcimers, that sort of thing." (Sylvan wasn't at all stuck up about his many talents, but he did like to keep the record straight.)

"'Tweedledum and Tweedledee agreed to have a battle,'" mused Olivier. "Raven, are you expected somewhere?"

The raven dropped the rattle. "*Cr-r-ruck!* Late. Date. Fired!" She began to flap her wings and lifted up into the air.

"Thanks for your help," Olivier called to her. "Don't forget the rattle!" He was sorry to see her go.

The raven circled and flew back down, passing so close that Olivier could feel a tickling brush of feathers against his cheek. "No problem. *Adios, amigo. Ciao.* See ya, pal!" She snatched up the rattle, which now had a hair-line crack in it from being dropped, and soared off again, this time disappearing into the Woods.

"They're expecting a monstrous crow, aren't they?" asked Sylvan.

"Hah, contrariwise. They'll have to make do. Things are totally mixed up because of that wind. I'll tell you about it on the way. Okay, Murray's stopped writing."

"Asleep, I think. Tired himself out." Sylvan handed Murray carefully to Olivier, who slid him gently back into his shirt pocket, so as not to wake him. He also pocketed the notebook and inkwell.

The boys then headed out, climbing through what used to be a window. Sylvan quickly surveyed the debris, confirming that most of his things were indeed gone, then said, "Who's *that*?" He nodded toward Alvis, who was now knee-deep in Sylvan's compost bin. Alvis hopped out when he saw them and came sauntering over, picking his teeth with an apple stem.

"A doorstop," said Olivier.

"Not something I need at the moment."

"You're right about that."

Olivier introduced them and they shook hands. Alvis' hand was slimy from stuffing rotten spinach into his pockets, and Sylvan said politely, "Pleased to meet you," while covertly wiping his hand on his pants.

Olivier told Alvis that he and Sylvan had to leave in search of some friends who lived in another part of the Woods. He secretly hoped that Alvis would take himself off to wherever it was he came from, but he claimed to be heading in the very same direction as they were.

"Might as well tag along with you fellas," he said, attempting a friendly grin that made him look more like he'd eaten another lemon, this one far less agreeable.

Olivier began to suspect that Alvis was hanging around him for some reason. He was going to be hard to shake off.

The three of them set out, following a path that Olivier had taken once before. Again, because of all the damage caused by the wind, he scarcely recognized it. Sylvan knew every bend of the path by heart, as well as every tree in the Woods, so they forged ahead confidently without any fear of getting lost. Olivier expected them to encounter more characters liberated from their stories, but the Woods were now eerily quiet and appeared to be completely abandoned. There wasn't even a faint breeze to disturb the leaves. Once, they heard a woodpecker *tap-tap-tapping* in the distance — *Hylatomus pileatus*, observed Sylvan — but no other sound except their own muffled footsteps on the pine needle path, or the noises they made scrambling over downed trees, occasionally snapping a branch while attempting to push it aside. They didn't even talk that much — something about the hush in the Woods silenced them, too — although Olivier did briefly fill Sylvan in on the curious events of the yard sale, and what the "plot twister" had done to the stories in the Dark Woods. Sylvan seemed troubled by the news, but if he had any theories as to what was going on, he kept them to himself.

Before too long, they passed an empty campsite with a burned-out firepit, where Olivier had previously encountered the gormless So-So Gang. He smiled, recalling how they had run around in a dither bumping into one another. What a crew! Shortly after this they entered the part of the Woods where Linnet's tree-boathouse was located. As they approached her tree, Olivier kept his eye trained on the branches above. The old ship, painted red and blue, was well concealed by the leaves of the great maple tree that it was wedged in. Usually at least some of the bow was visible from below, with the swan figure-head poked out of the foliage, especially if Linnet's wind-pals were playing around outside and rustling the leaves.

"I don't see it," said Olivier, puzzled. "This is the right tree, isn't it?"

"Positively," answered Sylvan, scanning the treeline and quickly noting the number of broken branches, big ones, too, that formed an arc of destruction, as if some-one had hurled an enormous boulder through the trees, leaving a great gap. "Don't tell me," he moaned, and pelted off, following the downward arc of the gap. Sylvan and Linnet didn't always get along, but he didn't want to see her getting hurt.

Olivier started running at the same time, yanking branches aside and snapping twigs underfoot as he tore through the trees. "I see it!" he shouted, catching a glimpse of the boat's red stern.

"Her place ... wrecked, too," Sylvan gasped, as they struggled through a dense patch of undergrowth to get to it. "Linnet might not have been in it when it came down."

"Yeah," said Olivier grimly. "Over there, it's Fathom!"

As they stepped into the small clearing where the ship had come to rest, they saw a boy who was wearing the kind of clothing a leopard frog might wear if it were a boy — an outfit similar in design to a wet suit, white on the chest and green with black markings on the back. The boy was pacing back and forth in front of the boat and run-ning his fingers through his golden hair. Hearing a noise, he turned, caught sight of them and cried out, "Olivier, you *made* it, and Sylvan! I tried to get hold of you, but the storm, it was *horrible*." Fathom, who was usually light-hearted and full of mischief, looked as if he might burst into tears, and given his watery nature, this threatened to be a virtual downpour.

Olivier hurried forward and touched Fathom's shoulder reassuringly, although he didn't feel all that reassured himself. This at least gave Fathom courage and the threat of tears receded. Olivier then turned to study the boat, trying to assess the damage. It hadn't suffered as much as Sylvan's cottage, although the swan figurehead lay in pieces on the ground, along with the steering wheel and a shattered trunk. Its sides had been badly scored and slashed — an ugly swath of red paint had been scraped off — and there was a jagged, gaping hole in the bottom. Most of the windows were either cracked or broken, but they had been battened down from the inside, which suggested some preparation before the wind tore the boat out of the tree.

"Where's Linnet?" he asked nervously.

"Inside," said Fathom. "She won't come out."

"Won't or can't?" asked Sylvan. He, too, was surveying the wrecked boat anxiously.

"Won't."

"She must be trapped," said Olivier. "Or too hurt to move, a broken leg or something. What did she say, Fathom. You *did* talk to her?"

"I tried to. I don't think she's trapped *or* hurt. She told me to go jump in the lake."

"She's upset about the boat," said Sylvan. "Can't blame her for that."

"SHUT UP!" a voice roared from within the boat. "GO AWAY, YOU CREEPS!! LEAVE ME ALONE!!!"

"What?" said Olivier. He and Sylvan looked at one another, shocked. Linnet could sometimes be testy and stubborn, and she liked to tease Sylvan, but she was never rude. Or unkind. Especially to her friends.

"Did someone call?" Alvis said, appearing through the tangle of treefall and brush, and walking casually toward them, hands in his pockets. "Cool boat."

"DROP DEAD!"

Alvis grinned. "Who's *that*?" he asked. "I think she likes me."

Five

Linnet wasn't coming out and that was that. They tried everything they could think of. Reasoning with her, pleading, even tricks. She was determined not to budge.

"*Are* you hurt, Linnet?" Olivier called to her through one of the covered portholes.

"No. So go away."

"I don't get it. What's wrong? Outside of the obvious, I mean?"

"Nothing. Will you guys just *leave me alone*."

"But we're here to help," said Sylvan.

"You *can't* help."

"We'll fix the boat."

"I can fix it myself. This doesn't have anything to do with the boat, all right?"

"What is it, then?"

"NONE OF YOUR BUSINESS."

"Linnet, quick ... run ... get out!" Fathom suddenly shouted. "A tree ... it's going to fall on the boat!"

"Dry up, Fathom. You think I'm dumb enough to fall for that?"

Fathom shrugged. "Worth a try."

"Stand aside," announced Alvis, swaggering up to the boat. "Girls find me irresistible."

"Hellooo, in there," he trilled in an affected, nasally voice. "It's meeeeee, *Alvis*."

"Yeah?" Linnet said, unimpressed. "Whoever you are, you sound like an insect. So BUZZ OFF."

Alvis turned to the others and whispered, "This won't take long. She's crazy about me."

Olivier was studying the side of the boat, thinking that he could easily scale it. The problem was barging into Linnet's cabin uninvited, and he might even have to break down her door. The even bigger problem was that she could use her wind powers to blast him right back out again, and probably would, given the foul mood she was in.

But then, another idea occurred to him.

"Fine, you win," he called to her. "We can't waste any more time here. Murray needs help."

She didn't respond right away, but after a moment called back, "Why, what's wrong?"

"Never mind."

"No, *tell me*, what is it?"

Olivier knew that besides being very fond of Murray, Linnet felt responsible for him, having once seriously damaged him with an arrow — by mistake, of course.

"He's starving," said Olivier. "Needs ink. Desperately." For all he knew this wasn't a fib, either. Feasting on invisible ink might be as substantial as eating an invisible hamburger.

"I have some," she said hesitantly. "If I bring it out, you have to promise not to ask any questions."

"We won't ask any because we're leaving. C'mon, everyone."

"*Wait*, don't go. I'm coming out. I have to find the ink first. Everything's a jumble in here."

The boys restrained themselves from saying anything, but there *was* some victorious air punching, and Alvis was strutting around, head held high.

They didn't have to wait too long before Linnet appeared on the deck, a small bottle of ink in hand. With her other hand, she tossed a rope ladder over the side and climbed down. Olivier thought she might have conjured up a windy helper and descended on a set of airy stairs, but she wasn't one for showing off her special ability. He always admired her for that.

Once she was down, he saw that her dark hair was more tangled than usual and she had a scratch on one cheek, but otherwise did seem to be all right. She didn't have any bruises or cuts or sprains, but she *looked* hurt. Injured in some inexplicable way.

"Here," she said, giving Olivier the ink. It was an emerald green colour and one of Murray's favourite brands.

"Thanks, Linnet. Hello, by the way. Haven't seen you for awhile."

She hung her head. "Sorry, Olivier. I didn't mean to yell at everybody, it's just that — "

They were all ears and leaning forward to hear what she had to say.

"Yes … ?" Sylvan encouraged.

But she only wrinkled her nose and said, "What's that *smell*?"

"That'd be me," Alvis piped up. He was standing as close to Linnet as he could get. "It's my macho, knock 'em dead cologne, straight from the sewers of Paris. *Eau de Ew*, it's called. Can't resist it, eh, eh?"

Beyond the odour of rotting spinach wafting out of the little guy's pockets, no one else had much noticed how very pungent he was, but Linnet had a keen sense of smell, and backed away from him.

"You must be Alvis."

"Himself," he agreed, waggling his eyebrows at her.

"We sure could use some fresh air here," said Fathom, holding his nose. "What d'ya say, Linnet, think you could scare some up?"

"NO," she snapped. "I *couldn't*. So don't *ask*."

"Okay, okay. Tadpoles! Keep your hair on."

"Wait a minute." Sylvan was wearing that *aha* look of dawning comprehension on his face that he frequently wore. "Is *that* what's happened? Your wind powers, they're — "

"*Gone*," she blurted.

"What!" said Olivier.

"Gone," she repeated, snapping her fingers. "See? See! Nothing happens, *nothing*." Normally, when she snapped her fingers like that, a breeze or two would immediately arrive and gambol around her, fluttering her clothing and lifting strands of her hair, idling while they found out what she wanted them to do. "I'm ... I'm useless ... and stupid. So go ahead and laugh."

Everyone protested at once, saying, "No, you're *not*." "Why would we laugh? That's dumb." "We're your friends, remember. This is horrible."

Everyone except Alvis, that is, and he *did* laugh. Loud and long and clutched himself so hard that a whole bowlful of potato peels rained down off his jacket. They all stood staring at him and giving him exceedingly dirty looks, until he finally stopped and protested, "She *said* to laugh. I'm just trying to be nice."

"You're nice, all right," said Linnet. "Nice and weird."

"Gosh, *thanks*," he responded shyly, toeing the ground with his blue shoe.

"This loss, Linnet, bet you anything it's temporary," said Olivier, ignoring him.

"A virus or something," added Fathom. "Wind chills."

"What happened, exactly?" asked Sylvan, who, after, all was the one with medical expertise.

"I don't know, but it happened during that windstorm, somehow. Fathom was coming over for a game of Watersnakes and Ladders." She glanced at Fathom and gave him a quick smile. "I was getting the board set up, and a couple of whiffs were tumbling around, playing in the boat. Next thing I know, there's a loud roar and this big bossy wind comes streaming in through one of the portholes and starts throwing my stuff around. Knocks over the game board, the chairs, blows pictures off the wall, rips through my books, flips open the trunk — "

"Happened to me, too," said Sylvan.

"Yeah? Really?"

"Seemed to be looking for something."

"That's what I thought. Boy, was I furious. Which is probably how I got rid of it. I summoned up so much energy that I punched it right back outside. It tore around out there for awhile, then grabbed the boat and sent it sailing through the trees. Then it gave up, I guess, and stormed off. I waited to make sure the coast was clear, then went outside to check the damage and raise the boat back up."

"Which is when you discovered — ?"

"Exactly. I couldn't do it. Couldn't even lift a stone."

"You strained your powers?"

"Or drained them. Totally. Kaput."

"You don't know that," said Sylvan. "You need rest, that's all."

"I hope it's as simple as that. Why do I have a feeling it's not?" Linnet looked so miserable, no one knew what to say. "Anyway, that's when I went back inside to think things through, not that it's helped any."

"Then Fathom came along?"

"Yup. Took me ages to get here," he said. "That crazy wind kept trying to pick me up and hurl me against the trees. I couldn't dodge it so I finally jumped in a pond and hid on the bottom underneath a rock. Scared a crayfish half out of her wits."

"That lousy wind," said Olivier. "You've never met it before?"

Linnet shook her head. "Lots of different winds in the world, Olivier, and not all of them good."

"What happened to the ... whiffs, did you say?"

"Yeah. Gone, too. Poor little guys. Might just be hiding somewhere, but I'm worried about them. They never stray far from the boat." All at once she thought of something and clapped a hand to her mouth. "Murray! He's starving, and here I am, whining about what's happened to me. *Olivier*, aren't you going to give him that ink?"

"Shoot! I forgot." He and Sylvan exchanged a glance as he hastily unscrewed the bottle cap, handed it to Linnet and then dunked Murray's nib into the green drink. Given his usual healthy appetite, Olivier trusted that Murray would at least be able to put on a good show of being hungry, and he did slurp half of it up.

"Why doesn't he take it all?" asked Linnet. "He must need it."

"Small amounts are better if you haven't eaten for a long time," advised Sylvan, in his most professional tone. "Why don't we see how he's feeling?"

"Good idea." Olivier readied the notebook and poised his friend for speech. This turned out to be not quite the speech they were expecting.

Hic! Nish saladdd. Caesar? Good schtuff. Hold the anchovies! Hic! HIYA Linnet, hic, got any more of those martinis, boysh?? Hic!

"Martinis?" said Linnet. "What are martinis?"

"Small Martians," said Alvis, knowledgeably.

"No, they're not," said Fathom. "Even I know that. What the H_2O has Murray been drinking? He thinks that green ink was a salad? He's looking kinda green himself."

Olivier and Sylvan glanced at one another again, only this time Linnet caught them. "All right you two, what's up? What's wrong with Murray?"

Hail Caesar! Hic! Hoc!

"Nothing much. You know what a clown he is," Olivier said.

Et tu, Brute?!

"Could be delirious from hunger," suggested Sylvan.

'Nother drop and I'll burst! Hic!!

"Oh, yeah?" She narrowed her eyes as she looked from one to the other.

"Well, you see, I kind of tricked you into coming out," said Olivier.

"Go on." Linnet folded her arms.

Ahhhhh . . . zzzzzzzzzzzzzz.

"Wait, Murray's crashed. He needs to sleep this off." Olivier settled him back in his shirt pocket, recapped the ink bottle and then told Linnet and Fathom about what had happened that morning up to their arrival at the boat. Both were astonished to hear about the wind pouring out of the conch shell and how it had disrupted the yard sale, and they speculated about who this Professor Blank was and what he was doing at Cat's Eye Corner. Olivier dug in his pants pocket and retrieved the crystal inkwell to show them, while Sylvan went on to explain about the invisible ink and what a potent one this one must be.

"Obviously," said Linnet. "You should never have given it to Murray. Although I suppose I would have done the same."

"You're not upset about being tricked?"

"Heck no, Olivier. I'm glad you got me out of there. Moping isn't going to help, is it? Besides, now that you're here, *you* can help me, right? You always have something with you that's useful, like the sunstone, and that remote thingy you had last time. So what did you bring?"

"Nothing much. Nothing special, anyway."

"Let's see."

While Sylvan held onto the inkwell and the bottle of emerald ink, Olivier reached into one pocket and pulled out the ten dollar bill his parents had given him for spending money (he had intended to buy the carpet with it) and some loose change. From his other pocket, he retrieved Blank's business card and the stone that he'd bought from the little girl at the yard sale. That was it.

After examining the stone thoroughly, passing it from hand to hand, they concluded that, true enough, it wasn't anything out of the ordinary — nothing like the sunstone at all. Olivier was tempted to throw it away, but thought better of it and slipped it back in his pocket. Blank's card provoked more speculation, especially when Sylvan said, "So that's why he wanted the inkwell."

"Why?" said Linnet. "This card *isn't* blank, you mean?"

"He's used invisible ink," said Olivier. "That's got to be it." He studied the card much more carefully, holding it in the direct sunlight. "Must be a terrific batch of the stuff, I can't see a thing. There aren't any giveaway scratches or marks or anything on the card. You think it's some sort of message, or the usual, his name and address and all that?"

"Who knows? Food for thought, though," said Sylvan.

"Speaking of food, Linnet ... got any snacks in the galley?" Olivier *had* to ask, he was beginning to feel woozy.

"Plenty. I guess I can't starve you just because you came empty-handed." She was joking, but there was an unmistakable edge of disappointment in her voice.

"Linnet, don't worry, we'll get to the bottom of this."

"*He* can't help," interrupted Alvis, with a dismissive snort. "*He's* only a kid. Here, glom onto this." He held out a ripped and crumpled piece of paper.

"What is it?" Linnet asked.

"Garbage," he said happily.

"Wonderful. Just what I need." She accepted the paper anyway, and straightened it out. She expected to see an advertisement for hair blowers, or windmills, or hot air balloons. But it wasn't an advertisement, and she began to read it with more attention, frowning as she did so.

"Where did you get this?" she said.

"Found it in the Woods, a bunch of them were blowing around."

"Were they ripped, too?"

"Nope," he said proudly. "I grabbed the best one."

She stared at him, then groaned. "Take a look," she said to the others, holding the paper up. It appeared to be a proclamation of some sort:

HEAR YE, HEAR YE!
BY ORDER OF THE DEPARTMENT OF AIR CONTROL
SYSTEMS, TOURISM AND FLAG-WAVING,
*LET IT BE KNOWN THAT **ALL***
*AND WE MEAN **ALL** GUSTS, BLASTS, BRE*
PUFFS, FLAWS, FLURRIES, ZEPHYRS, SCUDS, WIN
***MUST** REPORT FOR DUTY TO THE OFFICE OF TH*

"What's the Department of Air Control Systems, Tourism and Flag-Waving?" Olivier asked her.

"No idea. Never heard of it before," said Linnet. "You know, Sylvan?"

"No." Sylvan was as puzzled as everyone else (which didn't happen very often). "This might explain about your missing whiffs, though."

"Drafted!" exclaimed Alvis, chuckling.

"Could you please *get lost*," said Linnet, which only had the effect of drawing a delighted sigh from him. "Duty? What duty?" she continued. "Nobody *tells* the winds what to do. My people sure don't. And anyway, the whiffs are too young for whatever this is." She thought for a moment. "They were *stolen* by that blasted snoop of a wind."

"Why, that's dis*gusting*," quipped Alvis. Then, "Hey, watch it!" as Fathom scooped a handful of moisture out of the air and splattered him in the face with it.

"We'll find them," declared Olivier. "We'll go to this Department and get them back, and while we're at it find out what's been going on here. Could be the answer you're looking for, Linnet."

"I wonder," she said, thoughtfully. "It's worth a try. Worth it to rescue the whiffs, even if I don't learn anything else about, you know, my problem. Hold on, I'm going to get some food from the boat."

She climbed back up the rope ladder and reappeared in a jiffy with a bag of cheese sandwiches and another of peanut butter cookies. These she tossed overboard to those waiting below with outstretched hands. Simple fare, but they all set to with an appetite. Alvis set to with even more zeal than anyone else, for he stomped on each of his sandwiches before devouring them, and likewise pounded the cookies to pieces with his fist. The more wrecked things were, the better he seemed to like them. Fathom then teased an underground spring up into the open between a couple of rocks — one shaped like a basin — and they refreshed themselves by scooping up cold, delicious handfuls of water.

As Alvis was tucking the now empty lunch bags into his satchel, they began to discuss their next move. Everyone agreed that Olivier's plan was the best course of action, but how were they going to visit this Department of Air Control Systems and all the rest of it, when they didn't know where it was? He suggested asking the Wise Guys, Holy Moly and Holy Hannah, but Fathom said that they were away at the University of Hocus Pocus taking courses in Vapouring and Advanced Amphibology. This gave Fathom the idea of calling his mother on his shell (a much smaller version of the conch shell) and asking her. Big mistake, for when he did, Ma Flood insisted that he come home "AT ONCE, AND NO ARGUMENTS!!"

During the violent windstorm, their house in the river had been swept away by a fierce ocean-going current and she needed his help locating it.

"I *have* to go home," he said, crestfallen. "If I can find it. Ma's roiling, she's so worked up."

"You won't be missing much," said Sylvan. "This is bound to be a straightforward procedure. Sign a few papers, pay a processing fee. I suspect it's only some bureaucratic error."

"Boring stuff," said Fathom, hopefully.

"For sure," said Olivier. "What you have to do sounds like a lot more fun."

"I suppose," Fathom sighed. "Good luck, then. Call me when you're back, Linnet, and I'll skunk you at that game."

"You *wish*!"

With that and a wave (which *was* a bit wet) Fathom reluctantly hastened away and the others were left to make their plans.

"So what should we do?" asked Linnet. "Where do we start to look?"

"Ahh, umm," said Olivier.

"Ditto," said Sylvan, surprised to find himself so short on ideas.

"Since you guys have been so friendly," began Alvis, "I'll help you out."

They gave him a suspicious look.

"Come with me," he said. "To The Heap. You can ask Marv the Mangy. He's a mage, eh, he knows a thing or two, believe me. It's not that far, I'll show you the way."

"What do you think?" Linnet turned to her friends.

"We could check this Marv out. It's not as though we have any other plans, or sources of information," said Sylvan.

"True," said Olivier. He noticed that Alvis was watching him closely and vowed that henceforth he would do the same. He didn't trust the little guy. "We'll make a quick stop there," he agreed. "Then be on our way."

Alvis nodded, and beckoning them to follow, scuttled off into the surrounding forest.

"Better follow, he's fast," said Olivier.

Out of habit Linnet raised a hand to summon a helpful gust of wind. She intended to part some fallen tree branches that were in their way, but nothing happened, the branches didn't even quiver in response. "Rats!" was all she said, then turned her face away from Olivier and Sylvan, and insisted on going last in line.

Six

*S*ome baffling aspects of their guide's behaviour began to make more sense after the young travellers arrived at his village and saw what sort of place it was. *THE HEAP* read the town sign, although it could easily have read *THE DUMP*. It did, in fact, remind Olivier of just such a place he'd visited once with his rural-dwelling cousins. There he had foraged among castoffs of all kinds — junk no one wanted anymore — and had found a funky old typewriter, which he'd hauled home with the idea that he might become an author himself — the machine looked to be absolutely loaded with stories. His cousins jokingly called this dump their local mall, and the great thing about it was that everything was free.

The Heap was itself composed of a great many heaps, some double- and triple-decker mounds of broken furniture, discarded toys, wrecked appliances, tools, sports equipment, clothing, you name it. As they wove in and among these mounds trying to keep up with Alvis, who had bustled ahead, a car door that was propped up against one of them suddenly sprang open. A small woman emerged, wrestling a rusty, child-sized shopping cart with a wonky wheel into their path. This woman was dressed in a frayed, moth-eaten coat, oddly matched footwear — a fuzzy turquoise slipper and a red rainboot — and had on her head a sieve with a broken handle that served as a hairnet. When she noticed the children, she stopped abruptly to gape at them as though *they* were the ones who were so bizarrely decked out.

She soon rallied, though, saying, "Crappy day, eh, sprats? Me, I'm off to the Middenmart. Good riddance," she added, cheerily enough, then pushed the cart away, its one wheel wobbling and squealing loudly.

"Huh, these piles of trash are their *homes*," said Olivier, as they all watched her go.

"Who would have thought," said Linnet.

"Interesting," was all Sylvan had to say, and he did look very interested, intently examining the heaps as they moved on.

"So that's why Alvis prefers wrecked and broken things," Olivier said. "Makes sense."

"As much as anything here does," said Linnet. "And speaking of Mr. Irresistible, he's stopped at that massive pile of junk with the funny wire gizmo sticking out the top."

"A television aerial ... quaint. But TV, here?" This was the last thing Olivier expected to see.

"Has to be the mage's place," said Sylvan.

This mound was much bigger than the others, and had

better junk for the most part. Besides the TV aerial, which stood crookedly on top of the heap, there was also a tattered, night-black flag decorated with a silver crescent moon, a cracked magic lantern, a harp with no strings, a badly chipped crystal ball, a curling broom with bristles worn to a nub, a gargoyle with a broken nose and a missing ear, and a tarnished and bent caduceus with a brown bat dangling upside down from it, enfolded like a plump cigar and sound asleep.

Alvis had his hand on the doorknob. "Man, you kids are slow. Good thing no one was *chasing* you, eh? Okay, so let's see what Marv's up to." He gave the knob a twist.

"Shouldn't you knock first?" said Linnet.

"Knock?" He yanked the knob off the door. "Funny idea." Alvis hopped aside as the door itself came off its hinges and fell with a *whap* to the ground, raising a cloud of dust when it hit. Tossing the knob away, he hopped back onto the fallen door and strode into the heap overtop of it as if it were a drawbridge.

So much for being a doorstop, Olivier thought, rubbing the dust out of his eyes, yet following directly after Alvis without hesitation. Everyone did, as they were most curious not only about Marv the Mangy, but about the interior of these strange mounds. Once inside, they saw that it was much roomier than they had expected, which was a good thing, since it was no less cluttered. Again, there were piles of objects everywhere, and none of them new or in great shape. The place had a sort of yard sale decor, but with an exotic theme running through it. There were Aladdin-style lamps, and magician's accessories —

top hats, canes, scarves, capes — jumbled together with Christmas garlands, empty fishbowls, jewel-encrusted goblets, a seven-league boot (possibly, it was hard to tell), gaudy eyeglasses with different coloured lenses, a sundial, an exorcise video, and several armfuls of ancient, sepia-toned papers written in lost languages (lost on them, anyway) spilling out of a bashed-up cardboard box. Definitely some neat stuff, Olivier concluded, spying a pile of silk robes, crimson, saffron and sapphire-coloured, and patterned with mythological beasts, dragons, hippogriffs, birds of paradise. These were heaped onto a ripped and sagging armchair with bits of stuffing sticking out of it.

"Marv's watching TV," Alvis announced.

Olivier glanced around and saw neither a TV, nor a Marv. "Where?"

"Right under your nose, Roquefort."

"It's Olivier, if you don't mind, *Alvis*. All I see is that antique microwave."

The microwave, decrepit and soiled with food stains, was balanced precariously on a skinny plant stand a few feet in front of the armchair. As he was pointing it out, the robes on the chair began to shift and slide, and then a head popped out from beneath the pile. A head full of wild white hair.

"What's in, Marv?" asked Alvis. "Anything good?"

Marv sat up further and the silk robes slid to the floor like water. He was dressed in overalls, a plaid shirt and work boots, a getup more suitable for a car mechanic or a plumber, or Olivier's dad on the weekend. His wild white hair didn't exactly go with his wild red beard, but both were equally mussed-up and sproingy, and he had a kindly face, what they could see of it. His nose *was* a bit crooked, likewise his smile, and he had one blue eye and one green. Marv the Misaligned might have been a better name for him, Olivier thought, for he wasn't mangy at all. "Repeats," Marv said, turning back to stare at the microwave.

"Again?"

"That's the idea, Alvis."

"But it's not a TV," Olivier said. "How do you do, sir, by the way." Olivier introduced himself and his friends.

"Don't pay any attention to *him*," Alvis confided to Marv, while tapping his head. "Thick as a brick."

"Oh, I wouldn't say that." Marv got up from the chair and ambled over to shake hands, first with Olivier, then with Linnet and Sylvan. He was taller than everyone, but not by much.

"The boy may never have seen a Trash Viewer before. We're pretty advanced here, Alvis."

"Trash Viewer?" Olivier said.

"Yep, I'll show you." Marv walked over to the microwave, pressed a button, and the door sprang open. He then removed an empty sardine can from inside and threw it over his shoulder. It landed on the floor with a tinny clatter. "Ads," he muttered. Next he retrieved an apple core and a sheet of paper. The core he handed to Alvis, who immediately began to munch on it. The paper he handed to Olivier, who saw that it was an invitation. Or maybe not an invitation, but a decree. It was difficult to read because it was splotched and splattered with mud, as if someone had cleaned their shoes on it before sending it. He couldn't help but think of a dreadful person he'd met recently called Lady Muck, but this wasn't from her.

Come
You!
To the BASH
Dress Horribly
B.Y.O.B.
By Order of
HER HIGHNESS (phew!)
QUEEN BACTERIA

"What's B.Y.O.B. mean?" asked Linnet, who'd been reading it over Olivier's shoulder.

"Bring Your Own Bugs," said Marv.

"Oh."

"Third one of these I've received this week." Marv didn't sound entirely happy about this. "Important things do turn up in the TV, but lately, I don't know, really good garbage is getting harder to come by."

"What sort of bash is it?" asked Sylvan, who'd been reading it over Olivier's other shoulder.

"The usual kind. You'll see."

"We will? I mean, I'm afraid we can't stay," said Olivier. "We've come to ask your advice about something, and then we have to be going. No time to waste." He handed the paper back to Marv.

"Best thing to do with time, my boy." Marv crumpled the invitation into a ball and stuffed it down the side of the armchair. "How can I help you?"

"Alvis said you would know the location of a place called The Department of Air Control Systems, Tourism and Flag-Waving."

Marv stood looking thoughtful and running his fingers through his beard, until one got snagged. It took him a moment to pull his finger back out, and when he did there was a Chinese finger trap stuck on the end of it. He shook his hand vigorously until the thing flew off. "No," he finally said. "Never heard of it."

"How about this?" asked Linnet, retrieving the ripped proclamation from her pocket and showing it to him. "Did the other half happen to show up in your TV?"

"Hmm, let me see." Marv read the proclamation, then shook his head. "Sorry, no. Can't say as I've seen one of these around."

The children were doubly disappointed and they turned to stare accusingly at Alvis, who only hissed, "I said Marv knew a thing or *two*. Not *three*. What d'you expect?"

Frustrated, Olivier was tempted to ask Marv what two things he *did* know, but that wouldn't have been very polite, and the man was agreeable enough and did want to help.

"Why don't you kids tell me what this is about."

The three of them took turns explaining about the violent wind storm and how destructive and *snoopy* it had been, and how it had apparently stolen the whiffs from Linnet's place.

"You're a wind diviner!" Marv said to her. "Marvellous, my dear."

"Yes … I was," said Linnet, very quietly and looking down at the floor.

"Was?"

"That's why we have to find this place," said Sylvan. "For the whiffs, and … for Linnet. We're going to get this business cleared up. There's been a big mistake."

"I see," he said. "I do indeed." He closed his eyes and kept them closed. They waited what seemed a very long time for him to open them again, and had even begun to wonder if he'd fallen asleep on his feet, when he did open them. First the blue eye, then the green. "I *do* see," he repeated. Directly he turned and walked toward a tall library shelf that was leaning forward from one wall, but propped up by a long staff, forked at the top end, that kept it from falling.

Olivier remembered that his great-grandmother used to have one like it to prop up her clothesline. The shelves of this library were full of crumpled balls of paper, torn books, coverless books, chewed-up magazines, yellowed newspapers and paper airplanes. Standing on tiptoe, Marv rustled around on one of the higher shelves, throwing books and paper balls left and right. Finally, he seized a tiny wad of paper no larger than a postage stamp — "Here it is." He began to unfold it, and as he did so, it got bigger and bigger until, incredibly, it was the size of a tablecloth. Marv then gave it a shake, as if he were ridding it of crumbs. It wasn't crumbs that flew off it, though, but plump drops of water that somehow managed to splatter everyone in the face — except Alvis, who ducked in time.

"Gee, *thanks*," said Linnet.

"That felt like rain." Olivier wiped his face dry on his shirt sleeve.

"It *was* rain," said Marv. "Sorry about that. Not too sure how this thing works."

"What is it?" asked Sylvan, peering eagerly at the paper.

"A weather map. Found it in a dumpster near that new subdivision."

"Subdivision?" Like the TV, Olivier hardly expected to hear about subdivisions in this corner of the world. He couldn't think of anything less exciting.

"That's *math*, stupid," said Alvis, swallowing the last of the apple core and licking his fingers.

"Not quite, Alvis, and don't forget your manners," cautioned Marv.

"Those are my manners. How could I forget them?"

"Alvis, you're hopeless."

"Darn tootin.'"

Marv shook his head and continued. "The subdivision is a recent development, houses sprang up like toadstools only a few months ago. See here." Marv pointed to an area of the weather map on the left-hand side. "Up a ways on this mountain is where the Temple of Zephyrus is located. A ruin now, but I understand it was magnificent at one time. Around the base of the mountain is Nohow Town, where all the development is happening."

Olivier shifted position, partly to get a better look at the map, but also because snow was swirling off the north end of it, and he was getting chilly. Brushing snowflakes off his shoulder, he said, "You think the Department of Air Control Systems, Tourism and Flag-Waving is here then? In this town?"

"I suspect so. I could sort of *see* it, if you know what I mean. There's some connection with the Temple, although I don't know what. Could be that's the tourism part of the deal."

"It's a long way to this place according to the scale on the map, and look, there's a forest that covers a really big area. We'd have to get through that somehow." Olivier was liking the prospect of this venture less and less.

"It's a distance, yep."

"Why would anyone throw out this map?" asked Sylvan. He'd been studying it with fascination, watching as a storm cloud formed on the east side.

"Good question. It still works, as you can see."

The punchy cloud, dark as a crow's wing, suddenly zoomed across the surface, heading straight for Alvis. To everyone's amusement, it began firing tiny pellets of hail at him that pinged off his head.

"Ouch! Stop it!" He shielded his head with his arms and ran to hide behind Marv's armchair.

"Maybe it *is* malfunctioning some," Marv laughed, catching the cloud in a fold of the map.

"Can you show us the quickest way to get to this place?" said Olivier.

"Why, the quickest way would be to take a carpet. That's what I did."

"Pardon me?"

"Go see the Carpet Knight. He'll fix you up. You'll be there in no time."

"You don't mean — ?"

"A flying carpet," mused Sylvan. "I didn't know there were any of those left. Extinct, I'd heard."

"*Holy* cats," said Olivier. "Are you serious?" I knew it, I just *knew* it, he thought, Sylvia's carpet is one of them!

"Zephyrus," said Linnet dreamily. "The youngest of the wind gods. My dad used to tell me stories about him."

"You have a dad?" Olivier asked, surprised.

"Of course," she said. "And a mum. What did you think?"

"You don't live with your parents."

"Don't tell me you *do*?"

Olivier was about to respond that *yes*, he did, that was how it was supposed to work, when Alvis hollered from behind the safety of his chair, "What a *baby*. Not too swift, either, is he? Not like *me*."

"Yeah, you're swift, all right," agreed Linnet. "Especially when there's danger, you clear out fast."

"Aw, you adore me, don't you? Can't blame you for that."

Linnet laughed, but it was an edgy, unamused laughter.

Alvis was lucky that Linnet's powers were gone, Olivier thought, or he'd have more than a teeny hailstorm to worry about. Turning back to Marv, he asked, "Does he live here? The Carpet Knight?"

"Yes, indeedy." Marv closed his eyes again, but only briefly. "Whooa, stand back, everyone."

He motioned them to the other side of his heap, and not a moment too soon. One of the leaning, unsupported bookshelves toppled over, falling directly on the spot where they had been standing. Scrunched paper balls rolled every which way, paper airplanes were flattened and already damaged books landed on top of one another, bent and splayed. Marv gazed at the fallen bookcase, blinking. "Guess it was time to move some furniture."

"It's not very useful that way," said Sylvan. "Flat on the floor like that."

"Everything's useful, son. Makes a dandy table, and it's low enough so you don't need chairs." Marv shook out the map again, and this time they heard a low rumble, followed by a sharp **crack**, as a couple of lightning bolts the size of dinner knives leapt out. These vanished with a **hisss**, leaving behind a smell of burned matches. He then spread the map on the back of the toppled bookcase (now it *was* a tablecloth). "It'll keep my tea nice and warm if I set my cup on the southern parts, in this desert here. Say, would you weary travellers like to join me for lunch?"

"What are you having?" asked Alvis eagerly.

"The usual fare, junk food."

What a tempting invitation, but Olivier knew that time was short. A quick trip to this Nohow Town — on a flying carpet no less — and he figured they'd be able to get everything straightened out and be back home before dark. No one at Cat's Eye Corner knew where he was, not that Sylvia would worry, but Gramps might. He'd left in such a rush, he didn't know what had happened to them, either.

"I'd really like to," he said to Marv. "But we'd better get going." Sylvan and Linnet nodded in agreement, if regretfully.

"Me, too," piped up Alvis. He scrambled out from behind the chair to join the others. "Hey, who's hungry? Not me."

Olivier gave him a sharp look. It wasn't like Alvis to pass up food of any description.

"Another time, then," said Marv. "You're always welcome here. Alvis will show you the way to the Carpet Knight's heap. An amusing fella."

They shook hands again warmly and thanked Marv for his help. As they trooped out the door, he said, "See you at the Bash. You can't miss that." And with a rueful smile, he added to himself, "She'd never let you."

Seven

Olivier followed closely behind while Alvis once again led them through the narrow, twisting passages of The Heap. He was so excited about the prospect of seeing this flying carpet, and actually riding on it, that he wasn't giving much thought to anything else. Not even to Murray, whom he had completely forgotten about.

Murray, meanwhile, was experiencing his second rude awakening of the day. As Olivier leaped over puddles and swerved around scattered debris, he found himself being shaken and rattled and jounced around. In addition to the bumpy ride, he had a nasty hangover. It felt as if someone were screwing his cap on tighter and tighter. *Good grief*, he grumped to himself, *the boy's turned into a bucking bronco. And where on earth are we? The Augean stables? Grub Street? Was I consulted about this? Was I? For writing out loud! I've a good mind to bail out. Ohhh, my aching . . .*

Sylvan was also following along, at a slower pace. He was observing the individual style of each heap they passed and making mental notes for further reference. Already the title of a learned paper loomed in his mind: "Post-Structural Brick-à-Brack and Knick-Knack Shacks: The Trash Aesthetic in Architectural Design." He wondered if he could ask Murray to help get some of his ideas down on paper, and was humming with delight at the thought of the brainwork involved, whereas Linnet, lost in her own thoughts, was anything but delighted. Again, she was last in line and scuffling along moodily, hands plunged in her pockets, kicking garbage out of the way.

Thinking about Marv and his weather map had led her to thinking about Uncle Truckbuncle, another elderly advisor they had met recently who had also shown them a map, but a more ordinary one (except that north was the only direction on it). A long and dangerous journey had ensued, although *that* adventure had been a riot. At that time she had still been able to summon winds, and had even been carried along on one for a spell, cruising swiftly over fields and forests as though she herself were flying. Now she would have to rely on some smelly old flying carpet. How corny … and humiliating. Annoyed, she gave an object that was lying on the passageway a fierce kick, and then realized too late that she'd kicked the head off some kid's doll. The head bounced away, plastic eyelids clacking, and landed in a pile of muck. A little girl ran to pick it up, but before Linnet could apologize and examine the damage, the girl wiped the head on her shirt and exclaimed, "You fixed it!" Clutching the doll's head by the hair, she skipped happily away.

"I fixed it all right," muttered Linnet. "What a *screwy* place."

There was no doubt about that. When she caught up with the other two, they were standing before a heap that was the most peculiar one yet. It was heaped high as a tower and almost completely composed of odd bits of carpeting. There were so many different designs and colours and clashing patterns that it seemed to writhe with life. It drew the eye in the same way that a flickering, dancing fire does. Tendrils and vines wove in and among woolly fantastical creatures, flowers and medallions, all intricately figured and richly detailed in deep ocean blues, or fiery reds, or knock-your-eye-out yellows, greens and purples.

"That fragment is Egyptian," Sylvan was saying to Olivier. "You can tell by the — "

"Lecturing *again*, Syl?" said Linnet as she joined them. "Where's the carpet guy?"

Sylvan ignored the interruption. He was prepared to give her bad mood some leeway — *this* time. "Around back. Alvis went to fetch him."

"Sounds more like he's beating him up."

"It does?"

Both boys now began to pay more attention and heard a muffled, tinny protest coming from behind the carpet heap.

"Ow! Stop that." *Whap. Slap.* "I say, you can't … argh." *Whap. Slap.* "Youch!" *Slap. Slap.* "Why, I'll teach you … "

"You're right," said Sylvan. "Somebody's getting thumped."

"Better check this out." Olivier was already beginning to climb over a pile of rubber bath mats that were blocking the way, but then leapt back as the mats rose up like a startled flock of birds and took off in every direction. Pastel pink and green and blue bath mats flapped away, then began to settle farther off, once again in a pile, except for one black mat that wrapped itself around the base of an upended birdbath.

"Did you see *that*?" he said. "Amazing."

"Not so amazing if you're having a shower," observed Sylvan.

"True. But still … say, Alvis isn't the one getting trounced, after all."

"Too bad," said Linnet.

They had arrived at the back of the ruggy heap, and there was Alvis standing off to one side, arms folded and watching the Carpet Knight — who else could it be? — beating a carpet that was slung over a clothesline. Instead of a carpet-beater, the Knight was wielding an oversized whisk. Every time he whacked the carpet with the whisk, however, a corner of the carpet would rear up and slap him back. *Whap, slap. Whap, slap.* The defiant carpet wasn't taking this unpleasant treatment lying down (so to speak) and did seem to be getting the better of the Knight.

The Knight's gear, they noted, wasn't exactly standard issue. He was wearing a surcoat made of astroturf overtop a hauberk, not made of chainmail, but of paper clips. Instead of metal greaves or chainmail leggings, he had on

Argyll knee socks, and on his feet custard-yellow shoes shaped like sweet potatoes. His helmet was an extra-large soup can that entirely covered his head, which accounted for the muffled and echoey nature of his protests. The top of the helmet was decorated with a pompom on a spring that bounced around crazily every time he moved his head, which he did quite a bit trying to avoid the blows from the carpet.

Olivier was about to call out to him to attract his attention, when the carpet gave the Knight a particularly forceful slap and knocked him to the ground. The tin helmet flew off his head and clattered away, revealing a pale young man with a mop of dark hair, a boxer's nose and a droopy moustache. He was what you might call ruggedly unhandsome. He scuttled after his helmet on all fours, and Alvis, much entertained, giggled and snorted and slapped his knee, which sent a whole cluster of Brussels sprout leaves raining down. Olivier hurried over to help, with Linnet and Sylvan not far behind. He picked up the helmet — a wretched, dangerous thing, with the visor crudely hacked out of the tin — and offered it to the Knight, who hopped nimbly to his feet.

"Young page and fellow dude, I thank thee." He flashed a toothy grin (with what teeth he could lay claim to). "Most kind, most kind." He set the helmet down on the nearest pile of carpets and they shifted and jostled around, disturbed by the arrival of this inconvenient object. A few flicked their fringes with annoyance.

"You're welcome," said Olivier. "But why were you beating that carpet? It doesn't look dusty or anything."

"Well you may ask. It's the carpet snakes, you understand. They hide in the pile, you see. Most crafty they are and devilish hard to get out."

"Not really?" said Sylvan. He knew what a carpet snake was, a kind of python named for the diamond markings on its back. The name had nothing to do with carpets.

"Yea and truly, I kid thee not. Go for a spin on yon carpet, snake sticks his head out, bites off yon foot." He waggled his own foot by way of demonstration, lost his balance and would have toppled over, if Olivier hadn't grabbed him by the arm and steadied him. The pointy toes of his shoes helped, too, as he was able to dig them into the ground and stabilize himself.

"Thou art a scholar and a gentleman," the Knight said to Olivier. "Whooeee, I was feeling a titch lightheaded there."

"That's because your head's empty," hooted Alvis. "And *he's* no scholar!" he added.

"That's right, I'm not," said Olivier stoutly. "But my friend Sylvan is."

Sylvan gave a modest bow, and the Knight returned it. He also bowed to Linnet, saying, "Ahh, and this is your fair lady, is it not, your damsel in distress, your *girl*friend?"

"Um, no, Linnet's my — "

Before Olivier could say "friend," Alvis shouted "She's **MY** GIRLFRIEND."

And before Linnet could say, "**NO, I'M NOT! EHH!**" someone else, who had only then appeared in the yard, screeched, "YOUR *GIRLFRIEND*?!"

This someone was an unduly large someone for a resident of The Heap. She stood a good two heads taller than everyone else and was very solid-looking, like a shed in a dress. Not a very becoming dress, either. It appeared to be made of rat fur and was cinched at the waist (or circumference in this case) with a bicycle chain.

"Dear me, it's the beauteous Thrud," said the Carpet Knight, knees trembling.

Beauteous didn't quite capture it, Olivier thought. Bruteous was more like it. Plug-ugly was closer still.

"Shut yer gob," Thrud snarled.

The Knight did so, clamping his lips together so tightly that they turned white.

Thrud then stomped over to Alvis and bellowed, "*I'M YOUR GIRLFRIEND, AND DON'T YOU FORGET IT, PIPSQUEAK.*"

"Th-Thrud," he replied weakly. His cocky manner had utterly deserted him.

"Where have you been, you miserable roach? What did you bring me?"

Alvis hastily began to dig around in his satchel. A couple of lemons rolled out, and a brass bowling trophy that Olivier was sure he'd last seen sitting on a side table in Cat's Eye Corner. After scrabbling in the depths of his bag, he produced the glass slipper that he had picked up on the edge of the Dark Woods and offered it to Thrud with a hopeful, if anxious, expression.

She snatched it out of his hand and examined it greedily. "Hmph, it's *pretty*," she sneered. Evidently this was not a desirable quality. "Give me the other one, dummy."

"Only found one," Alvis said in a very tiny voice.

"ONE?" she roared. "Are you SAYING that I'll only have ONE lousy shoe for the BASH!?"

The children were staring at her in wonderment. Dainty of foot, Thrud was not. Surely even she realized that? She was no Cinderella, and was even stiff competition for the Ugly Stepsisters.

"What are you dopes looking at?" She glared hatefully at them. "WHO are you, anyway? You don't belong here!". She continued to glare, as though the very sight of them offended her deeply. "I'M TELLING."

With that, she grabbed Alvis by the scruff of the neck and stormed off with him clutched in one huge hand and the glass slipper in the other. He didn't kick or squirm or even shout in protest, but hung limp as a rag as she carried him away, feet dragging.

"Charming," said Olivier. He wasn't sorry to see Alvis go, but he did feel sorry for him having to go *that* way. "Quite the girlfriend."

"No wonder he likes you," Sylvan said to Linnet. "*Anyone* would be better than her."

"*Thanks* a lot."

"Who is she going to tell?" Olivier asked the Knight, who had turned somewhat bluish from holding his breath during Thrud's interrogation.

"Why, the Queen, my man," he gasped. "'Tis her auntie, you know."

"What will she do?" asked Linnet.

"Fair question, fair one. Same old, same old. Clap you all in irons, cut off your heads, nothing untoward, not at all."

"Oh!" they all said.

"About your carpets," added Olivier quickly. "Do you think we could borrow one, er, right away?"

"Why, you may have one, my fine fellow!" The Knight bowed to Olivier, his chin pointing like an arrow toward the ground. "Sure, why not, yea and all that."

"Really? That's fantastic."

"Watch out!" said Sylvan. "Face plant."

As the Knight began to fall forward, the black bath mat instantly unstuck itself, making a loud ripping noise as the suction cups on its bottom half let go of the birdbath. It zipped over to the Knight and not only saved him from falling splat, face first, onto the ground, but continued to hover before him, acting as a kind of ledge to prop him up.

"How about this one?" he said.

"Too small, I'm afraid," said Olivier. "It has to carry the three of us."

"Righto, gotcha, excellent point, well thought out. You *could* each have one, but true, true, they can be hangers-on and clingy sorts, and if there's a bathroom in sight, well, say no more."

Leaning on the bath mat with one elbow, the Knight chewed on the end of his moustache and surveyed his yard. There were carpets of all kinds everywhere, some draped over logs and lawn chairs, some piled high like stacks of pancakes, some stretched out flat sunning themselves and others rolled up and snuggled together in companionable groups. "I have a shag carpet that might do. Only a pup, but a goodly size and plenty of zip."

He put his fingers to his lips and whistled. A white shag carpet with black polka dots came bounding up to them and almost knocked them over. It jumped around, pleated and unpleated itself like an accordion, flipped over on its back and spun in circles.

Olivier didn't see how anyone would be able to ride on it for more than a second. "I really like this one, but do you have one that's ... more mature? Trained, I guess, more settled? I'm just a beginner myself, haven't ridden on a magic carpet before."

"Bound to, must have, take your pick," said the Knight, shooing the shag carpet away.

"Scoot, back ye go, time for a vacuum!"

The shag carpet paused in mid-spin, doubled itself up and shot away out of sight.

"What about the one you were beating?" Linnet asked. It was an exceedingly handsome carpet and she felt it wouldn't be too shabby to ride on that one, if it had to be done at all.

"Oh, dear me, my stars and garters, and furthermore, what can I say," said the Knight, greatly alarmed. "That one is much much too dangerous. What with the eggs, don't you know."

"Eggs?"

"Snake eggs, my lovely. Yea and truly, why else would I be using a whisk?"

"I see." She couldn't help but smile. "That could be a problem."

"Hurry, let's decide," urged Sylvan. "Or we'll never get away from here." He strode over to a carpet that was mostly hidden behind a pile of others. "How about this one? It looks broken-in. Experienced, but obedient, I'd say, and the ride should be fairly smooth. You know, it even reminds me of the Persian carpet I have at home. At least, the one I *did* have before that wind blew it away."

"Unbelievable," said Olivier, walking over to have a look. "It might look like yours, Sylvan, but it's *mine*. Or almost mine. This is the carpet I was going to buy at the yard sale, I'd recognize it anywhere. That twisty flower pattern, the coffee stain in one corner, the cat scratches, the ink splotches. What's it doing here? Where did you get this?" he asked the Knight.

"Couldn't say, couldn't say. Show up here all the time, they do. Drifters, runners, low lifes, ha ha. You're welcome to it, my friend, but I have to warn you, it's infested. It's more of a crawling carpet than a flying one, eh what."

It was, too. Examining the carpet more closely, they could even see them, hundreds of fleas hopping up and down on the rug as though it were a trampoline.

"A whole flea circus," said Sylvan, unhappily. "More fleas than carpet."

"Yea, and it's going bald," added the Knight.

"Okay, sure, there *are* a few fleas on it and some threadbare patches, " Olivier admitted.

"Furthermore and in addition," continued the Knight, "it's depressed, saddened, feeling down, you might say, and I will say."

"Depressed?" said Olivier.

The carpet lifted a single fringe despondently and let it drop.

"Won't fly, I fear, nay, no way. No get up and go."

"That's terrible," Olivier said, not wanting to believe it. The carpet was lonely, that's all, here among these strangers. It was probably homesick for Cat's Eye Corner and would cheer up when it remembered him. Or it was depressed about the fleas. Who wouldn't be? He would give it a good shake — gently, though. Maybe a pep talk, some encouragement and praise. He would —

"TERRIBLE, EH? Ya haven't met 'Er yet, have yez. Ya buncha flippin' cleanies."

Cleanies?

Someone shoved Olivier hard from behind and he felt himself falling forward onto the carpet. There was a sudden clamour of voices, raucous, crude ones, and Sylvan and Linnet shouting out, followed by a burst of bullying laughter. It all happened so fast. They were attacked and knocked down, and before they could fight back — or scramble to their feet and run — the three of them were rolled up in the carpet, hoisted in the air and carted off. They squirmed and wriggled, all squashed together like the filling in a cabbage roll, and strained to listen, desperate to figure out what was going on. Roughly bumped up and down, all they could hear was the heavy *tromp tromp* of footsteps as they were borne away, and in the distance, the diminishing voice of the Carpet Knight, exclaiming, "Dear me, oh double drat, avast, what to do, *goodbye*, what to do?!"

Eight

What to do, indeed? As soon as Olivier hit the ground after they'd been unfurled from the carpet, he began slapping his pockets in a flurry of agitation. He knew it wasn't going to help, but he did it anyway. While they had been packed together so tightly, he realized that something dreadful had happened — something even more dreadful than being abducted. With his one arm pressed flat against his chest and against his shirtfront pocket, he knew for sure that it was empty — Murray was gone! But where, and how, and *when* had it happened? Olivier hadn't been paying the least bit of attention to his friend. He'd been so preoccupied with the novelty of The Heap and with the prospect of riding on a magic carpet that he'd been treating Murray like an ordinary, dumb pen that was stuck in his pocket, useful when needed. True, Murray had been sleeping off the effects of the invisible ink, but Olivier hadn't even checked to see if he was awake and

restored to his usual funny self. He tried to think back.
Murray could be lost anywhere in this place, and it was so
cluttered with junk … and if someone else found him,
someone like Alvis, they might stomp on him, or worse.

Olivier felt sick with shame, and not only that, he was
itchy. So itchy he thought his skin was going to tear off
and run away. During their suffocating ride in the carpet,
the fleas had been having a banquet. All three of them
were now ferociously scratching themselves and squirm-
ing and scrunching up their faces in agony.

"What in Scum's name is wrong with them, Trattles?"
asked Queen Bacteria, whose own face was scrunched
up, but that was her usual look. "Are they *mad*?" She was
standing on an overturned orange crate, which brought
her to eye level with her captives.

"Undoubtedly, yer *High*ness (phew!), it's the washing
that does it. Dries 'em out, their skins, eh, and they go
crazy with the scratchin'. All that soap." Here Trattles shuddered, partly out of distaste, but mostly because it was
thrilling to use such bad language. "It slimes their noggins,
eh."

The Queen gazed at them with disgust. If they hadn't
been so busy scratching and wriggling with discomfort,
they would have returned her very look. Queen Bacteria
was not a washer herself, nor at all acquainted with what
was considered here to be a highly dangerous substance
— soap. Washing? Soap? Both dirty words in her books.
Her face was slick with grease, her straggly brown hair
filthy and matted, and her clothing looked like the latest
from the rubbish bin. Rank in her case did not signify

her exalted position, so much as her heightened odour. A rotten eggs, decaying matter and piquant, outhousey, *je ne sais quois* fragrance radiated off her in noxious waves. Her attendants held their noses as they approached her, which was the proper protocol, but made for some nasally announcements. Such as when the thuggish guards arrived with the rolled carpet, "Yer badjesty, here arr duh strayngurs!"

These guards were now standing some way off, as was her assistant, Trattles. She was a *powerful* ruler, and no one dared come too near. Many had been known to faint in her presence, and besides the agony of the flea bites, the children were also struggling not to gag. This did make for some unusual facial expressions on their behalf. But it also afforded them the opportunity to do some thinking and observing, while attention was focused more on the spectacle they were making of themselves.

Olivier for one was very much engaged in sussing out the situation, probing it for weak spots. Escape was his primary objective — he couldn't wait to get out of this place — but not without Murray. While the malodorous monarch was observing them with undisguised horror, he twisted around to scratch his back, and saw that they were in a compound fenced with boards, chainlink, barbed wire and broken glass. The yard within was strewn with the usual garbage, but a royal amount of it. At the farthest end sat the largest, messiest, most festering and flyblown heap yet — the Queen's residence, presumably. In front of her place was a colossal mound of stuff — everything and anything you could think of, from chairs to china to children's toys — and the mound was growing in size as citizens of the Heap streamed in through a gate at the other end of the compound, marched up and tossed items onto it. Situated beside this gate were four burly guards, who were keeping an eye on everyone as they entered and making sure that they had the price of admission — an object for the mound. The guards' uniforms consisted of various car parts and other hardware: hubcaps, upholstery, fenders, metal pipes and wiring. They were gruff and snarly, taunting and bossing the people who were coming in, and from their voices, Olivier recognized them as the same guards who had shanghaied them.

Turning back to face the Queen, he caught her baleful eye. She was giving him the once-over, and evidently not much liking what she saw.

"Is it true that you w-a-s-h?" she demanded.

"Wash? Of course," answered Olivier. "Most days, that is, your Highness."

This damning admission caused horrified gasps from the gathering crowd, and a wave of whispers passed through it, growing louder and louder, "He washes washes washes washeswasheswasheswasheswashesWASHESWASHES …" Some parents clapped their hands protectively over the ears of their children.

"Halitosis! You ARE mad, then," said the Queen. "My dear husband did that very thing once. We tried to stop him, but he would w-a-s-h. He had to find out what it was all about." She paused, and glared at Olivier, as though this foolhardy act was his fault. "Do you know what happened?"

"No. What?"

"He *dissolved*, that's WHAT. He stepped into the bath and was GONE in two quivers of a rodent's whisker."

Fortunately, the Queen failed to notice the children trying very hard not to laugh at this, for she had stuck a finger in the corner of her eye and was mining it for a tear. "Boo hoo," she said, rather matter-of-factly, then flicked the extracted teardrop at Trattles, who, perhaps a frequent recipient of the Queen's condensed grief, dodged it by leaping deftly aside. She returned her attention to Olivier, squinting at him as though his state of cleanliness was simply too radiant for her to handle. (He was hardly what you'd call pristine, and his one hand was still blue from reaching into his book.) "I know what you are," she said. "A SPY."

"No, I'm not." Actually, he *was*, but only at Cat's Eye Corner, where he was trying to keep track of his step-step-stepgramma's suspicious activities. This didn't seem like a good time to mention it.

"You're ALL spies," she accused, glaring next at Linnet and Sylvan. "You're working for THAT MAN."

"If we were spies, we'd be undercover," countered Sylvan. "Under a cover of grime, in this case. We'd all be as disgustingly filthy as you."

Olivier thought this impertinence very brave of Sylvan, although it was only him being clever, as usual.

"Ho ho, aren't we *high* and mighty? Don't flatter yourself, my boy. Or ME, for that foul matter." The Queen tried to suppress a girlish smile.

"What man?" said Linnet. "We're not working for anyone."

"Are you giving me a dirty look, young lady?"

"Yes," answered Linnet, defiantly.

"Very nice, dear, but it won't help. However, to show you that I have a heart as big as a dumpster, I'm going to have you buried up to your necks in offal until I decide what to do with you. That way you'll be able to watch the games."

"Awful what?" Linnet said in a low voice.

"You don't want to know," answered Sylvan.

"Games!" said Olivier, trying to stall for time as he continued to survey the yard even more urgently for a way out. "Sounds like fun. What sort of games?"

"Oh, they *are* fun." The monarch clapped her hands together and a puff of dust rose up into the air. "Let's see, there's Pin the Tail on the Skunk (a real skunk), Catch the Disease, The Hundred Yard Rash, The Sick in a Sack Race, Count the Maggots in a Jar, Tiddly Stinks and the Banana Peel Slide, followed by a gross feast of leftovers served on genuine, used aluminum pie plates and in old pizza boxes."

"And there's a grunge band for entertainment," added Trattles.

"Yes, yes!" In her rising excitement the Queen was moulting flecks of dried mud and soot. "THEN I get to break all my gifts! I'll pummel and crush everything, SLASH and SMASH and BASH the whole lot. Then everyone gets to join in, until there's NOTHING left but shreds and shards and broken bits."

"What a waste," said Olivier. This explained the baseball bat, golf club, sledge hammer and other whacking equipment that formed a smaller pile beside the mound of goods.

"Exactly. It's magnificent!"

The Queen turned toward a newcomer, who was thundering heavily toward her. "Why, if it isn't my miserable, ugly niece. Hello, dear, you look positively toxic, what did you bring to my Bash?"

Thrud thrust out her hand to show the Queen her glass slipper. "*This*. But look, Auntie, you old bag, my dopey, dingbat of a *BOYFRIEND* here already fixed it." She nodded sharply at Alvis, who was cowering behind her. "Not only *THAT*, but there's only *one* of 'em."

"Tsk. Fool! You know I get first crack, Alvis."

"It was supposed to be a present for Thrud," he said weakly.

"She might as well KEEP it, then. It's no good to ME, is it?"

Thrud gave a little smirk of satisfaction and stuffed the glass slipper in her bicycle-chain belt.

"You better find me a replacement," the Queen snarled at Alvis. "FAST."

"How about this?" Bolder now, he reached into his satchel and pulled out another offering that made the children gasp with shock as soon at they realized what, or rather, who it was. *Murray!*

The Queen snatched him out of Alvis' hand, grimacing as she looked him over.

Olivier was appalled. He could imagine all too well what Murray was feeling ... and thinking. Something along the lines of *Ewwwww, get your filthy paws off me, you hag!!*

"It's not worth much, is it?" the Queen complained. "An inferior product. What's it made of? Tin? It won't take much to destroy it, but it will have to do, I suppose." She tossed him back to Alvis. "Throw it on the pile."

"With pleasure, your majesty." He bowed, and before running off to do her bidding, gave Olivier — who was glaring furiously at him — an amused, sidelong look.

Olivier had to bite his tongue so as not to call out for him to stop, or say something rash and put Murray in even more danger. Since the Queen was the one who got the first crack at everything on the pile, and the games hadn't started yet, there was still time to rescue him.

"Whatya gonna do with this bunch?" Thrud now wanted to know. "Bury 'em in mud? Run 'em through the garburator?"

"I'll take care of them for you, your Highness," a voice from behind offered. "I have just the thing for spy infestations."

"Well, badness me, look what the cat dragged in," said the Queen.

Olivier jerked his head around and saw that it was Marv who had spoken. Wearing one of his slithery satin capes and attempting to wear on his face a cruel expression (not too successfully), he was brandishing what appeared to be a can of hair spray, although there was no identifying label on it.

"You received the invitation, I see," said the Queen. "You don't always *dis*grace us with your presence, do you, Mage? But since you are here, and since my subjects *and* my objects are ready and waiting for the festivities to begin … "

"And since no one else wants to touch 'em," added Trattles.

"That, too." Queen Bacteria shivered at the very thought. "Do what you will," she ordered Marv. "But *do* it thoroughly. Or else! Come Thrud, come Trattles, I declare the games officially open and festering." She reached for her sceptre — a mucky, obscenely dripping plunger — and, stepping down off the orange crate, stabbed it repeatedly into the air as she marched toward the buzzing and excited crowd. Trattles and Thrud followed obediently behind.

"Shhhh," Marv cautioned the children as he led them away from the gathering, toward the opposite side of the compound.

"See here," he pointed out a slash in the chain-link fence. "I snipped this after I came in." He lifted aside his cape to show that he'd come armed with more than a spray can — there were a number of tools sticking out of his pockets, including a pair of wire cutters. "Practical magic, eh. If you lift it aside, you can squeeze through. As soon as everyone's involved with the games, I'll shield you from view with my cape and away you go."

"Marv, thanks so much," Sylvan whispered. "But you'll get into trouble."

"Nah, I'll just say I made you all vanish. No lie, either."

"There's one problem," said Olivier.

"Yeah," the other two agreed.

Olivier explained. "On that mound of stuff she's going to wreck, there's, um, a pen we *have* to take with us."

"A pen?" Marv blinked slowly a couple of times. "Yep, I see, right you are. I noticed that when you were at my place. A *special* pen."

"At least someone in this dump appreciates him," said Linnet, squinting as she tried to see where exactly Alvis had thrown Murray. "Look, Thrud's sneaking over to the mound of stuff … what's she trying to pull? You know, with one lick of wind I could have Murray here in no time, snatch him right from under her fat, ugly nose."

"I'll go," said Olivier. "You two crawl through the fence and I'll run up, grab Murray and run back."

"Won't work," said Sylvan.

"You'll get caught and Marv *will* get into trouble."

"Leave it to me, kids," said Marv, rubbing his hands together. "Nothing easier." Before he could do whatever it was he had in mind, though, he faltered, "*Tarnation.* She's got him."

"She's stealing from her own aunt," said Linnet. "*Stealing* Murray. Alvis must have told her about him. The sneak!"

"That *does* it!" said Olivier. "She'll hurt him."

Before anyone could stop him, he was off, swerving through the crowd, running full tilt toward Thrud.

"All righty. Time for Plan B," said Marv. "You two stay here and make your move when I tell you." Then he took off, too, but skirted the crowd as he hurried back toward the Queen's upturned crate, where Sylvia's carpet still lay, immobile and about as unmagical as they come.

"We can't just stand here and do nothing," Linnet said.

"Hang on," replied Sylvan, placing a hand on her arm to hold her back. "Blazes, did you see that?"

The "that" Sylvan was referring to involved Olivier. It just so happened that he had dashed away at the very moment that the referee for the Banana Peel Slide had dropped a fresh, well-rotted peel for the next contestant, but it was Olivier himself who stepped on it. When his foot hit the banana peel he'd been tearing along at top speed, and so slid a remarkable distance, arms flailing and one leg waggling, as he tried to regain his balance. It was an unexpected, although mightily impressive performance. He only stopped when he smacked into Thrud ("*OOOF!!!*"she gasped), which was like hitting a rubber wall. He bounced directly off her and landed with a *whump* on the Queen's mound of gifts, at the same time that Murray, launched by the impact, flew out of Thrud's sweaty grip and shot like a rocket over the fence.

"Double *blazes*," exclaimed Sylvan. "There goes Murray!"

Thrud was not at all happy about this turn of events, and was especially enraged about losing her newest acquisition. While balling up both fists and stomping over to give Olivier a major thrubbing, she was, however, stopped short by her aunt.

"Contamination! Caught you *clean-handed*, you thieving minx," growled the Queen as she leaped in front of her brandishing the drippy sceptre.

Marv, meanwhile, had joined the Carpet Knight, who had arrived late, but was trying to be helpful by poking at Sylvia's carpet with a serving fork, and saying, "Come on, old thing, buck up, be a sport, it's not that bad, life is full of ups and downs, what?"

"Especially for a carpet of your fine nature," encouraged Marv. "Here, this should do the trick." He gave the spray can a shake, took aim and pressed the nozzle. A sparkling blue cloud emerged and settled on the carpet in a misty, evaporating shower that smelled lovely, like a rainy day in the woods. The carpet began to shudder and shake. If it hadn't been so noisy, with everyone still cheering wildly for Olivier, astounded by his record-breaking slide, and the Queen giving Thrud a royal blast, a chorus of tiny voices, sputtering and coughing, might have been audible emanating from the carpet itself.

"Holy jumpin', what was that?!"

"Jig's up gang, let's hop it!"

"Be there in a tick, I'm a mite slow."

"Very funny, fleabrain."

"C'mon, I've never seen so many human hotels in my life."

"Swell digs, and all you can eat!"

As its tiny residents fled, the carpet gave itself a slow, luxurious stretch. Once that was accomplished, instead of rising off the ground and waiting patiently for passengers to climb aboard, it furled itself up tight as a log. It then began to roll away, picking up speed as it went. Soon the carpet was barrelling through the crowd, knocking people off their feet as it spun toward the gate. The guards tripped over themselves rushing to get out of its way, one honking the car horn on his fender breastplate — the carpet was speeding along unstoppably. Even more surprising, Alvis broke free of the crowd, darted over and hopped on top of it.

"Dear me!" said Marv, watching Alvis scramble to keep his balance like a log-rolling lumberjack. He and the carpet disappeared through the gate. "That wasn't supposed to happen."

"No, nor *that*, no, not at all," said the Knight, gazing up at a strange object that was flying overhead. "By my stars and garters! My gift to the Queen, oh dear, oh dear, I reckoned it was a goner, and it is, it *is*. Looks awfully like a tea tray, don't it?"

"Triple *blazes*!" said Sylvan. "There goes Olivier!"

Suffice to say that the new world champion of the Banana Peel Slide was, incredibly, also flying through the air. His newfound fans below were going wild, roaring with delight — what would the boy do next?

The reason he was making his exit in this unlikely manner was not because Thrud had finally managed to get her hands on him and had given him a walloping send-off. No, she couldn't have done that, for she was at present too busy staggering around, bellowing, with the Queen's plunger stuck on her head. The cause of Olivier's rapid departure was even more curious: on hitting the pile, he'd landed on top of a bristly doormat that had no intention of being treated like one. It wasn't going to stick around to be pummelled to shreds, and, taking Olivier's arrival as the first blow dealt, and indignant to the very fibres of its being, it gathered up its strength, blasted off the mound and cleared the fence with plenty of space to spare. This was not quite what Olivier had in mind when he had for so long imagined the thrill of riding on a flying carpet.

"Aaaaaaaaaaaaah," was the only comment he had to offer on his way over the fence.

"We're next!" said Linnet. "Marv is signalling us to go." She tugged aside the snipped section in the chain link fence. "We've got to see where Olivier lands."

"And Murray, too."

They turned briefly to give a thumbs-up and a quick, happy wave to Marv and the Carpet Knight, who both waved cheerily back. Then, with everyone at the Bash still shouting and staring with wonder after their vanished champion, Linnet and Sylvan squeezed unnoticed (or so they thought) through the gap in the fence.

Nine

What a tumultuous ride! After the doormat cleared the fence and the tangle of stunted trees and bush that surrounded The Heap, it skimmed over a swamp — Olivier made alarmed eye contact with an equally alarmed frog — crashed through a stand of dried reeds, flew, with no space to spare, through the gap in a jagged outcrop of rocks, then shortly after came to a sudden stop by crashing into a large tree trunk. He tumbled to the ground and lay there for a few minutes catching his breath. It had been an express delivery out of trouble, no doubt about that, but was he in even deeper trouble? He groaned and rubbed his head as he sat up. Where *was* he, for instance? And *where* was everyone else? He checked his arms and legs — he was a bit banged up and sore, but luckily hadn't broken any bones. Brushing a tuft of cattail fluff out of his hair, he turned to the doormat, which was lying beside him, motionless except for a couple of twitching bristles.

"Um, thanks," he said. He *was* grateful to it for getting him out of that scrape.

WELCOME, the doormat said.

Naturally, doormats often *do* say exactly that. Their vocabularies are extremely limited. But when Olivier looked again, the block letters that were emblazoned on the mat had changed to **GOODBYE**. With that, it rose off the ground, readied itself in a take-off position and sped away, swerving and dipping as it navigated around thistles and rocks and tree stumps.

Olivier watched it go with a sentiment that was one part amazement and two parts misgiving. It *is* hard to get used to everyday objects leaving you in the lurch, and now he was completely alone. He estimated that he'd travelled quite a distance from The Heap and knew that it would take the others some time to catch up with him … if they could find him at all. There wouldn't be any swift rides on a magic carpet, either. So much for accomplishing their mission and getting home before nightfall, he thought dismally.

"Linnet!" he called out. "Sylvan?"

No answer. He wondered if they were searching for Murray, which was what he should be doing. He *could* try to find his way back, although staying put was likely a better idea. Sylvan would pinpoint his whereabouts by calculating the direction the mat had flown and the speed at which it had been travelling. Or something like that.

Olivier stood up to take a look around. He was facing a rocky field, with a few trees and clumps of bushes growing here and there, but behind him loomed yet another forest. The trees in it seemed to be mostly white spruce and were enormous. He couldn't even begin to stretch his arms all the way around the one he'd crashed into, not that he felt like hugging it — he'd get sap all over his shirt. He stared beyond it, into the forest's black depths, hoping there weren't any hungry wild animals roaming around in there, nor wild anythings, for that matter. And on the subject of hunger, he seriously regretted not taking Marv up on his offer of lunch. A bag of donuts, or chips, or cookies would hit the spot right about now.

Olivier sat back down and leaned against the tree, prepared to wait. To pass the time, he went over some of what had happened on their journey so far. He thought about Murray, and about how much he missed him. He thought about Alvis, and about how much he *didn't* miss him, the little wretch. He squirmed, and slunk down farther. The tree bark was rough against his back and it was hard to get comfortable. He waited and waited. Where *was* everyone? It was getting late, afternoon turning into evening, the air tinged with darkness. As he strained to listen, thinking that surely they'd be coming along soon, it occurred to him how quiet everything was, how utterly still — no wind at all, nor any of the usual outdoorsy sounds. No birds (he was half-hoping that the raven would show up again), no bugs, no rustling leaves, no ... what was that? There *was* a sound, faint but growing louder. It was someone singing, although he didn't recognize the voice. Same with the tune, which was familiar, but the lyrics weren't quite right. He listened attentively:

My body lies over theeee oceannnn

My body lies overrrr the seeeeeeea

My body lies over the ocean,

Oh bring back my body to meee

Ohhhh bring back, bring back

Bring back my boddddddy to meeeeee, to meeeeee

Bring back, bring back, bring back my body to ME!!!

"AHHHHHHH!!!" Olivier screamed.

Terrified, he jumped up, stumbling in his rush to hide behind the tree. He had never in his life seen anything more horrible!

A singing, severed head floated out of the woods. Spying Olivier, it skimmed over and began bobbing in front of him, grinning ludicrously.

"Aww, don't do that, don't scream," the head begged, following Olivier around to the other side of the tree. "You'll give me a migraine."

Olivier couldn't speak. All he could do was stare at the head, which was staring back at him, albeit in an encouraging enough way.

"Oh, come *on*," it said. "I'm not going to hurt you, am I? What would I do, bite your nose? Give you a head-butt?" It chuckled at this. "Being a boy, I suppose you *do* want to wrestle, don't you? You'll get me in a headlock, I fear. Although I have to warn you, I *am* headstrong. Look, do cheer up, the worst I'll do is call you a name. What is your name, by the way?"

Olivier managed to respond, stammering his name,

and then, courteous even in the face (as it were) of fear, he asked the head its name.

"Why, I'm The Horseless Headman, you must have heard of me."

"Er, sort of."

"Some of my friends call me Einstein, because I'm such a brain, you see, and others call me Bob, which I seem to do a lot of these days, and for short, which I now regrettably am, you can call me Max, which, on the other hand, *not* that I have one, is a nickname that makes me feel like the *most*. Like Maximum, don't you know, like Maxi-million."

With this, he zoomed up to the top branches of the tree and then zoomed back down again, settling in an empty bird's nest not far above Olivier's own head. This resting spot gave him the advantage of resembling an Elizabethan gentleman wearing a twig ruff (or at least he more resembled an Elizabethan than he did a large, talking egg), and once he was stationary, he seemed less frightening. Also, Olivier had to admit, Max hadn't gone in for a gory dismembered look, but was neatly groomed with a tidy moustache, a soul patch fuzzy as a burr beneath his lower lip, and his longish hair tied back in a ponytail.

"A most agreeable view," Max observed, gazing around with an affable expression. "It's not so bad really, my condition. A bit shocking at first, naturally, but then again I don't have to wear a tie to work, do I? Not that I have a job at the moment. It *has* been a bit of a setback, but believe you me, there are plenty of opportunities out there for a person with brains. They say it's hard to get ahead these days, but here I am! And wasn't I head boy in school, always head of the class. *You can be anything you set your mind to*, Ma used to say, *son, use your head*. I intend to, yes sireee ... figurehead, head count, talking head, head of state. Or headliner in an improv show, you know the sort, where you talk off the top of your head. Not to rule out head hunter, headmaster, why, head of the corporation — I could wear a headphone! How would I look in a head-dress? Silly, I suppose. "

"What happened to your, ahh ..." Olivier didn't want to be indelicate.

"Body? Yes, noticeable, is it? I mean to say, that it's not noticeable, not being there and all. Well, it can happen to anyone, can't it. You see, I was galloping through these woods one fine day, and didn't I whack the old noodle clean off on a low-lying branch. Next thing I know, and I *did* keep my wits about me, no horse, no extremities, nothing left below the chin line. It *was* liberating, and didn't it just fix my bad knee, although I must say I had a raging headache for days. You wouldn't happen to have an aspirin on you, would you? Or a head band, wouldn't that be chic?"

"Sorry."

"Not at all, just thought I'd enquire."

"How do you eat, anyway?"

"Face in the plate, my boy. Not entirely convenient, but what's a gentleman to do. Dinner, now that reminds me, I'm here to give you a heads-up."

"Really? About what?"

"I forget."

"Oh."

Max continued to smile pleasantly, completely unperturbed by this lapse. "I do have a good head for numbers. Ten, for example. Or thirty-seven. Fifty-three is a robust and lively number, wouldn't you agree?"

"It's all right, I suppose," Olivier said, a bit exasperated. "But look — "

"Where? Yes, yes, right you are, I see it!" Max was gazing off across the field. "A mawworm, fancy that."

A *what?* Olivier looked, too, and although it had grown darker as evening settled in, he spotted a sinuous creature streaking across the field, flying erratically up and down, over rock piles and through the tall grass. Every once in awhile it gave itself a good shake, apparently trying to get rid of something that was clinging onto the back of it.

"No, no, not a mawworm," Max decided. "A moondog, perhaps?"

"I think I know what it is," said Olivier.

He *did* know for sure when the thing flew closer. It was the carpet, *his* carpet, and who was clinging onto the back end of it, grasping it by its fringe and hanging on as tenaciously as a flying crab, but Alvis. Alvis was about the last person Olivier wanted to see, although as it turned out, he didn't see him for long. The carpet did a backflip and careered past them, with Alvis now also upside down, but still determinedly hanging on.

"Arrrrrrrrrrrrrrrrrrrrrrrrrrrrrrrgh," he cried, as both of them disappeared into the forest.

Olivier was beginning to understand why Sylvia had claimed that the carpet would be unhealthy for him. More likely, Alvis simply didn't know how to control it.

Olivier was positive it wouldn't give *him* any problems.

"My," said Max. "What a peculiar occurrence. It *is* hard to credit some of the beings one encounters in these parts. Makes one feel light-headed." With this, he levitated out of the bird's nest and pointed his nose toward the forest. "Well, young man, this has been most diverting, but I'm going to head out. I shall try to make some headway, for, as you are undoubtedly aware, it is always prudent to get a good head start. Especially before heads begin to roll, ha ha. *Bon soir,* my friend. Try to keep your head above water, and your nose clean." He gave a brisk nod and began to float away.

"Hold on," said Olivier.

"To what?" Max called back. "That *is* a rather insensitive request, wouldn't you say?"

"I didn't mean … well, sorry, but before you go, can you tell me where I am?"

"Certainly, you would want to know that, wouldn't you?" Max had turned back toward Olivier to answer, but had done so too quickly, and spun around several times like a top (which he *was*, in a way). "Whoa, no brakes," he said, wobbling dizzily from the spin. "You're at the edge of the Nameless Forest. There's a sign posted over yonder, explaining the situation. I really must pop off and, ah yes, I remember now what I was to tell you. You're invited to dinner."

"I *am*? Where?"

"Witch's house."

"A witch? *No thanks*, then." He shuddered. "I know what they like to eat — their guests."

"Ah, but this witch is different, you'll see."

"She isn't a wicked witch?"

"She has a wicked sense of humour."

That didn't sound promising, either. A jokey witch. "I'm not going," Olivier said finally.

"I shall convey your regrets," said Max. "To her, and to your friends."

"What! My friends? My friends have been captured by a witch!?"

"Enraptured is more like. And stuffed — she makes a mean bread pudding. Very mean, and crusty. I wouldn't touch her head cheese, if I were you, though. Toodle-ooo!"

"Where does she live?" Olivier had to shout after him, for Max had accelerated, and was sailing away like a hardball hit out of the park.

"Halfway There," he answered, and was gone.

Halfway there? What's that supposed to mean? Halfway to where? Or was he already halfway to where she lived? Which direction? he thought. Had to be into the forest, isn't that where witches always lived? Max had come out of the forest, after all, and had gone back that way. He should have waited and then they could have gone together. When Max tells this witch that he isn't coming to dinner, she'll be on the lookout for him anyway, crafty as her kind are. Witches! This corner of the world, the Cat's Eye Corner of the world, seemed to be riddled with them.

Olivier continued to grumble to himself as he walked over to find the sign that Max had mentioned. It was obscured by a low branch, which he held aside as he read:

NO TRESPASSING, TRAIPSING, OR TRIPPING THE LIGHT FANTASTIC!
ENTRY ABSOLUTELY FORBIDDEN, JUST FORGET IT, DON'T
EVEN THINK ABOUT IT, YOU PEDESTRIAN PEDESTRIAN!

TRESPASSERS WILL BE PROSECUTED, PERSECUTED, PUMMELLED,
PINCHED, POACHED, POMADED, PETRIFIED, AND PUT IN A BOX
IN AN UNPLEASANT PLACE!

SO THERE! NYAA NYAA NYAAA!!

He found this sign very hard to take seriously. It *did* go overboard — there wasn't a spare inch of space on it for further taunts and threats — and was decidedly lacking in the stern, no-nonsense wording that a proper, self-respecting sign should possess. Possibly this was a sample of the witch's "wicked" sense of humour. Or possibly ... it meant business, and not one he much wanted to get involved in.

Undecided as to what to do, he stared again into the gloomy depths of the forest. Even darker now, it wasn't exactly the best time of day to go wandering into it. He turned around and gazed across the field in the direction of The Heap. If he walked back that way, he could ask Marv for help and search for Murray. Although if Linnet and Sylvan had already found Murray, and had entered the forest farther along, then all three of them this very moment might be the witch's prisoners. Olivier turned back toward the forest. *That's* the way he had to go, and that's what he did, first bending down to grab a hefty, knobbly stick for protection, and then stepping boldly into the Nameless Forest.

Ten

At least there was a path to follow, however faint, and Olivier was sticking with it, careful not to go astray. Every so often, he encountered a sign posted on a tree that said things like, **"YOU'LL BE SORRY"** or **"BOO!"** or **"WRONG WAY, GOOFBALL!"** He hurried past these — they were too dumb to trouble him much — but, as the signs were getting harder to read in the encroaching darkness, he had no choice but to hurry. How he wished he had brought something *useful* with him, like the sunstone that had once guided him through the Dark Woods. An ordinary piece of gravel wasn't much good for anything — and he had even paid for it! (Olivier did have a tendency to thrift, but he also had a greater tendency to generosity, which balanced things out nicely in his nature *and* in his bank account.)

He realized now that he was in the vast forest that he'd seen on Marv's weather map, not at all a cheering thought.

What got him thinking about the map was the fact that this forest didn't seem to have much in the way of weather, outside of a rain shower that fell at predictable intervals. About every five minutes it would start to rain abruptly, and then a minute later stop, just as abruptly, as if someone above were turning a tap on and off. Although these sudden showers fell here and there, willy-nilly, they were easy enough to avoid since they also fell in circumscribed areas, circular or square, and precisely measured. The rain didn't smell like proper rain, either — rain that fell in a forest, anyway, which usually evoked a fragrance of leaf mould, evergreen needles and wet earth. This rain left behind an artificial odour, like a deodorant, and this he found both irritating and unsettling. The witch's idea of a joke, no doubt. It was one thing to have an uncle who was a practical joker — like Uncle Fred who greased every doorknob in his house — but quite another to have to encounter a witch who was one.

Max had called this place the Nameless Forest, and Olivier began to worry that this meant it was the kind of wood he'd read about in stories in which your memory faded and you forgot everything, even your own name. To see if his own memory was holding up, he tried recalling a few dates of vital importance — when the zipper was invented, or what year Paul Henderson scored his famous goal, or his own birthday — April 23rd — which was the same as Shakespeare's, as his mother loved to remind him. His mum was a great believer in memory work. She felt that everyone should have an emergency supply of memorized poetry available in case they got stuck in a dreary situation, like having to sit and listen to Uncle Fred, who, besides finding plastic vomit endlessly useful and hilarious, also had many excruciatingly long stories about plumbing repair in his conversational repertoire. Well, this situation was certainly dreary enough … and … and thinking about his mum, Olivier suddenly felt a pang of homesickness and loneliness and … his anxiety about what lay ahead deepened. Night in an unknown forest with no food, no friends, his parents too far away to help, and a witch's house as his destination. Fear, yes, he felt that, too.

But *come on*, he thought to himself, determined not to let fear devour him. He'd be useless then. *Focus on something … anything!* He decided to try reciting one of his mother's favourite poems.

"How happy is the little Stone," he began, right enough. "That rambles in the Road alone … And … and doesn't care about Careers … And … um, something … what is it? … something … never fears …"

"Exigencies."

Yeah, he thought, that's it, *exigencies.* He'd always meant to look that word up. He liked the sound of it.

"And Exigencies never fears … " a voice, not his, continued.

Wait a minute. "Who's there?" he asked softly. "Max, is that you? Alvis?" That little rat had to be around here somewhere, he figured, and even Alvis might be a welcome sight, given the circumstances.

The response to this query was much longer than he expected and perfectly jumbled and very strangely spoken, as though the speaker were gargling and talking at the same time.

"Nor pleasantries, nor pastries, minnows eels hogwash, do you have any idea, why, he's wet behind the ears, or will be, with this coupon, I thee wed, or is it a capon, row row row, one never knows, one sand dollar off, life is but a dream, if it doesn't rain ..."

The voice was close by, but because of the dense undergrowth and the failing light, Olivier couldn't see who was speaking. Nor did he really want to, despite feeling that he could use the company and some directions. Just his luck to run into some kind of nut. His hand tightened around the stick he'd picked up at the edge of the forest.

"Rain, rain, go away ..."

Which it did, but it didn't go far, because one of those instant downpours, a perfect rectangle of rain, all at once fell where Olivier happened to be standing. "Ack!" He hopped aside out of its range, but not before getting doused. *Great*, he thought, now I'm soaked and I stink of deodorant and there's someone hidden in the trees jabbering like a madman.

"Too bad, too bad, a rose by any other name, they're mad not me, here's rue for you, and pond slime, Sweet Thames run softly, Mississippi mud, in your eye, they're coming, crayfish leeches alive-alive-o, she bought a lovely, watch out, let's play find the fish, 'til I end my song, they're coming, watch out ..."

The rain had driven Olivier off the path, and he hastily took cover behind a clump of ferns, because "they" *were* coming. He could hear them running hard, feet pounding on the path, and screaming shrilly. There were four of them, women wearing ragged dresses, feet and arms bare, thin hands either reaching out beseechingly or pulling at their long, tangled hair. As they surged by, he saw that their faces were distorted with distress, mouths open wide, their screams terrible to hear.

"Screaming Mimis ..." said the voice, lightly, with a gurgle of amusement.

"*Who* are you?" Olivier looked all around, annoyed. "*Where* are you?"

"I'm here, I'm there, I'm a dashing sparkling fellow, I'm H_2O, don't you know, a veritable stream of consciousness, beware, I'll brook no interference, care for a drink ..."

"You're a ... *no*, I do *not* believe it," said Olivier. He had walked farther off the path and the only thing he could see making any kind of sound was a small stream. As it tumbled over and flowed around several mossy rocks, it gurgled and splashed, and actually did seem to be making noises that could be taken for watery words and phrases. Olivier crouched down to take a closer look. Possibly it was some bewitched creature hidden among the rocks that was speaking.

"Are you a frog?" he asked.

"Get 'em in my throat sometimes, betimes, time after time, silt in my mouth, sand in my pockets, small fry in my eye ... "

"Let me get this straight. *You're* a river?"

"A beck, a burn, I'm only a kid, a rivulet, a streamlet,

a rundle, a mere creek, a trickle, a branch, a brook, a brook ..."

"Oh, brother, don't tell me. You're a *babbling* brook." More of the witch's jokes!

"And you're all wet." The brook splashed at his shoes, but fortunately missed, as Olivier was wet enough already. "A big drip ..."

"Er, that's poetry, you know. Babbling brook?"

"Sure, sure, yeah, yeah, tell me another, and another ... "

Olivier quickly changed the subject. He'd already been conversing with a free-floating head, so why not a body of water? "Who were those women?" he asked.

The brook made a deep glugging sound, possibly its version of sighing. "Trouble, trouble, trouble, worry, worry, worry, listen, listen, listen ..."

Olivier sat down beside it and did listen to what it had to say, although it wasn't easy to make sense of it. The brook did go on and on (it was sort of like his Uncle Fred in that way), and he had to pick out the significant shreds of information and try to piece them together.

Apparently the Screaming Mimis appeared in the forest when there was a disturbance in the natural order, when something was seriously wrong in the world — their distress was a warning and a lament. Olivier might have pointed out that a talking brook was itself a sign that things were a bit out of whack, but he politely kept this observation to himself. He did ask if this trouble was the witch's doing, and the brook said *no* — actually it said a stream of them, *no no no no no*, bouncing the word along its length like a ping-pong ball. She didn't like it "at all, at all, at all," it said, with an Irish lilt.

"I have to go there, to her house," Olivier said, trying not to sound nervous. "Am I going the right way?"

"The right way, the bright way, my way … " answered the brook. "Follow me, go with the flow … "

"The bright way?"

The brook began to glow with a greenish phosphorescence.

"Oh, wow, how do you do that? You're not polluted, are you?"

"Haven't touched a drop, I swear …"

It grew brighter and brighter, creating a path of light through the dark.

"Follow, follow …" it continued. "Let's go, let's go, eh, I'm all aglow, shake a leg, it's my chemistry, shall we say, my excitable molecules, my *joie de rive*, pretty fluent, eh, for a little guy, *eau de vie, fleuve de bouche,* don't mean to gush …"

Olivier couldn't decide which was more uncanny — the fact the brook seemed to know more French than he did, or that it had begun to glow with this ghostly light. In the book Sylvia had given him, he'd read about a phenomenon called St. Elmo's fire — a luminous corona that appeared sometimes around ships before a storm — and he supposed this could be an example of that. The air didn't feel as if it had any storm potential in it, but anything was possible here, and he didn't want to get caught in an even bigger downpour. He didn't like the idea of leaving the other path, but decided that he'd better follow the brook. Not that there was much choice, since night had truly fallen and visibility had decreased to nil.

He walked along beside it for quite some time, his feet bathed in its green light as he picked his way through tangled roots, clambered over rocks and circled around low-growing juniper bushes. The brook prattled on about this and that, and that and this, and Olivier tuned in and out, only half-attending to what it had to say. He was hungry and weary and his flea bites itched. His smelly clothes also chafed and grew even more uncomfortable because they were shrinking as they dried. Still, the brook had a soothing effect on him. At times he caught snatches of the poem he had started to recite earlier, and it reminded him again of home, and of what a cozy, happy place it was. Even *with* Uncle Fred visiting. What's a little plastic vomit on your plate when you sit down to dinner, after all?

After trudging what seemed like *forever*, Olivier began to notice that not only was the brook's guiding light growing weaker, but so was its voice.

"Are you tired?" he asked.

"Going under, my friend … "

The brook had been growing narrower and narrower, and now seemed to be taking a detour, vanishing right into the earth.

"I'm here, you're there …" its voice a mere trickle.

"Don't go," said Olivier, although he knew that it was a dumb thing to say.

"No choice, can't be late, not a shallow fellow, but look, look there, over there, there you go, courage, courage …"

Olivier looked around and saw, off to the left, a light

shining through the trees. "Is that it?" he asked. "The witch's place?"

The brook said nothing in response, or nothing outside of a faint burble. Olivier stood watching it for a minute more, until even its glow faded away. It was still there, naturally, it hadn't dried up, but was flowing quietly now, like any ordinary brook.

Before turning toward the light in the forest, he bent down and laid his hand lightly on its surface. The temperature of the brook changed from cool to warm. Olivier smiled and said, "Courage." Then he rose to his feet and made his way toward the witch's house.

Eleven

Olivier proceeded cautiously through the forest. Indeed, he was almost breathless with caution (this may have had more to do with his rapidly shrinking shirt), but you could hardly blame him. He wasn't afraid of meeting a bear or a lynx — the Nameless Forest didn't appear to be inhabited by animals of any kind, not even the usual squirrels, chipmunks or hares. But the woods were no longer silent. He kept hearing odd, spooky noises that didn't seem to have a source. As he himself crept along quietly, treading on the soft, springy forest floor, he heard a shout echoing in the distance, then a snatch of music, followed by the sound of someone scuffing through dry leaves. Next came an unearthly hissing close by, a half-whistled tune, a bark of laughter. Then, directly behind him, a firecracker *exploded*, which so startled him that he jumped in terror and popped most of the buttons off his shirt. He ran to take cover behind a mossy stump, then peered around anxiously for the culprit who'd thrown it, but saw no one.

As he was about to continue, he heard a different noise — the sound of someone tearing through the forest — and he slunk down farther behind the stump. He thought at first that it might be the Screaming Mimis again, and he definitely didn't want to get in their way — they gave him the creeps. Besides, they'd probably trample over him without a moment's hesitation.

He ventured a quick look when the commotion neared and saw not the screaming women, but a lone figure making an equal amount of racket. It was a man who was completely covered in hair from head to toe. Long, bushy, knotted, twig-infested hair. A wolf man? No, he had a bulbous, fleshy nose poking through the shaggy hair on his face. A wild man, then? A wildly annoyed man, at any rate. He was hopping up and down as he ran, tearing leaves off the trees, snapping branches and hollering at the top of his voice, "I'M FREAKIN' OUT HERE, I CAN'T TAKE IT, THE FLAMIN' NERVE, BOY OH BOY, DOESN'T THAT JUST TAKE THE CAKE, SHEESH, SOMEBODY'S GONNA PAY, YA HEAR ME!!!"

A daunting performance, but Olivier didn't think that the fellow was much of a threat, for he was too involved in his own grievance. He watched him go, watched him blaze a trail through the forest with his indignation, then crept out from behind the stump and moved on with even more misgiving. This witch must *really* be causing trouble, he thought.

His conviction was only strengthened by what happened next. The light he had been following started playing tricks.

It shifted position, moving slowly up and down, then back and forth. Next it began to lead him in circles, in and around the trees, then vanished altogether, only to reappear behind him. It hovered in place just long enough to make him think he was on the verge of arrival, before it receded again, dwindling in size until it was no bigger than a pinprick glimmering through the wood. Olivier gritted his teeth with frustration and thought, *Now* I'm *freakin' out here!* He wondered if the wild man was someone who'd been invited to dinner years ago and never could find the place. This thought reminded him that he *had* been invited, after all, and he decided that he wasn't going to budge another inch until the light settled down and started to behave. He crossed his arms and tapped his foot with impatience, like a teacher facing down a rowdy class of loudmouths and spitball-throwers. Amazingly — it worked! Gradually the light stopped moving, held in place by *his* glare (or so he wanted to think), and it stayed that way, fixed in position.

A dozen steps farther and he was there. What a surprising there it *was*, too. For one thing, the light he had been following was issuing from an ordinary post lantern, solidly planted in the ground. It was similar to the one at his own house that illuminated the front walk, nothing special or tricky about it. The walk at home was made of interlocked brick, whereas this one was made of fieldstone and led up to a house that could have doubled for Cat's Eye Corner. In fact, it would *have* to double to be truly like Cat's Eye Corner, for it was only half there. It wasn't the first time that Olivier had encountered a replica of Sylvia's place, but this one was the strangest yet. It had been sliced right down the middle like an enormous cake, and only half of the usual front steps led up to half the front door, upon which appeared only half of the lion doorknocker. *Halfway There*, Max had said when Olivier asked him where the witch lived, and it was beginning to make sense. *Some sense, not a lot!*

On the other side of the front walk opposite the post lantern was a purple mailbox, upon which the following appeared in silvery letters: Miss Mayhap's Academy for the Undecided.

The witch ran a private school? Leaning up against the mailbox was a very large letter, too large to fit inside, and Olivier crouched down to have a look at it. Beyond its size, it seemed to be a regular letter and was addressed simply to "Betty." The stamp affixed to it depicted a man with a long head and a wide grin, some figure of importance in these parts, Olivier supposed. He considered picking up the letter (picking up the mail in this case might require some effort), as it could offer a diversion once inside. While the witch was reading her mail, he could read the situation. (If this letter *was* intended for her, and not a student named Betty.) He could use it as a shield if things got dicey, or inflict a few paper cuts with it. *Feeble*, he told himself, and continued up the fieldstone walk without it.

He was about to ascend the half-steps to the front door, then veered left instead, deciding go around to the side of the house. Surely the witch knew he was here, but in case she didn't, he might as well see what he could find out by doing some snooping. The front of the house was dark, except for a weak light in the front window, but near the back, where the kitchen would be at Sylvia's place (unless it was on vacation!), the window was brightly illuminated and casting a warm, yellowish glow onto the grass outside. Olivier edged up to it and peeked in. It *was* the kitchen, and very like the kitchen at Cat's Eye Corner, only bigger, and decorated differently, except for the cat clock on the wall. These details Olivier took more note of later, because at the moment he was transfixed by the social scene within. Everyone was there! Sylvan, Linnet ... (*groan*) Alvis ... and (*hooray*) Murray!

Murray was on the table, reclining on a plush, red velvet tea cozy, and beside him was a champagne flute, half-filled with a sparkling light blue ink. He was *safe* ... or so Olivier dearly hoped. He was immensely relieved to see everyone, but his friends were obviously enchanted, under some terrible spell. They were chatting and laughing and having what looked like a fabulous time. Impossible. If they were being their usual selves, they'd be worried sick about him, discussing how to find him, or out searching for him. It had to be magic. Even Alvis wore a contented smile on his face as he munched his way through a platter of eggshells, watermelon rinds and hulled pea pods. The only thing that didn't look cheerful was a bread pudding that sat in the middle of the table. It bulged out of its bowl, two raisins stuck in its puffy bulk, like eyes. Weirdly, it seemed to be staring right through the window at him, and it wore a remarkably baleful expression for a pudding.

The witch was at the counter, busily preparing ... what?

Likely some vile, vaporous potion. Her back was to him, so he couldn't really tell, but something about her ... her clothes, her shoes, *something* struck him as being familiar. When she turned around, she was holding not a potion, but a lopsided layer cake slathered with slapdash wavelets of icing (one half of the cake was vanilla, the other half chocolate), and he realized with a shock that she was the tall woman who had been at Sylvia's yard sale. *Her*, a witch?! *But ...* he thought in confusion, *she was the one who had told him about Fathom's call, and she had helped him escape from that irate Professor Blank.*

If Olivier hadn't been so surprised by this discovery, he would have ducked below the sill to buy a little thinking time. As it was, though, his face was hovering in the window in full view, and as the tall woman approached the table with the cake, she caught sight of him.

"Max!" she said. Then, "No, dear me, it's not Max. I believe it's Olivier. So it is! Come in, dear, come in," she spoke up so that he could hear, addressing him through the glass. "You poor boy, you must be starved." She held up the cake as if to entice him in.

"Olivier!" exclaimed Linnet, and both she and Sylvan jumped up from the table and waved him in.

There was nothing for it — he *had* to go in now. Nothing could have stopped him at this point anyway, for not only was he thrilled to see his friends, but it was clear they needed his help. If this was a trap, they'd lost sight of it, and he was determined not to let that happen to him. He gave them a wave and walked around back in search of the kitchen door.

When he entered, a clamour of voices greeted him.

"Geez, Olivier, what took you so long?" asked Sylvan.

"You look beat," said Linnet. "What happened to your clothes? Did you have a growth spurt or something?"

"Whew," Alvis pinched his nose with two stubby fingers. "What a stench. Deodorant. I can't stand that smell."

"Glup!" added the bread pudding.

"But where on earth is Max?" asked the tall woman, setting the cake down beside the pudding. The pudding seemed to find this insulting, for it began to bubble and steam. "Please do have a seat, Olivier. My name is Betty, by the way, Betty Mayhap, although sometimes it's Nightingale, Margarita Nightingale, isn't that swish? I only use *that* name when I get dressed up and go out on the town. We didn't meet properly last time, did we? Did you like my poncy act? I'm not really that stuffy, you know. It was a perfectly lovely yard sale, I only wish … but, where *is* Max? He's such a scatterbrain, his mind does tend to wander. Unless … he got caught in a brainstorm. He was *supposed* to accompany you here. Don't tell me you came all by yourself!"

"I did," said Olivier.

"I *told* you." Linnet turned on Sylvan. "I knew something wasn't right. Gosh, Olivier, we should have been out looking for you. We've been here for ages."

"I thought you were in good hands," shrugged Sylvan.

"You obviously haven't met Max," Olivier said. "That's okay, I'm here now." He couldn't help but think his friend *could* have been a tad more concerned, but Sylvan was just being his logical self. "Oh man, it's so good to see you guys."

"Sit down, sit down," ordered Betty. "I'll bring you a bowl of soup and some homemade bread. We'll wait and have our dessert when you're ready. You poor thing, tell us all about it, what a brave lad you are. Here, you look shivery." Betty draped her black, feathery shawl over Olivier's shoulders, and patted his arm kindly. "Mercy me, I do hope Max hasn't gotten himself into a fix. He needs sufficient head room, you know. Only last week he got wedged in some branches and I had to take a pole out into the forest and give him a brisk clip on the chin to dislodge him. He wasn't pleased at all ... he can be a bit of a hothead."

"Who *is* this Max person?" asked Linnet.

"You wouldn't believe me if I told you," Olivier said, pulling the shawl tighter — it was wonderfully warm and soft. He sat down at the table, taking a chair that was the closest to Murray. He so much wanted to reach out and scoop Murray up and have a happy, chatty reunion, but he also didn't want to disturb him. For the moment, he was content to be near him.

When Betty slid a steaming bowl of savoury vegetable soup under his nose, along with a plate heaped with buttery slices of bread and thick wedges of cheddar cheese, Olivier thought he was going to faint with longing. The food smelled fantastic and he was famished. His friends honestly didn't seem to have been poisoned or enchanted for having eaten it.

"What's wrong, dear?" said Betty. "Should we tackle the cake first?"

"It's only that ... " Olivier toyed with his spoon, catching sight of his own reflection in its bowl. *Go on*, his reflected self seemed to say, *spit it out*. "Max said you were a witch."

"Did he? *Bah*, his head is full of nonsense. I'm a librarian, retired. Does this look like a witch's kitchen?" Betty extended her hand toward the sink, and several dishes hopped out of the sudsy water and slotted themselves into the drying rack. "Don't mind them, they do that all the time. That soap is much too slippy. Must change my brand."

"Right," said Olivier, digging into the soup. A *bad* witch probably wouldn't bother to do the dishes, he reasoned.

"So fill me in," he said to his friends. "While I fill me *up*."

"Yeah, eat," encouraged Sylvan. "We want to get at that cake." He then proceeded to tell Olivier about crawling through the break in the fence, after Olivier had zoomed away on the doormat. ("That must have been *some* ride.") He and Linnet decided to look for Murray first, and it wasn't long at all before they found him stuck like an arrow in a birch tree.

"Is he *okay*?" asked Olivier, glancing at his pen pal.

"Fortunately, birch wood is softer than some. His nib's a bit out of joint, but Betty has been giving him the royal treatment, as you can see."

"That's when we heard those guards coming, shouting for us to stop," said Linnet. "Somebody must have seen us leaving. That sorehead Thrud, maybe." Linnet smiled, "Plunger- head, I mean. Anyway, we took off, running like anything, and they almost had us. But then Betty just sort of *appeared*. She climbed down from a big poplar tree and motioned us to follow her."

"Happenstance. I was hunting for beetle larvae," said Betty, taking a seat at the table. "Lovely on toast. Not bad on ice cream, either."

The children all grimaced. Not one of them had been able to face ice cream after their last adventure, let alone ice cream with beetle larvae on it.

"Wasn't that awfully far from your place?" asked Olivier.

"I know a shortcut, dear."

"Does she ever," said Sylvan. "We were here in no time."

"I bet," said Olivier. "How about you?" He then turned to Alvis, while finishing off the last bite of cheddar. "Hope you haven't turned anyone into cheese lately," he added.

"Very funny," said Alvis. He had several watermelon seeds stuck on his face, which *was* funny.

"Betty rescued him, too," said Sylvan.

"Did not!" Alvis protested.

"Don't be a doofus. That carpet would have been the end of you, and you know it, if Betty hadn't stopped it and unthawed your grip. The thing was orbiting the house here and Alvis was screaming his head off."

"Thought it was Max," said Betty.

"I was not!" countered Alvis.

"Where is it now?" Olivier said, thinking, *My* carpet.

"The naughty thing flew off somewhere," Betty waved her hand. As she did so, a cake server flew off the counter and landed on her palm. She stared at it for a moment with mild surprise, then continued. "Yes, that rascally carpet. I could tell it had some feral threads woven into it when I examined it at your yard sale. I bought the water alarm clock, by the way, Olivier. Marvellous, what a time-saver. I don't have to wash my face when I get up in the morning. I hit the alarm and *whooosh*."

"Betty, how did you get to my step-step-stepgramma's place, anyway? And what was going on with that Professor Blank?" Once he'd gotten started, Olivier realized that he had about a hundred questions to ask his genial, but somewhat mysterious hostess. Such as, *Where is the other half of your house?* And, *Why does it resemble Cat's Eye Corner?* And, *If this is a school, where are the students?*

"Dear, why don't you tell us about your adventures first, while I serve out the cake. Unless … would anyone care for some bread pudding? It's one of my specialties."

"NO THANKS, BETTY!!!" they chorused.

"I *was* going to make a marble cake, but I seem to be fresh out of them. Marbles, that is." She began to serve out thick, wobbly slices of chocolate *and* vanilla cake to every-one. Two fat slices each. "Go on, Olivier, we're all ears. No, wait, I take that back! Let's just say we're all listening." She muttered to herself, "*All* ears, wouldn't that be a sight?"

So, between mouthfuls of super-delicious cake, Olivier described his crazy ride on the doormat, how it ended, and about waiting for them by the tree. Then he told them about meeting Max, the Horseless Headman.

"*Gross*," said Linnet.

He described Alvis shrieking past, unable to control the carpet.

"Not *true!*"

He told them about wandering through the forest, and about the unnatural rain and the Screaming Mimis.

"*Tsk*. Very worrisome," said Betty. "How do you know what they're called, dear?"

"I met a babbling brook, I mean it *talked*, and was really helpful, giving me directions and everything."

"A talking *what*?" said Linnet. "Are you feeling all right, Olivier?"

"I'm fine." He pulled the shawl closer around him, mostly because he could feel his shrunken pants starting to give way at the seams. Too much cake. "There were all these scary noises in the forest."

"Oops, my fault," said Betty. "It's a little system I have set up to discourage intruders. Same with the signs posted on the trees. I have electronic devices and whatnot installed. The moving light, did you find it maddening? All very up-to-date and scientific."

Electronic? Scientific? Olivier doubted it. "Was that wild man there to scare off intruders, too?"

"Wild man? What did he look like?" she asked.

"A hairball with legs."

"Heavens, that would be a Hairy Conniption. There's been a plague of them in the forest lately. Such irritable fellows, never satisfied, always complaining. But then, these are troubling times." Betty sighed and did look troubled. "Well, we won't let it ruin our dessert."

The bread pudding sighed, too, and sank lower in its bowl. Possibly it had been wanting the other dessert ruined.

"Say, I almost forgot," said Olivier, hoping this might cheer her up. "You have a letter out front by your mailbox. A very large letter."

"Why, marvellous. That would be from Heath."

"Heath?"

"Yes, you'll like him. He's a giant."

"A *giant*?"

"Mmm. Heath Magnusson-Whittier-Throxmorton Jr. Only a young giant, but he's making quite a name for himself. Perhaps you've heard of him?"

Olivier shook his head.

So did Sylvan, but for a different reason. "That's an awfully *big* name for a giant. Usually they're called Throp, or Glop, or …"

"Glup," went the pudding.

"Yeah, or Glup. Names to match their brainpower."

"But, Sylvan," said Betty. "Heath is an intellectual giant."

At this, Sylvan laughed dismissively. "No such creature."

"Don't be too hasty to judge. You can decide for yourself when you meet him."

"A *giant* is coming here?" said Linnet. "First, I'm supposed to get *my* head around the idea of a talking head, then a babbling brook, and now a *giant*?"

"Yes, I trust that's what his letter is about," said Betty. "We, all of us, have some important matters to discuss when Heath arrives. But at present, children, I'm going to put the kettle on for tea. Would you like green tea, black tea, pink tea or purple tea with orange spots? Think about it, will you, while I nip out and collect my mail."

One minute Betty was rising from her chair, and the next she was gone. No one had seen her do it, but the kettle was on the hob and starting to hiss and pop as it heated up.

Olivier was thinking less about what kind of tea he wanted than about these "important matters" they were to discuss. "I wonder what's up?"

"A giant, that's what," said Linnet.

"Yeah, an *intellectual* giant," sneered Sylvan (which he never usually did, and it wasn't at all becoming). "Sounds like an oxy*moron* to me."

"Wait." Now Olivier *was* thinking about tea. "Betty will want to use the tea cozy, right? So it's wakey-wakey, Murray! Rise and shine." He struggled to retrieve the notebook that was wedged in his pants pocket, and lifting Murray up, he then positioned him over the page, ready to write. Murray felt surprisingly cool, and Olivier certainly didn't get the reception he was expecting.

Soooo, it's YOU is it? Murray was giving him the cold shoulder (though strictly speaking, like Max, he didn't have one to give), and was so indignant he could scarcely write. Although he managed. *If it isn't my erstwhile and former and so-called friend. Where were YOU when I needed you, eh? EH? Too busy following your own nose, galumphing off into the sunset, leaving me behind in the dust and mud and slop! Poor little ME, lost, alone! THEN almost trodden on by Dopey there. Or is it Grumpy?*

"Does he mean *me*?" said Alvis, who'd been sneaking a peek at Olivier's notebook. "That stuck-up piece of junk is lucky I found him."

And if that wasn't horrific enough, that hideous troll friend of his practically crushed the life out of me!!

"What troll?" said Alvis. "Thrud?! *My* Thrud? Huh! He's got a point there."

Of course I've got a point, melon-face! I'm a pen!! A MOST distinguished one. I hail from a long, well-connected line, and I can write one, too. But as for you, Olivier, I'm not writing YOU another word!

This announcement was followed by several hundred words, many of which were not very nice words, either.

Linnet and Sylvan both gave Olivier looks of sympathy and encouragement, as if to say, "Never mind, he'll get over it once he's gotten it out of his system."

Murray didn't, though, and he kept on ranting about the injustices he'd suffered and the danger he'd been in after falling out of Olivier's pocket on the way to the Carpet Knight's heap. The more he raged, the more sorry he felt for himself, until finally he got so worked up that he began to talk himself silly.

Woe is))) me!) ((Dear (oh dear oh)()()((I ((don't)))feel so)))) hot ...

Betty re-entered the kitchen, wheeling her mail in on a dolly, and happened to glance at the notebook.

"Mercy!" she said. "He's not well. Not well at all. I don't believe I've ever seen such a bad case before."

"Case of *what*?" said Olivier, aghast.

"Parenthesitis, dear." Then she added, "It's not *usually* fatal, *if* one catches it in time."

Twelve

"Will it *work*?"

Olivier was pacing around the kitchen, too fidgety and anxious to sit still. He pulled Betty's shawl tightly around himself as he paced.

"I'm afraid we'll have to wait and see, dear," she said.

Murray was stretched out on an oblong butter dish, encased in a poultice that Betty had concocted. It resembled a mucky, edible sleeping bag made of flour, mustard, herbs and who knows what else (edible for Alvis, maybe). Only Murray's nib was visible, its usual bright gold tarnished and dull with illness.

"Good thing he didn't fall into a *comma*," Alvis said, grinning. "Maybe he got caught in a second *draft*. Hey, you should give him some *pen*icillin. Or put him in a holding *pen*. Better yet ... a *pen*itentiary." He was on a roll. "Give him a life *sentence*, eh? Get it?" He glanced at Linnet to see if she was impressed by his wit.

She wasn't.

"Actually, I'm going to put him in the larder," said Betty. "He needs peace and quiet."

And a painless, punless environment, she might have added.

"Yeah, clam up, Alvis," said Olivier. "This isn't funny, you know."

"All this fuss over a stupid pen," Alvis grumbled, flicking a watermelon seed at the bread pudding.

"GLUB!" The seed stuck to the pudding's side, but not for long. The pudding sucked itself in as if it were deflating, then sharply puffed itself back out, sending the seed zinging back to Alvis. It bounced off his nose.

"Watch it! *Stupid* pudding."

"Smarter than you," said Sylvan.

"Everyone, *hush*. I believe we have company," said Betty.

They all fell silent and strained to listen, hearing only the *tick-tock* of the cat clock and the soft, insistent sound of a moth batting against the window ... and then, the sound of footsteps approaching. A very large sound, which was followed by a booming knock on the kitchen door.

Betty hurried over to open it. "*Heath*, you made it. What a relief, come in, dear, watch the door frame there. Heavens, I am *so* glad to see you."

The children didn't know if *they* were all that glad to see a pair of extra-large hands grabbing the door frame and giving it a stretch, as one might stretch the too-tight neck of a sweater before putting it on. They watched with appalled fascination as a foot — fashionably shod in polished, size 24 brogues — appeared over the threshold.

The giant was crouching down, stepping through, and then he was *in*.

There was a moment of awed silence, which Alvis broke, saying, "Hah! You're *not* so big."

"Regrettably true," agreed Heath, his voice deep and plummy. "I am the runt of the family. Lilliputian in comparison. Terribly sorry to disappoint you, my friend."

This unexpectedly polite response stymied Alvis, and he did clam up, silenced more by Heath's suave manner than his size.

Olivier himself was speechless, staring up at the new arrival. The room seemed to expand in order to accommodate him — he had a formidable presence, and not only because of his height. He seemed to radiate a benign power, and he didn't at all fit the image Olivier had of giants. So much for the ragged tunic belted with a length of rope, the bare callused feet, the filthy hair. Heath was clean-shaven, had a trendy haircut and stylish clothing — a lime-green linen suit with a darker green handkerchief folded neatly in his breast pocket and a matching silk tie with a beanstalk motif. He was also carrying a briefcase, which he set down while Betty made the introductions.

He greeted them all with a bow and a friendly word. Linnet's cheeks coloured, as he was very handsome, and it was a handsomeness writ large, you couldn't miss it. Sylvan, on the other hand, was regarding him with disdain, and repeated his own name when Betty introduced him, saying it more loudly, as if Heath were hard of hearing or too slow to catch it the first time.

"SYLVAN BLINK," he said. Then added, "Ph.D."

"Ah, yes. Heath Magnusson-Whittier-Throxmorton Jr.," responded the giant genially. "Ph.D., LL.D. *So* pleased to meet you."

"Yes, quite," said Sylvan, a bit sourly. And not to be outdone, added, "LL.D, Sc.D., M.L.S."

"D.D.S., D.Ed., M.B.A., Mus.D.," said Heath.

"D.D.S., D.Ed., M.B.A., Mus.D, *MD*!" trumped Sylvan.

"Boys, boys," interrupted Betty. "Let's save the duelling doctorates for later, shall we. I suggest we retire to the library and have our tea there." She already had a laden, rattling tea tray in hand. "Have you eaten, Heath? I have some lovely vegetable soup ..."

"I have, Betty, thank you." Heath picked up his brief-case and smiled warmly at his friend as he extended his hand in an *after-you* gesture.

"Heath is a vegan," she explained to the others as they followed her out of the kitchen.

"So am I!" said Sylvan, who, as far as Olivier knew, was no such thing.

The library was an attractive room, cozily furnished with squashy-looking armchairs and a big couch, a field-stone fireplace, paintings, candles, and shelves and shelves of books, some with intriguing bindings. One book, with the title **GRRRRRR** running along its spine, was covered entirely in black fur, another on the subject of dermatology had a bumpy red rash crawling all over it (Olivier was keeping his distance from that one in case it was contagious), and yet another, a cookbook, appeared to have been baked, for its binding was crispy and nicely browned — and still warm, Olivier noticed, when he touched it lightly. Sylvia's *Enquire Within Upon Everything* must have come from such a library as this, he thought.

The room was a little *too* cozy for Heath. He promptly remedied that, though, by doing a little hands-on, instant renovating. Reaching up, he pushed the ceiling upward a good arm's length, and did the same to a couple of the walls. Olivier thought he might try this himself later to see if the house was as rubbery and malleable as it seemed.

"Hope you don't mind, Betty," the giant murmured.

"Not at all, Heath, make yourself comfortable. Everyone, do have a seat. Sylvan, dear, would you be so kind as to light the fire while I pour the tea?"

"*Yeah*, sure." Then he added, more graciously, "My pleasure." He knelt down by the hearth and began wadding up sheets of newspaper and checking the kindling supply.

"I'm so glad you're attending to it," said Heath, as he lowered himself into a super-duper-sized chair that was obviously meant for him. "I'm hopeless at that sort of thing."

Hearing this, Sylvan went to work with a concentrated effort, and ended up building a terrific, roaring fire that everyone — except Alvis — gazed at with admiration. It snapped vigorously, shot out sparks like glowing handfuls of jewels (fortunately, there was a firescreen), and even smelled sweetly fragrant, as the wood he'd selected from the log pile was apple. Sylvan himself stood admiring the fire for a moment, then slipped into a chair beside Heath, whereupon they immediately fell into conversation about thermonuclear dynamics, string theory and how to make the perfect risotto.

Betty served the tea, which turned out to be a somewhat confused colour, like a psychedelic Scottish tartan, since everyone had requested a different kind. When Olivier received his cup, he saw that the tea was even more curious than that. It was very unsettled for a drink, swirling around in the cup and splashing up against the sides.

"Tsk," said Betty. "I must have stirred it too much." She gave the teapot a reproving look. "I believe we have a tempest brewing in there." Sure enough, muffled, stormy sounds were issuing from the pot and drips of tea were flying out of its spout.

"The only place you'll find one these days," said Heath, taking a sip. He was holding his own large cup like a demitasse of espresso. "*Most* refreshing."

Olivier hazarded a sip, too, taking care not to get splashed in the face, and found that it *was* refreshing. It tingled on the way down his throat like an effervescent mint tea, and somehow made him feel as if he were standing at the edge of a lake facing a bracing wind.

Linnet was about to try it, but then carefully set her cup down, and said, "Why? Why is the teapot the only place you'll find a tempest?"

Heath set down his own cup and glanced at Betty. She gave him a quick nod, and he said, "It's against the law, Linnet."

"What? Tempests?"

"Yes, tempests, squalls, gales, typhoons, extreme and unruly winds of any kind."

"But that's ... nuts," she said. "It's impossible. No one controls the weather, the winds."

"You did," said Heath, gently.

"*Did*, yeah." Linnet kicked the leg of the coffee table and it gave a soft groan of dismay. "Only, I didn't, really. I mean, it was more … friendly than that. Control isn't the right word for it."

"So *that's* what the Department of Air Control Systems and all the rest of it is about?" said Sylvan.

"That and more." Heath turned again to Betty. "Did you receive my letter?"

"Oh drat, I *did*, but in all the excitement, I set it aside."

"No matter. I found out a few things, but didn't want to say much in the letter in case it was intercepted. What excitement might that be?"

Betty filled the giant in on Murray and his condition ("Parenthesitis!" he frowned "Dear, oh dear."), and then went on to tell him about some of the children's travels, and in particular about Olivier's trek through the forest.

"That rain?" said Olivier, shifting uncomfortably in his constricting clothing.

Heath nodded. "Fake. Harmful, obviously, if it shrank your clothes, and potentially lethal if the formula is tweaked, more acid or solvents added to it."

"Or deodorant," complained Alvis.

"But *who* is doing this?" said Olivier. "It's crazy."

"And how are they doing it, and why? All good questions, and yes, it is crazy. Mad, in a very well-disguised way. Betty and I can supply at least some of the answers, but not all, I'm sorry to say." Heath rubbed his chin thoughtfully. "Linnet, when you were a child do you remember hearing stories about those old duffers, the wind gods?"

"Er, I am a child, Heath."

"Right, goodness! I suppose I meant a much younger child. I was thinking of myself as a boy, sitting on my grandmother's knee — "

"Broke her legs, I bet," said Alvis.

Heath paused for a beat, then continued, " ... *sitting on my grandmother's knee* listening to tales about them, the wind deities. Of course, no one believes in that sort of thing anymore."

"Boreas, Notus, Eurus," said Linnet. "And Zephyrus, my favourite. I loved hearing those stories, and *I* believed them. Still do, sort of."

"Don't say it too loudly, then. That's also against the law. Look, it's like this ... a short while back, a new government came into power in this corner of the world. The leader is a man named Sleek, although he calls himself The Facilitator, and it's been his mission to normalize everything."

"Huh?" said Sylvan. Not his most eloquent statement, but it neatly summed up the general feeling.

They all leaned forward to listen, except for Alvis, who leaned forward to kick the table, trying to make it groan again.

"He was elected 'fair and square,' as he says, on a platform of promoting clean streets, decent wages, plain speaking, sensible clothing ... everything in moderation."

"That sounds all right," said Olivier.

"It *does*," said Betty. "But moderation is best in moderation, dear."

"I guess."

"His reforms started out well enough," said Heath. "People were happy with the way things were going, but not *too* happy. That wasn't allowed. Then more and more laws were codified and a police force was established to enforce them. Locally they're called the Control Freaks."

"Fireworks are a no-no," said Betty, with a sigh. "Ditto chocolate pie, big hair and nonsense poetry. We're not permitted to stay up late, have second helpings or even second thoughts. Indecision is considered a very bad thing by the administration, and my Academy for the Undecided has been closed. I don't suppose you noticed, but my house was so vexed that half of it left in a huff."

"Ah," said Olivier. "I wondered about that."

"The only insects that aren't being sprayed into extinction these days are humbugs. You know the kind, they alight on your shoulder or crawl into your ear and hum the most appalling muzak!"

"Dreadful," agreed Olivier.

"What do these Control Freaks do if you break the law?" asked Sylvan.

"Lawbreakers are sent to a 'finishing' school in Nohow Town where they learn how to toe the line," said Heath. "In Facilitator-speak, they're 'processed.' Some people disappear altogether. I suspect that the ancient temple up on the mountain is being used as a prison of some kind. Linnet, it's interesting that you should mention Zephyrus. The temple was supposed to be an actual haunt of his."

"I know, I've heard about it. Zephyrus got fed up living in that cave in Thrace with his brother Boreas, who's a real slob."

"Okay, so this guy is a tyrant," said Olivier. "But an *ordinary* one, isn't he?"

"Or a tyrant of the ordinary," said Betty.

"I mean, he doesn't have special powers, does he? I don't see how he can control the weather?"

"Nor do we," Betty replied. "That's why you're here. To help us find out."

"Oh?"

Linnet spoke up, "He's *not* a diviner, but he sent that windstorm, right? The wind that stole my own powers and my whiffs. Yet, aren't rough winds supposed to be against the law?"

"He makes the rules, Linnet, but he doesn't obey them himself," said Heath. "He's above all that. Take his house in Nohow Town, for example. It's a model of restraint and simplicity, minimal decoration, contains very few possessions. Every citizen is expected to do likewise. Simplicity is commendable, can't argue with that (and no one does). But everyone is encouraged to buy things to help the economy, and then, by law, they are required to throw out whatever they may have bought a couple of weeks before to make room for the new purchases. A modest balance has to be maintained. What happens to these things? They're collected and sent to a recycling facility, so-called. I suspect that they're simply diverted to Sleek himself. Somewhere, he has a colossal hoard of confiscated goods and treasures."

"My flute," said Sylvan. "My new lacquered pen."

"Indeed," nodded Heath. "He wants it all."

"Ouch! Your vicious table stepped on my foot," exclaimed Alvis.

"Don't be silly," tutted Betty, and with a barely concealed smile, turned to Olivier, "Your job here won't be easy, dear, because Sleek has a particular interest in you."

"*Me*? I don't even know the guy."

"You met his agent at the yard sale."

"Professor Blank?"

"That's right, and he gave you his card. Why don't you get it out and we can try to decipher what it says."

Olivier dug down, pulled the crumpled card out of his pocket and flattened it out before handing it to Betty.

"Perfect," she said. "Let's see if this works." She clamped an edge of the card with the sugar tongs, raised the lid of the teapot (a tiny roar of wind gusted out) and dipped it in. After swishing it around in the tea, she took it out and gave it a shake, then set it on the table. Everyone stared at the card as it turned a creepy, blood red colour, and watched closely to see if anything else would happen. Gradually, *it did*. Letters and words slowly began to appear in a black gothic script, until finally the whole thing was readable:

Professor Carnifex Blank
Executions, Hangings, Limb Removal Service
No Muss, Some Fuss (depending on victim)
Tel: 000-0000
(Don't call 911. It's too late!)
Eeeeeee-mail: cblank@yrtoast.ha

"Hmph, it's only his business card," said Heath, turning the card over. "Wait, what's this?"

On the other side of the card, in Blank's own hand-writing presumably, were the words,

This is the ONE.

"He's marked you, Olivier. By carrying this card, you're incriminating yourself. If the Control Freaks stop you and do a search ..."

"Let's burn it," said Linnet, snatching the card up and hurrying over to the fireplace.

"Good idea."

"Toss it in."

"Go ahead, do it, Linnet."

Linnet threw the card into the fire, where it landed on a burning log and began to sizzle like a slice of bologna in a frying pan. It smoked, belched, popped and finally turned black, curled up and disintegrated into ash, although it left behind a nasty smell in the library, like burned hair.

"Peachy," said Alvis, taking a deep breath, while the others were screwing up their faces in disgust.

"I don't get it," said Olivier, feeling distinctly uncomfortable, and it wasn't from the stink in the room or his shrunken clothing. "How do they know about me? What's it supposed to mean that I'm the *one*?"

Heath flipped open his briefcase and pulled out a poster, which he held up for everyone to see. Depicted in pen and ink was a remarkable likeness of Olivier, and above the drawing were the words, **WANTED (but not much).** And below, it said,

If seen, report at once (proceed in an orderly and measured pace) to Facilitator Headquarters.

"Good heavens!" said Betty. "Where did you get it, Heath?"

"They're posted all over Nohow Town. I snuck in at night after curfew — or as the administration calls it, Beddy-Bye — and tore down as many as I could find."

"That's taking quite a chance!" She explained to the others, "No one is allowed to be taller than Sleek himself."

"But who's gonna stop a big lunk like you?" Alvis said to Heath. "You could punch them out, stomp on 'em, fix 'em for good."

"Not my style, Alvis. I'm working a different angle, brains not brawn, eh, and they do have some very inventive weaponry at their disposal. Blank is involved in developing that, as well, I understand. But Olivier, sorry, I know this poster doesn't answer your question."

"It does say that I'm not wanted *much*." There was a glimmer of hope in his voice.

"Oh, they want you, all right, but can't sound too eager about it. That would be setting a bad example. *Why* they want you, I'll get to in a minute, if you'll bear with me. Sylvan, you said something about losing a pen."

"Yes, a Japanese lacquered pen. You know the makie technique?"

"A design using sprinkled coloured powder? Inlays of iridescent shell?"

"That's right. Her barrel's decorated with a sky dragon done in gorgeous colours — red, blue, green — and the dragon is shown soaring through a golden cloud clutching a *tama*, a sacred pearl. She vanished during that windstorm. You really think this Sleek guy has her?"

"Undoubtedly. He collects pens, secretly and probably as an investment. How do I know? Let's just say a little bird told me. Because of this hobby of his, he's managed to get his hands on an extremely rare fountain pen called a Sibyl. You're all acquainted with a remarkable pen yourselves, so I don't think you'll find it beyond belief that this pen of his has prophesying powers. When you write with it, the Sibyl makes predictions, and it has warned Sleek about 'a stranger bearing a stone,' a stranger who stands to do him great harm."

"I ... I do *have* a stone," admitted Olivier.

"Good," smiled Heath. "I thought you might."

"But it's nothing special. I mean, look." Olivier produced the stone from his pocket and set it on the table.

"Hmm," Heath frowned. "True. Still, you never know. It could be a pantarbe, a touchstone, a *Lapis lineus* in disguise."

Olivier was thinking about these mysterious-sounding stones when the word "disguise" triggered another thought altogether. "Betty, you said that Professor Blank was looking for something that was wearing 'a coat of elemental brown.'"

"I did, yes. I figured you'd catch the reference."

"I didn't. Until now. It's from a poem, right?"

"Exactly so," she said, and began to recite:

> "How happy is the little Stone
> That rambles in the Road alone,
> And doesn't care about Careers
> And Exigencies never fears —

Whose Coat of elemental Brown
A passing Universe put on … "

Olivier continued:

"And independent as the Sun,
Associates or glows alone,
Fulfilling absolute Decree
In casual simplicity — "

"Let's just say that a little brook told me that," he said
to his friends, who were gaping at him, nonplussed by this
unexpected talent of his. "A stone. That's what Blank was
looking for when he was digging through those fossils, and
then when that little girl gave me this one, he started to
chase me. I thought he was going to brain me with that
walking stick of his."

"He would have," said Betty.

"So *this* is it, what they're so worried about?" It was
indeed a humble little stone. "Hard to believe. What does
it do, do you think? How am I supposed to use it?"

"No idea, dear." Then she added, kindly, "But I'm sure
you'll know when the time comes. And speaking of time,
it's getting late. I for one could use some sleep. Why don't
we call it a night and put our heads together in the morning? We can decide what to do next, and … speaking of
heads, where *is* Max? He was supposed to join us."

"Max? Most likely he snagged his ponytail on a
branch," said Heath. "It's happened before. Don't worry,
Betty, I'll go out and have a look for him."

"*Would* you, while I show everyone to their rooms? I'd very much appreciate it, Heath."

That settled, they all rose and stretched, and said their goodnights to one another. All except Alvis, who claimed he needed a bedtime snack.

"You know where the garbage can is, help yourself," said Betty, gathering up her shawl from the chair where Olivier had left it. "Make sure you close the lid when you're finished. Your room is on the right, at the end of the hall."

Heath headed out the front door in search of Max, while Linnet followed behind Betty as she started up the stairs. Sylvan stayed behind briefly to choose a book. He always read something before going to sleep, and selected one with a plain cardboard cover called *I Think Therefore I Wrote This Book: An Exceedingly Long and Excruciatingly Detailed History of Modern Thought and This and That with Biographical Musings and Asides, Not to Mention a Complete Index, Extensive Footnotes, and a Few of Mummy's Favourite Recipes*. "Dead Boring!" screamed the blurb on the front cover.

"This should do the trick," said Sylvan.

"Yeah, I'd be sound asleep before I got halfway through the title," said Olivier.

He yawned as he grasped the banister and started up the stairs, and even though the evening's discussion had given him plenty to think *and* worry about, Olivier didn't expect that he would be awake much longer.

Well, he was certainly wrong about *that*.

Thirteen

After experimentally adjusting the walls, Olivier's room in Halfway There looked less like his room in Cat's Eye Corner than it did when he'd first entered it. Here was a curious feature of Betty's house: you gave a wall a firm push and it shoved off a short distance. It was like pushing a boat away from its mooring at a dock. The house was boat-like in other ways, too, in that he could feel it rocking as he lay in bed. He hadn't noticed this earlier in the evening and supposed the house rocked at night to help you sleep — not that it was helping him any. Linnet might enjoy it, reminding her of her boat at home, but he found it annoying. Everyone else was probably sleeping soundly in their rooms down the hall, while his own sleepiness had deserted him the moment he slid under the covers.

The bed itself was snug enough, as were the flannel pyjamas he'd discovered neatly folded under one of the pillows. He wondered if they had been left behind by one of Betty's former resident students (perhaps this student, advanced in Indecision Studies, couldn't decide whether or not to take them with him). Olivier hadn't worn pj's to bed for a couple of weeks and they felt great, especially after stripping off his own sorry, shrunken, smelly clothing. Before retiring, Betty had promised to find him some other clothes in the morning, and so he had emptied his pockets before climbing into bed, setting the inkwell that contained the invisible ink on top of the headboard (Sylvan still had the bottle of green ink), along with his notebook and money. His jeans had been baggy to start with, but it was still a relief to unload these things, especially the awkwardly shaped inkwell.

As he was settling in under the covers, he remembered the stone. *Crumb*, he'd left it downstairs in the library and wasn't much inclined to go back for it, either. He was leery about what this house got up to during the night (it seemed to be an even stranger house than Cat's Eye Corner, if that were possible). Not that anything was going to happen to the stone. This *was* Betty's place and most likely secured by some sort of magic, despite her pretending to be a retired librarian (not that one can't be both a librarian *and* a witch). It could wait until morning, he decided. As far as he was concerned, it could wait forever, since the stone only seemed to be bringing him the worst kind of attention.

Olivier shuddered, thinking of Professor Blank and his weird hat, but as Blank was not much of a sleep inducement, he sensibly put him out of mind. Instead, he started to count dachshunds jumping over hedges, and even though they were very low hedges the dogs kept getting stuck and barking with frustration. The next thing he knew he was thinking about Murray, who should have been beside him dreaming away on the next pillow instead of ailing in the larder, encased in a glop suit. He wished he'd brought a book upstairs, too, or had taken Betty up on her offer of a bath. Raising his arm, he pushed down the pyjama sleeve and looked at his inky blue hand and forearm, visible, if a bit ghostly, in the moonlight that was flowing through the window. Funny that it hadn't worn off or faded by now — the ink, not his hand. This made him think of a story he'd read about a severed hand that had crept up the wall of an old house during the night and in through the open window, scuttling along, over the bedclothes ... Olivier glanced nervously toward the window, which *was* open. *Stop it!* he told himself. *Go to sleep.* But he didn't. He began to wonder where Max was and if Heath was having any luck finding him. He listened for the giant's return, and heard only a bird singing its heart out somewhere deep in the forest. What kind of bird sings at night? What a pretty song it was, too, but unfamiliar, he'd never heard anything like it before. The bird kept repeating its song at intervals and he was attending closely, waiting for the next installment, when in the room he heard another sound. A *scratching* noise that was coming from the closet.

It so happened that this was a noise Olivier had become familiar with of late. But here? How could that be? He had already checked out the room before getting into bed, looking in all the corners, the bureau drawers, the wardrobe,

the headboard, the closet, even the waste-paper basket …
and all had been empty. (Curiosity, nosiness, caution, call
it what you will, Olivier was at least thorough.) There had
been another occasion at Cat's Eye Corner when he'd
heard such a noise at night and suspected that a rat might
be making it, but now he knew better. He hoped he did,
that is. Hopping out of bed, he tiptoed over to the closet,
hesitating only a second to listen again to the *scratch-scratching* before gripping the cold, marble knob and
pulling open the door.

What he expected to see was a cat, some shy or nervous
companion of Betty's who had not put in an appearance
at dinner. And he *did* see a cat, and a shy cat, too. But it was
a cat he knew — she was the smallest and most retiring
of the Cat's Eye Corner clowder.

"Emily? It *is* you, isn't it?" As she emerged out of the
closet, he bent down to give her head a light scrumble
with the tips of his fingers — she had silky mist-grey fur,
not as dark as Eliot's, except for the darker ring markings
on her tail. It *had* to be her. "What on earth are you doing
here? *How* did you get here?"

He didn't expect her to answer; cats never *did* humour
their friends in this way. Emily accepted his greeting,
purred briefly, then began to switch her tail back and forth
impatiently, signalling that this was a business call rather
than a social one. She moved toward the bedroom door,
and it was then that he noticed her limping. Her front paw
was hurt, and she was stepping on it gingerly.

"What happened, Emily? Was it that horrible Professor
Blank?" The last time Olivier had seen her, she'd had

a firm grip on the Professor's ankle.

She glanced up at him and her eyes, catching the light, flashed a luminous yellowy-green. She then turned her gaze to the door, and stood staring at it, waiting for him to do the honours. Which he did, and in a wink she was out in the hall and moving swiftly along it, despite her injury.

Olivier followed, as he knew he must. In the dimly lit hall — it was lit by a succession of bloodshot eyeball nightlights — he passed doors that were firmly closed, as they always were at Cat's Eye Corner, and others that stood ajar. One of the partially opened doors was Sylvan's, and in hurrying past it, Olivier heard his friend talking in his sleep. The snatch of speech that he caught was thick with consonants, and for all Olivier knew could have been Anglo Saxon (it was). He would have liked to listen to more, if only to tease Sylvan in the morning, but kept on, moving farther and farther down the hall — this *was* an elastic property — until finally Emily slowed down. Her slight feline figure melted into the shadows ... and a much larger figure stepped out of them.

"Sylvia!" he said, astonished. "Step-step-stepgramma?"

"Hello, Olivier," she said, pleasantly, as if they had met at midday in the hall at her place. "You know, I rather like that step-step-step business. It's fun, isn't it?"

"Am I dreaming?" This question was mostly directed at himself, since he couldn't quite believe what he was seeing.

"*Are* you?" she asked. "I *could* give you a pinch." Instead, to his relief, she reached up with a bandaged hand to pick a shred of papyrus out of her mussed-up hair.

"That wind! Honestly, I've been excavating items out of my hair for days. It's like an archeological dig." She tossed the papyrus onto the floor (Sylvia wasn't much for housework).

"What happened to your hand?" He was very surprised to see her left hand wrapped in a black bandage, with only three of her long fingers poking out.

"Oh *that*. I got into a bit of a scrap with that odious little man who was trying to break into the house."

"I hope you squashed him."

"Indeed. He's positively one-dimensional now. I put a stamp on him, you might say, and dropped him in the mailbox. I kept his hat, however. It makes a most cunning trash can."

This sounded too good to be true. "Are you sure this isn't a dream?"

"Hmm. I for one happen to be feeling particularly awake at the moment, not to mention real. How about you?"

Olivier shrugged. "The usual."

"Excellent. In that case, I have a message to deliver. You see, it wouldn't do if you were dreaming, and then woke up in the morning and couldn't remember it."

"What is it? This message, who's it from?"

"It's ... oh!" Sylvia's eyes widened. "The little *devil*," she exclaimed. "It will have to wait, Olivier. *Go*, hurry, you must *hurry*. There's a *rat* in the larder."

"A rat?" Then, "No!" he shouted, comprehending her meaning. He turned and bolted, running back along the hall to the top of the stairs, then he practically flew down them, almost taking a tumble. On the ground floor he peeled past the library and the front parlour, following the lower hall to the kitchen. He bounded over to the larder and hurled open the door. There was an ear-splitting *crash* as something fell to the floor and shattered, and at the same time a short figure, obscured by the dark, scrambled past him and out the kitchen door, which banged loudly as it shut. Olivier panicked, not sure whether to chase the intruder or check first to see if Murray had been harmed — or if he was still there!

His shout had roused the others and they weren't far behind.

"What is it, dear?" Betty was cinching her purple plaid bathrobe, curlers bouncing in her silver hair, as she hurried into the kitchen and flicked on the light. (Actually, all she did was snap her fingers and the room lit up.) "Goodness." She came up behind Olivier and peered into the larder. "My pickled mandrake." The crashing noise had been caused by a huge jar of preserves that had hit the floor.

"A rat," Olivier answered. "A *little* rat. I startled him and he must have knocked this off the shelf, or dropped it." He couldn't see Murray anywhere, so got down on his knees and began picking through the shards of glass and moving aside the plump, wobbly roots.

"Alvis?" asked Sylvan, rubbing the sleep out of his eyes and surveying the damage.

"Yeah, I'm pretty sure it was him. If Murray's hurt, or *gone*, I'll …"

"I'll *get* him," said Linnet, heading toward the door.

"No problem. I'll run like, ahh … like …"

"A girl?" said Sylvan.

Linnet flashed him a murderous look and then pushed through the kitchen door, slamming it shut behind her.

"Well, she *is*," Sylvan said sheepishly. "Maybe I'd better go help." He ran out the door, too.

"Careful with that glass," warned Betty. "There he is! Under that pile of elephant garlic. I always put lots of garlic in the mandrake pickle."

"Yes!" Olivier quickly brushed it aside, scrunching up his nose as he did so — the vinegary smell from the preserves was strong enough without the garlic. Murray lay fully exposed except for a few soggy bits of flour and some pickling spices that were sticking to him. The poultice, which had hardened during the course of the evening, had broken open like a cast when he hit the floor. Olivier lifted him up with extreme care in case something *in* him was broken, as well.

"Not to worry, the poultice will have cushioned his fall," said Betty, offering Olivier a damp cloth to tidy him up with. "He'll need a good restorative tonic and I have just the thing."

While Betty was preparing this, Olivier cleaned off the gunk and polished Murray on his pyjama sleeve. He spoke to him in a soothing, upbeat way, knowing that Murray would be highly indignant, even traumatized by the experience.

Betty set a sherry glass down on the table along with a blank sheet of paper. The glass was half-full of a concentrated black ink, thick as molasses. It was the blackest ink Olivier had ever seen, and when he slid Murray in, he was concerned that it might inspire in his friend an equally black mood. Even worse than the one inspired by his illness.

The drink didn't disagree in any event. Murray knocked it back with one big noisy slurp.

"My, I hope he doesn't get gas," said Betty.

"Euw. Me, too." said Olivier. "Do you think the parenthesitis will be cleared up?"

"Let's see, why don't we?"

Olivier raised Murray out of the glass and positioned him at the top of the paper that Betty had provided. He didn't know what to expect. His hand trembled slightly and he was holding his pen friend more slackly than usual. This normally might provoke Murray to say, *Get a Grip, eh, lad.* But Olivier didn't want to put him under any pressure, or make him suffer an undue amount of stress.

Woo-hoo! I'm baaack! Murray's script was bold and feathered with whimsical flourishes. *Scrivens, but didn't I just have the strangest dream. I dreamt I was an enchilada, of all things! Ándelay, ándelay! Arriba! Arriba! So what's new, what have I missed — besides you, lad? Tell me, who is your delightful companion, I don't believe we've met.*

Not only was Murray himself sparkling from the buffing he'd received, but his words sparkled as well. A big smile spread on Olivier's face. Murray was back to normal (normal for Murray, anyway). Betty was cheered, too, for it's always pleasant to be appreciated and called delightful. She introduced herself and they all chatted excitedly, giving Murray a sketchy update on what had been going on. For his part, Murray said that after he'd tumbled out of Olivier's pocket at The Heap and smacked into a broken coal scuttle, things had gone a bit fuzzy, his memory splattered with ink spots.

Bless me, but I recall being sharp with you, Olivier, my apologies, the old nib was clogged. I fell into a swoon and the next thing I know I'm in the larder impersonating a food item when that deranged elf sneaks in, grabs me off the shelf and drops me on the floor. Kersplat! Does anyone else smell garlic, by the way? You know, I have the strangest yearning for a Caesar salad.

"So it *was* Alvis, I thought so. He was going to steal you, Murray, but I got here in time, thanks to Sylvia. She warned me."

"Sylvia? Your step-step-step-step … ?" Betty lost count. "You must have been dreaming, dear."

"Only three steps. And no, it wasn't a dream, I'm sure of it."

"Ah, an undream. They're most convincing."

An *un*dream. This was a new one on Olivier, but before he could ask about it, Sylvan and Linnet arrived back in the kitchen, and with a noisy fanfare. They slammed the back door hard as they entered one after the other, and they were shouting.

"I did *not*," said Sylvan, clearly exasperated.

"You did *too*," countered Linnet.

"DID NOT!"

"DID TOO!"

Hello you two, here I am. It's me, your old pal Murray! I feel terrific. I am terrific!!

Linnet and Sylvan were too busy staring daggers at one another to notice Murray, even when he wrote a little louder, then a lot louder.

I bet you missed me. You were so worried about me, I know, I know. Ask me how I am now. Just ask, go on!

"OAF!"

"STUMBLEBUM!"

Excuse ME, but —

"DUMMY, KNUCKLEHEAD, PEABRAIN!" Linnet had been leaning on a waist-high stick, using it for support, but as she spoke she raised it and pointed it at Sylvan, jabbing it emphatically with each fresh insult.

Sylvan was growing very red in the face. If there was one thing he did not take kindly to, it was insults to his intelligence, and it looked as though he was about to whip the stick out of her hand and clout her with it.

"*Please*," said Betty. "Let's not bicker, you'll upset the house. Relax, take a deep breath and then tell us what's happened."

"Yeah, what's going on?" said Olivier. There was often tension between his friends, but it usually didn't erupt into outright argument and name-calling.

With the aid of the stick, Linnet limped over to a kitchen chair and sat down, scowling as she leaned the stick against the table, and then bent over to undo the laces on one of her shoes. "Ouch!"

"My dear, you've sprained your ankle." Betty immediately crouched down to help her ease the shoe off her right foot.

"It's Sylvan's fault."

"You're bats! I *said* I had nothing to do with it. You tripped and fell, simple as that."

"You pushed me."

"I wasn't anywhere near you."

"*Someone* did."

"Alvis?" said Olivier, trying to intervene. "Yikes, your foot's really swollen."

"Yeah, *ow*, and no to it being Alvis. He was ahead of me and I'd almost caught up to him. I called to him and, he likes me and everything, so I thought he might stop. That's when somebody bumped me from behind. My foot caught on a tree root and I took a real dive."

"Don't look at me," said Sylvan. "I got there after you went down. And a fat lot of thanks I get for helping you."

"Maybe it was that Hairy Conniption guy," suggested Olivier. "You must have seen something, Sylvan, if you were directly behind."

"No, nothing. I saw Linnet fall, but I didn't see anyone push her."

"You're blind, then," said Linnet. A liar, too, she might have added if Betty hadn't glanced at her and shaken her head, dissuading her from pursuing it any further.

For his part, Sylvan was convinced that Linnet was so accustomed to skimming swiftly along easy as the wind that she wouldn't admit to doing something as clumsy as tripping over a tree root. She had to blame someone for pushing her.

"The tree roots in this forest *are* rather active sometimes," admitted Betty. "On rare occasions wanderers have been entirely wrapped in roots and then plunged into the earth, never to be seen again. So consider yourself fortunate, both of you," she said brightly as she got up and walked over to her fridge. She dug around in her freezer for a bag of peas, which she then carried back to Linnet, applying it gently to her ankle, now as swollen and purple as Betty's bathrobe.

Linnet didn't feel fortunate. "How will I be able to travel to Nohow Town like *this*?" she said, miserably. "If only my winds, if only … *forget it*!"

"Has Heath returned?" asked Sylvan.

"Not yet," said Betty, plainly troubled by this.

Everyone fell to thinking their own thoughts, and the atmosphere in the kitchen grew gloomy and overcast with worry. Even the bread pudding seemed to be frowning, having developed a cascade of wrinkles as it sank deeply into its bowl. Olivier struggled to come up with something heartening to say, and then it struck him. "On the bright side, we *have* foiled Alvis, because Murray's safe, and Murray's recovered from his illness. Cause for celebration, I'd say."

"Oh, hi, Murray," said Linnet, with zero enthusiasm.

Everyone turned their gaze upon him.

Finally it was Murray's turn to receive his due, to get some well-deserved attention. The trouble was, he'd waited so long for someone to notice him that he'd fallen into a brown study, and when Olivier readied him to write, he moved as mechanically as a sleepwalker across the sheet of paper, saying in a dreamy, sepia-toned ink, *An enchilada, my word!*

Fourteen

The stone.

As soon as Sylvan said, *He didn't manage to steal Murray, but I wonder if he took anything else?* Olivier knew that Alvis had, and he knew *what*.

When the boys raced to the library, they saw that, sure enough, the stone was gone from the coffee table, which also happened to have powdery blue footprints leading up to and away from it. It was obvious that Alvis had also searched Heath's briefcase. Papers were strewn over the floor (mostly research papers, Sylvan confirmed) and oddly, a snowball was resting on the arm of Heath's chair. A snowball with a bite taken out of it.

"Alvis must have sampled it," said Olivier, touching the snowball to find out if it was real. It felt cold enough, but wasn't melting in the heat of the room.

"He also opened my letter from Heath," said Betty, entering the library with a large sheet of writing paper in hand. "Heath was wise in not revealing anything much in it. Although, as you know, even the weather can be a dangerous subject these days."

"The little wretch is a spy." Olivier sank onto the couch. "I knew he was up to something. This Sleek guy collects pens, right? That's why Alvis tried to take Murray. And if Sleek gets his hands on the stone, he'll be safe from … from *me*, I guess, and whatever it is I'm supposed to do with it."

"Let's go, then," said Sylvan. "We've got to nab Alvis before he gets to Nohow Town."

"It's the middle of the night," Betty reminded them. "You're also in the middle of a forest. You'd be lost the moment you stepped out the door, and there are those tree roots I mentioned. The forest is plainly disturbed at present, and dangerous. Besides, Linnet is in no condition to go anywhere."

"She can stay here with you," said Sylvan.

"No, I can't, and *won't*." Linnet had limped into the room with the help of her stick, which Olivier now looked at more closely, then more closely still.

"That's Professor Blank's," he said. "It's the staff he almost clouted me with." He looked at it again. "Wait a sec, maybe he was the one who knocked you down."

"He'd have to be so *blank* as to be invisible," said Sylvan.

Olivier thought about what Sylvia had said about stamping Blank and dropping him in the mailbox. If she'd been serious (and it was always hard to tell), surely he wouldn't have been able to follow them here? "Could be an identical staff, I suppose. Where did you find it, Linnet?"

"It was propped up against a tree. Sylvan found it for me." She cleared her throat. "Um, thanks, Syl. It's perfect. I can get around easily using it for support."

"No, you can't," chided Betty. "But if you're determined to go, I have an idea. Linnet, come with me, dear, I want to try something. In the meantime, you two run upstairs and get dressed. Olivier, you'll find a change of clothes laid out on the bed, best I can do on short notice, I'm afraid. Let's meet in the kitchen in, say, ten minutes."

"Got it."

Since Betty had been downstairs with them the whole time, Olivier didn't see how she could have set out clothes for him. Although if she did so by means of witchery, he also didn't see why she gave him *these* clothes. A little magic laundering would have been appreciated — they were filthy — and they could have used some tailoring as well. The jeans were what his mother called high-water pants, for the cuffs rose far above his ankles, and they were also ripped at the knees. Conversely, the shirt was big enough to fit his father, and might have qualified as a regular dad-shirt if it weren't for the smudges of mud and grease on it, and what looked like dried cake icing or ice cream all down the front where someone had wiped his hands. More student castoffs, but since there wasn't much choice, Olivier zipped, buttoned, rolled up his sleeves, filled his pockets with the objects he'd set on the headboard and ran downstairs to collect Murray. Sylvan was already in the kitchen, sipping coffee and munching on the scones that Betty had also set out.

"Not much sleep, but this helps."

"None for me," said Olivier. "Sleep, I mean. At least, I don't think so." He slid the snoozing Murray into his shirtfront pocket and helped himself to a scone.

Before long Linnet appeared with Betty directly behind her. Linnet was grinning and walking with scarcely any difficulty, although she was still using the staff. "Whoa, cool duds," she said, sliding into a chair beside Olivier.

"Yeah, eh." What really *was* cool was seeing Linnet in brighter spirits. "Is your ankle better!?"

"Betty fixed it with this ointment gunk she rubbed all over my foot. Smelled revolting, but it worked!"

"I only *improved* it," corrected Betty. "Linnet, you still have to go easy on it, which is why you'll have to travel by boat, rather than on foot."

"Sounds good to me. It'll be faster," said Olivier. "But it also sounds impossible. Like you said, Betty, we're in the middle of a forest."

"Not impossible, Olivier, but *very* tricky. Let me explain."

—•—

"I've caulked it as best I can," said Betty. She was standing on the bank of a stream she called Sly Creek and was handling a flashlight like a laser as she scrutinized the small rowboat in which the children were seated. She scanned every single seam and crevice of the boat. Finally satisfied, she handed the flashlight to Linnet.

Olivier was trying to be optimistic, trusting that Betty had given the boat a magical caulking, since it was clear they were going to need it. The waters they would be travelling over evidently had an attitude. "Sly Creek shouldn't be a problem," Betty had said while guiding them through the forest. "Only a bit of a nuisance."

"How so?" Olivier had asked. "Does it babble, too?"

"No, not that. Although it does make rude noises sometimes. Your best policy will be to ignore it. It's the lake you have to watch. Remember, be as quiet as you can crossing it. Don't say a word. If … *when* you get to the other side, you will have saved yourselves hours of trudging around it and you'll have a much better chance of catching Alvis."

If? Olivier definitely didn't like the sound of that *if*. "What's so bad about this lake?"

Betty hesitated. "It's unpredictable. It can get a tad, how shall we say, ahh, rough. But most of the time the lake is calm and perfectly safe. Keep that in mind, dear, and it will come to pass."

Sea monsters, Olivier thought. All the ones he had ever read about crowded into his head — Scylla and Charybdis, the kraken and remora, even Scotland's Nessie, along with other nameless, nightmarish creatures with serpentine necks and groping tentacles and teeth like knives. This was more what he was keeping in mind when they finally shoved off from the bank in Betty's rowboat and waved goodbye. The plan was that she would search for Heath and Max, and once assured of their safety, would meet the children in Nohow Town and help them do battle with the bureaucracy, along with some spying and intelligence gathering of their own. *If* they got there. Olivier was experienced enough in this adventuring business to know that there was a certain predictability to the unpredictable. If there was one thing they could count on in the journey ahead, he felt, it was trouble.

All went smoothly for the first twenty minutes or so. The boys were working the oars, while Linnet sat in the bow waiting for her turn to row and watching the scenery pass by. What she could see of it, for it was altered, night-time scenery, buried in darkness or touched with a faint wash of moonlight. Birches gleamed ghostly white, and along the bank, sedges and rushes formed tall, ragged clumps and willows rose up like wild-haired amazons.

"You know, this reminds me of riding in Sharon's boat," she said, shivering in the cool night air.

"On the River Stynx? No comparison," said Olivier.

Linnet turned and gazed thoughtfully at him. She had flicked off the flashlight earlier, and now turned it on again, letting the beam play over him.

"Hey, stop it."

"Maybe it reminds me of that because you're wearing Sharon's clothes."

"What!" Olivier glanced down at his shirt and jeans, and had to admit that he'd seen their like before when he and Linnet and another friend, not Sylvan, had travelled to an unsavoury ice cream factory and palace. A girl named Sharon had ferried them over.

"You're wearing *girls'* clothes?" Sylvan smiled.

"Sharon was wearing *boys'* clothes," said Linnet.

"And stop snickering."

"I'm not snickering," Sylvan was indignant. "I've never snickered in my life."

"C'mon you two, don't bicker," said Olivier. He *liked* that word. Bicker, it sounded like what it meant.

Linnet and Sylvan clammed up and all was silent, except for the oarlocks squeaking and the oars plashing in the water and the … snickering.

Olivier stopped rowing and peered around. Was it Alvis, hidden away in the dark, behind a rock or clump of reeds, making fun of them? Was it only the water lapping — but not *laughing* — against the boat?

"Okay, I give up. Who is it?" said Linnet.

"Seems to be a what, not a who," said Sylvan, looking over the side. "Uh-oh."

"What?"

"We're sinking. I mean, see, the water level is going down."

All three stared in disbelief as the creek's level swiftly diminished like water draining from a bathtub, and with all the accompanying sound effects. A few *glug glugs* and it was gone, leaving the boat mired in mud, along with a couple of wriggling sprats and an annoyed snapping turtle that was clacking its jaws angrily.

"Betty did say that this creek was a nuisance," offered Linnet, shining the flashlight in the turtle's eyes, which did not improve its temper any.

"Sly Creek, right enough," said Olivier. "What do we do now?"

"Sit here," said Sylvan. "Not much else we can do, is there?"

So they sat, glumly, anxious to be on their way, and also anxious about the snapping turtle, which was struggling through the mud toward them. Something below the boat — the turtle's unfortunate mate, perhaps — had begun to gnaw on the keel. About the same time as this, they heard a low roar in the distance, and the turtle hastily ducked its head into its shell.

"Here it comes!" said Sylvan, pulling in the oar.

Olivier wasn't as fast with his oar as Sylvan, and the sudden rush of water that tumbled and frothed along the creek bed caught it and snapped off the blade. He didn't have time to worry about it … the boat was instantly swept along, twisting and turning on the surge. Incredibly, they weren't capsized, although the flashlight flew overboard when Linnet let go of it to grab onto the gunwale. They were carried along a good distance before the water settled and began flowing along as before.

"Why is this called a *creek*?" said Linnet.

"The oar," Olivier groaned, gazing at what was left of it — a ragged-ended shaft. "My fault."

"Don't blame yourself, that happened so fast," said Sylvan. "After all, Linnet lost the flashlight."

"You would point that out, wouldn't you? But for your information, Sylvan, it *isn't* lost. See, it was washed along with us." Linnet was pointing at the submerged flashlight, still glowing under water. "All I have to do is reach down and … eek!"

When Linnet had plunged her hand into the creek to retrieve the flashlight it jerked away from her, and then began to circle the boat, the wavery beam of light pointing up at them. Once, twice, three times it went round. Nothing appeared to be holding it.

They looked at one another, more than a little unnerved, until Olivier spoke, "Ignore it, remember. It's only the creek acting up. We'll have to use the oars like poles. Let's keep going."

Sylvan nodded, then stood and struck his oar into the water. Olivier did likewise with his broken one, giving the boat a shove forward when the oar touched bottom. He felt like a Venetian gondolier, but not a very adept one because the boat kept switching directions on them. When they pushed it ahead it would swing back around, pointing to the way they had already come. Then after awhile, the boat refused to budge at all. The water itself seemed to have thickened like glue and both oars stood straight up in it, stuck fast.

"Brother, what next? And this is the *easy* part of our trip?" said Linnet.

Olivier plunked himself back down on the seat. "We could walk there faster, and skip the lake crossing altogether."

"Good idea. How's your ankle, Linnet?" asked Sylvan.

"Better, but I know that without catching any wind I couldn't jump as far as the bank." Very lightly, she touched the surface of the creek with her staff. When she raised it up, a viscous, stretchy gob of water came with it, stuck on the end. "Ick. I sure wouldn't want to fall in this stuff, either."

"So," Olivier concluded.

"So," Sylvan agreed with a sigh.

So … they sat and waited again. And sat and sat and sat and sat. Glued to the spot, the only drifting they did was into sleep. While the other two began to nod off where they were seated, Olivier finally curled up on the floor of the boat near the stern, using the lunch bag Betty had provided as a pillow. This wasn't such a bad thing. It had been a long night, and he was desperately tired. He dropped into sleep like a stone and sank to the very bottom.

Olivier was so profoundly asleep that he had difficulty rousing himself when he felt something soft and woolly brushing against his face. Then it was slapping his face, tickling his nose, chucking him on the chin. "Go away," he murmured, opening one eye only. What he saw with his one eye made him open the other one immediately. It was the *carpet*! But something terrible had happened to it, for it was tiny now, a dollhouse carpet, a mini-mat about the size of a chocolate bar. Olivier rubbed his eyes to make sure he was seeing straight, while it orbited his head and dove at him like a horsefly. The *rain*, he thought. That blasted rain shrank my carpet! His hand shot up to grab it and it evaded him, scooting aside. He tried again and missed. The carpet flew around and around, dipped down to skim lightly over his hair, then took off into the forest. Gone.

He was still staring after it, when he realized that the boat was moving. Glancing quickly overboard, he saw that the water was behaving like water again, except for some strange sounds it was making — rude, wet, raspberry noises and loud *hyuk, hyuk, hyuks* that woke Linnet.

"It's morning!" She stretched and yawned, then gave Sylvan a nudge with her uninjured foot. "Wake up. We're on our way."

"We're really on our way," said Olivier. The boat was picking up speed as the creek began to flow faster and faster.

Sylvan straightened and blinked groggily as he looked around. "The oars are gone, not that it matters. At the moment, anyway."

The little boat was zipping along more like a speed-boat than a rowboat.

"I guess Sly Creek is sick of us." Linnet was hanging onto the gunwales, beginning to enjoy the ride.

"The feeling's mutual," said Olivier, watching the forest thin as they entered a marshier stretch of land. They whipped past stands of osiers, then individual osiers, and then no osiers as the creek's banks began to widen. It was now more a full-bodied river than a creek, and soon they were at its mouth. (A big mouth, appropriately enough.)

They passed a lopsided, half-submerged sign with a legend on it that read: **YOU ARE ENTERING THE LAKE FINGERS TOURIST AREA. ENJOY!!**

"Fingers? What a funny name for a lake," said Linnet. "I wonder why it's called that?"

Olivier only sighed, and braced himself.

Fifteen

"We —" Sylvan began, but was instantly hushed by his friends.

Olivier mimed zipping his lips and Linnet shook her head strenuously, eyes wide with alarm.

Assuredly, *all* their eyes had widened with alarm after they had been launched onto the lake proper with a final, propelling shove from Sly Creek. With no oars and no wind, they were soon adrift and practically motionless. This gave them plenty of opportunity to silently observe the great number of wrecks piled up on the shore. Sailboats, skiffs, rafts and cabin cruisers — all had some-how come to grief on this lake, and their smashed remains — hulls, masts, jibs, keels — were scattered far and wide. It was a sobering sight and they were taking Betty's advice seriously — no talking.

Olivier wanted to tell the others about his carpet sighting, but that could wait. He also wanted to consult with Murray, but didn't dare in case his pen pal's nib squeaked while they were conversing. (*I do NOT squeak*, Murray would have insisted, as indignant as Sylvan had been about the snickering accusation.) Linnet longed to point out Nohow Town, the skyline of which was visible on the other side of Lake Fingers, and she particularly wanted to point out the Temple ruins that rested on the side of the mountain rising above the town. She restrained herself from doing this and instead ran her fingers lightly along the side of the boat, touching wood for luck … if *only* they could drift to the farther shore unnoticed by whatever it was in Lake Fingers that did the noticing — and the boat bashing.

For Sylvan, however, speaking was more of a habit and a need. He had so many thoughts and ideas percolating in his head that they were difficult to contain and tended to spill out uncontrollably. What he'd been going to say wasn't all that significant, though, more a combination of nervous chatter and second guessing: *We should have taken the long way around*. And all that he did say was *We,* which is such a small word, hardly a troublemaker, and yet …

Olivier had no sooner mimed zipping-his-lip than he heard that *splish splash* sound.

And again, *splish splash*.

He didn't think it was issuing from the inkwell in his pocket this time.

Then … a short distance beyond the boat a *hand* shot out of the water. A *blue* hand. It was slightly larger than an adult's hand and had long tapering fingers, which it wiggled a little. It quickly vanished, sinking back under the waterline. Then two more hands, identical to the first, appeared on the other side of the boat. They were smooth and blue and had no fingernails, only fingernail impressions. They wiggled and fluttered their fingers as the first had done, then also slipped back under. Then five more hands shot up out of the water, then thirteen, then many, many more. These did not go back under, but remained above the surface to form a dense, blue finger-wiggling barrier around the boat.

The children were paralyzed with fear. If someone had asked them to speak now, they could not have.

Like a gang of bullies in the schoolyard, the hands next began to push the boat around. They shoved it one way, then the other, then back again. They did this for a while, then began twirling it around, faster and faster, in dizzying circles, clockwise, then counterclockwise. When they tired of this game (and before anyone could throw up on them), they started rocking the boat. Blue wrists and forearms were now visible, as they reached up to latch onto its sides. They jerked the boat roughly up and down, again and again, almost overturning it.

"Stop that!" Linnet broke out of her cowed trance. She snatched up her staff and began whapping the fingers to make them let go.

The hands backed off. The ones that had been hit shook their fingers in pain, while the others waggled their index fingers at Linnet, giving her a *no-no-no* warning.

Linnet waved the staff threateningly at them, but they moved back in regardless and with balled-up fists began to punch the boat — *bam, bam, bam* — evidently trying to knock it to pieces. (So far, Betty's superior caulking held.) One of the hands reached in and swiped the bailing can, which it then used to splash them with water.

The boys had no weapons to fight with, so they plundered the lunch bag for fruit. They pelted the hands with apples and flung bananas at them like boomerangs. Olivier fired an orange at the one that was wielding the bailing can, but another hand intercepted it before it struck. Instead of firing the orange back, as some of the other hands were doing with the fruit, this hand vanished underwater with it. Seconds later an array of orange peels floated up to the surface.

This gave Sylvan an idea. "Offer them something, Olivier." He ducked as an apple sailed toward his head, only to take a hit of water full in the face. "Plah!" he gasped. "A token, a gift, something that might appease them. Before they sink us!"

"Yeah, Olivier. It's worked before." Linnet knocked the bailing can flying with her staff. "Score! Ha! You're all thumbs," she taunted the hand.

Olivier knew that it was worth a try and likely the only thing he could do that might save them, but *what* could he offer this rowdy pack of digits that would placate them?

He didn't get a chance to puzzle over this for very long. The hand that had been dousing them, possibly stung by Linnet's taunt, reached up, grabbed hold of Olivier's long shirttail and yanked him out of the boat. All the hands then streamed toward him, and poor Olivier, struggling and kicking, was tossed around among them like a beach ball.

His friends watched, helpless and horrified, as he was borne beyond their reach.

"They'll drown him," Linnet whispered.

What the hands did instead, or rather what they did first, was frisk him. Fingers crawled all over him. Exceedingly cold fingers, soft and wet as clay and smelling strangely sweet, like hyacinths. They plucked Murray out of Olivier's shirtfront pocket, passed him around, and then one of the hands plunged below, disappearing with him into the depths.

'Oh, *no*," groaned Sylvan.

Next, the notebook, the inkwell and Olivier's cash — everything, even some lint, was picked out of his pockets and whisked below.

Olivier was all too aware that he would be next. He took a deep breath, preparing to hold out as long as he could. He had never liked putting his head under water and figured he was going to like this even less. Especially if his head never broke the surface again. As he waited, rigid, holding his breath, eyes clenched shut, he sensed a rustle of excitement pass through the fingers, like a breeze passing through a stand of tall grass. The hands stopped digging in his pockets and crawling over him (*and* they'd stopped pinching and poking, as some had been doing). Olivier heard his friends calling to him, saying something he couldn't quite understand. He let out his breath — before he turned as blue as his captors — and opened his eyes. Warily, he looked around. *No*, he thought, *non possumus*.

Although it *was* possible. The evidence of this was glinting in the sun, held high by one of the hands. It was the *doit*, a coin Olivier knew well. The doit was made of solid gold and had a huge nose embossed on one side and the Latin words *Non Possumus* inscribed on the other.

You might call it a saving currency (rather than the kind one saves) because it seemed to turn up whenever Olivier needed it the most. The last time he'd used it as fare to pay for their passage across the River Stynx. He'd given it to Sharon, who had put it in her pocket and … *yes*, his tatty old jeans. Sharon's tatty old jeans … Linnet had been right. The doit had been there all along, but he'd been too absorbed in their journey to dig into his pocket and discover it.

He couldn't begin to guess why the blue hands wanted the doit and what it might mean to them. The main thing was that they not only wanted it, but seemed to revere it. All the hands, except for the ones that were grasping him, were swarming around the one hand holding the coin, either straining to touch it or wiggling their fingers excitedly. Even better, Olivier himself was suddenly getting a lot more respect. The hands that had been holding him so roughly and pitching him around turned themselves palms upward and began to rock him back and forth, soothingly. It was like swaying in a hammock made of pliant flesh and interlaced fingers — unnerving still, but not as unnerving as their previous shenanigans had been.

At this point something truly odd occurred. A hand appeared out of the water that was different from the others. It was the same size and shape, but it wasn't blue. It was more a glowing, pearly white. This hand reached up, lightly grasped Olivier's elbow, then began delicately to peel off that inky stain Olivier had gotten from plunging his hand into his book. The stain rolled easily down his arm and when it was completely removed it resembled a long, filmy glove. With help from one of its mates, the hand then slipped this on, stretching and tugging and flexing its fingers to get a tight and agreeable fit. This accomplished, it was as blue as all the others. With a pleased salute to Olivier, it sank back under the water.

While Olivier stared wonderingly at his own, now perfectly clean, hand and forearm, the hand-hammock carried him back to the boat. Gently, carefully, they tipped him into it like a serving of some rare and delicate dish they had just cooked up. As his friends hugged him and patted him on the back, the hands began clicking their fingers, cracking their knuckles and giving each other high fives.

While its fellows were celebrating, the hand holding the doit sank below with it. Surely, Olivier thought, he could use his newfound popularity to rescue Murray, but he didn't need to. Instantly Murray soared out of the water like a flying fish and landed with a noisy clatter in the bottom of the boat. They gave a shout of surprise, then cheered with delight! Olivier scooped him up, dried him off with his shirttail, and with a reassuring and grateful pat, slipped him back in his shirtfront pocket.

The rest of his things (except for the lint and the loose change, which they must have kept as a tip) followed promptly, tumbling into the boat soaked but undamaged, the ten dollar bill scrunched into a muddy ball. A few extras even appeared, a questionable bonus from the depths: a rusty spike, a toothbrush with a leech clinging to the bristles, a slimy bottle of cod liver oil and a child's yellow plastic shovel. And *then*, a final and *much* more desirable object was tossed into the boat. It hit the thwart and would have bounced back into the water on the other side, if Olivier hadn't made a grab for it and caught it.

"*Non possumus* squared," he said. "Feast your eyes on *this*. It's the stone!"

"No way," said Linnet, giving it the once over. "It does look like it, though. How did they — "

"Get real, Olivier. How many zillion ordinary stones like yours are there in the world?" said Sylvan.

Olivier was unswayed. "It *is*. I know it." He dropped it into his pocket and began gathering up everything else, except for the other bonus items. "I'll keep it anyway until we catch up with Alvis, then we'll know for sure. Um, I wonder what happened to him? If this is my stone, then — "

Linnet picked the writhing leech off the toothbrush and dropped it overboard (no one else wanted to touch it). "Do you suppose he's down *there*? With *them*?"

"Nah, he wouldn't have tried to cross the lake, how could he?" said Sylvan. "Which proves it isn't your stone."

But it is, Olivier thought, as he gazed out at the hands. They were waving at him, trying to get his attention. He wasn't happy with Alvis, and more than once had thought about how satisfying it would feel to thump him one, but he wouldn't really, and he sure didn't wish this watery fate on him. The hands were now pointing to the farther shore, posing a question. He turned to Linnet and Sylvan.

"I think they're going to give us a hand."

"I hope not," said Linnet.

They gave several. As soon as Olivier called to them in agreement, it was all hands on deck and everywhere else, and the boat began moving swiftly along the lake's surface. Anyone standing on the shore watching its arrival would have run away in terror to see it being propelled by this blue ambidextrous monster.

The hands guided the boat to a small, weather-beaten dock. After Olivier jumped out and secured the rope, they slid back under and vanished, their shadowy underwater forms gliding smoothly away into deeper waters.

"What *are* they, exactly? Do they have bodies, or what?" said Sylvan, as he and Linnet also climbed out onto the dock.

"I'll ask Murray. He was down there with them, after all." Olivier reached for his notebook. "But not right now. Notebook's still too wet."

"We don't have time for that, anyway," said Linnet, gingerly testing her sore foot. "Besides, I feel exposed standing out here. Let's check out this town, and we'd better be sneaky about it, especially you, Olivier. They'll haul you off if you're recognized."

They soon discovered that sneaky was going to be difficult to achieve. As they walked along the narrow road that led from the lake to Nohow Town, what they noticed most of all was what *wasn't* there. The landscape was bleak. The fields that stretched away on both sides of the road consisted mainly of dead grass, tree stumps, skeletal bushes and, alive at least, clumps of poison ivy.

There were no wildflowers springing out of the ditches, no insects buzzing around, no birds in the sky. Nor was there anywhere at all to hide if need be.

"You'd think there would be *some* trees left standing," complained Sylvan. Like Linnet, he was a forest-dweller and felt distinctly ill at ease in open areas, especially ones scoured of all interest.

"You would," she agreed. "When Betty was fixing my ankle she told me that getting rid of trees is part of The Facilitator's 'Equalization Project.' He thinks there are too many of them, and he doesn't like them being taller than he is, either."

"Too many trees? What a weirdo." Olivier sniffed the air. "Do you smell smoke?"

Nothing ahead of them appeared to be burning, so they turned to survey the forest that skirted the far side of the lake, the side from which they had come, and spotted tendrils of smoke twisting up into the sky. "Forest fire," he said grimly. "The lake may have been our only option, after all. Will Betty be all right?"

A loud rumble of thunder rolled overhead.

"I'm pretty sure she has more than a few tricks up her sleeve," said Linnet. "Gol, did you see that? Lightning. That must be what's starting the fires."

Even though it was a cloudless and perfectly fine day, a fork of lightning that actually did look like a big shiny fork had appeared in the sky and was stabbing at the trees in the woods.

"Thunder, *then* lightning?" said Sylvan. "That's messed up."

"Both are fake. That thunder sounded like a recording," said Olivier. "*How* does this Sleek guy do it? It's got to be him."

"That's for us to find out, I guess." Linnet was pointing ahead with her staff. "There's the town sign."

**nohow town
"home of the average citizen"
population 1,000, whatever
have an ordinary day**

"Sounds like a fun place, eh?"

"Really. A barrel of laughs."

"Can't wait."

They trudged on, their spirits a little lower, their hearts a little heavier, and worry beginning to nip at their heels like a yappy little dog.

Sixteen

When the three reluctant adventurers entered Nohow Town, they attracted the attention of a real dog (so much for being sneaky), although it wasn't a yappy one. He whined and wagged his tail when they encouraged him to come closer, but was too timid and kept a safe distance in following behind them. The dog was medium-sized and of no particular breed, with medium-length beige fur, a wan expression and a listless bark. Altogether, he was sadly lacking in pep and doggy enthusiasm. Olivier felt sorry for him, especially when he ambled past a bag of garbage set out on a curb and didn't even stop to sniff, let alone tear into it with true canine zest.

Leaning up against this bag of garbage was a bicycle in perfect condition, almost new.

"Don't tell me someone's throwing *that* out," marvelled Linnet.

Apparently so. As they continued down the street,

past identical boxy houses, they saw other bags of garbage (one per household) with bicycles, tricycles and skateboards set beside them, waiting for collection.

"Something tells me that the wheel is being uninvented here," said Olivier.

The beige dog soon lost what interest it had in them and wandered off, and shortly after they entered the downtown area in search of the Tom, Dick & Harry Pub, where they were to meet Betty. Olivier knew they were being too open, and that a stealthier approach would be wiser, but the place just seemed to be too boring and ultra-normal to be dangerous. Besides, they encountered very few people, and the ones they did paid them no mind, as if they were scarcely worth noticing. The citizens of Nohow Town had a preoccupied air and tended to look neither up, nor down, nor around, but straight ahead as they advanced down the street. Some people walked with hunched shoulders, squatting slightly as they moved along, while others tottered along on tiptoe. It looked ridiculous, but no one was laughing.

"Trying to conform to the height requirements," whispered Sylvan. "At least we're below their radar."

"Everyone wears the same thing, too," said Linnet, glancing at the cheap, grey business suits on offer in The-Man-on-the-Street Clothing Store — "One Size Fits All" — and The-Girl-Next-Door Boutique.

They passed other stores that were equally dreary, like Humdrum's Travel Bureau that offered Middle-of-the-Road tours, and that had an oddly contradictory slogan — "Just Don't Go!" They saw a bookstore with only one book in it for sale — *My Uneventful Life* by Lester Trite, and a movie theatre called The Run-of-the-Mill — "Now Playing: *The Blahs.*" Hurrying by Plain Jane's Shoes, they caught a snatch of conversation between two women who were staring in at the window display, which featured a "selection" of sensible, brown no-loafers.

"Nice shoes."

"Yes, nice."

"Very nice."

"But not *too* nice."

"No, no, they're moderately nice."

"Nice distinction."

"Yoiks," said Linnet when they were beyond hearing range. "This place is unreal."

"Agreed," said Olivier. "So is this." He had spotted a poster like the one that Heath had shown them — Olivier's "Wanted (but not much)" poster. It was taped to the window of Norm's Non-Variety Store, beside an advertisement for a cereal called Ordinario's — "*Guaranteed to have no sugar, no flour, no flavour, no nuthin'!*"

"It's a good likeness of you, Olivier. Too good," said Sylvan. "Maybe they're more aware of us than we think. Let's find this pub and make ourselves scarce."

"My ankle's sore, anyway. I could use a rest." Linnet limped ahead. "Sure hope Betty gets here all right."

Finding the pub was the easy part, since it was only a few doors down from the non-variety store. Betty had instructed them to wait for her, not inside the pub, but around back. They slipped down the narrow alley beside it, which led to a small enclosed yard, fringed with scrubby lilac bushes. Empty wooden crates were stacked near the pub's back door, and they carried three of these over to the most leafy of the bushes and arranged them so that they could keep an eye on the door and the alleyway.

The hard part was waiting for Betty to arrive, because she didn't.

They chatted to pass the time, Olivier telling the other two about his surprise visit from the shrunken carpet while they were stuck on Sly Creek. "It's so tiny, it's useless. Not that I'll ever see it again. It's turned into an outdoor carpet, a stray."

Linnet wondered aloud about Fathom, if he'd been able to find the Flood homestead, a watery speculation that led her to wondering about whether or not Sharon had been a student at Betty's Academy for the Undecided. "How else would you end up with those clothes?"

"Got me," said Olivier. "But as I recall, Sharon was plenty decisive."

Olivier got out the stone to take another look at it — still an ordinary stone, no different from any other chunk of gravel scattered in the yard. "It's so hard to believe this is any kind of threat."

"Maybe it's not," said Sylvan. He then told them about other stones he knew of, magical and powerful ones, madstones, wishing stones, or the kind that Heath had mentioned — the *Lapis lineus*, which is said to prophesy by changing colour, and the pantarbe, a precious stone that acts as a magnet for gold.

"This Sleek guy sounds totally greedy, so maybe that's what your stone does, Olivier, it attracts gold," said Linnet.

"Too bad the doit's gone, we could've tested it."

"But I do have some gold. Or Murray does." Olivier set the stone down beside him on the crate and drew Murray out of his shirtfront pocket. "His nib." He then held Murray nib-first near the stone. They watched closely to see what would happen, and what happened was … nothing. Except that Murray started heating up, which was not a good sign. It occurred to Olivier that Murray had been stuck in his pocket for quite some time, so he fumbled for the notebook to give his friend a chance to say something. In drying, the book had fattened up and the paper was crinkly. It made a rattling and agitated noise as Murray briskly recorded his thoughts.

Well, well, well. What do you know. SOMEONE has managed to recall that I exist! Even if it's ONLY as an experimental subject. NO, no, make that OBJECT! What if that boulder had knocked me out? Given me a CONCUSSION? Eh, EH? Did anyone think of THAT?!

"Um, gee, sorry, Murray."

"We didn't mean — "

And furthermore, if you lot had your wits about you, you wouldn't be maundering on about nothing … yakking and blathering away, and, and … where was I?

"You were going to tell us about what you saw in Lake Fingers, weren't you?" Olivier offered. "We'd love to know." True enough.

"Yeah, Murray, did those hands have bodies?" said Sylvan.

Couldn't say, my boy. It was dark down there. Heads and legs were in short supply, although they may have had bodies as they were wearing neptunics.

"Seriously?"

No. That was a joke.

"Ha, not bad," Olivier grinned. "But you must have seen something."

I did, to be sure. On the lake bottom there was a monumental stone head, an Easter Island job that was adorned with a colossal stone nose. The hand that nabbed me stuck me up one of the nostrils, which regrettably did impede my view of the proceedings.

Hearing this, they all tried very hard to keep a straight face, so as not to cause Murray further umbrage.

"Yuk," said Olivier, biting his lip. "That's why they wanted the doit, I guess. Nose worship, or something."

A most frightful experience. The nostril into which I had been so rudely plunged was stuffed with slimy algae, and there was a most uncouth eel residing in one of the eye sockets who kept poking his hideous mug in wanting to make my acquaintance.

Murray's language bristled, but his mood had improved greatly. He might have gone on to embroider his tale further, if he hadn't been interrupted by the arrival of a bird, which swept in over the pub's roof and settled in the topmost branch of the lilac bush.

"Oh look!" said Linnet. "Too cool, I've never seen one of those before."

Never seen a bird! And you being named after one. Linnet, you must get out more, my dear.

"I've never seen that *kind* of bird, Murray. It's a nightingale, I swear. And here in drab old Nohow Town, of all places."

"You're right," said Sylvan, gazing up at it. "*Luscinia megarhynchos*. What used to be called a nightsinger in

Old English." (He much preferred to be the one dishing out information.) "It's sure a long way from home."

"So are we," said Linnet.

Olivier was staring at the bird and murmuring to himself, "A nightingale. A *nightingale*?" The bird was about the size of a robin, but with a greyish white breast and reddish brown feathers on its back. With its bright black eyes it was returning his look, angling its head as if it were equally curious about him. Clamped in its beak was a thin strip of material.

"Is that birch bark? She must be building a nest," Linnet said.

"No, it's papyrus," answered Olivier.

"It *is*?" Linnet didn't sound convinced.

"Uh huh." He was certain that this was the same strip of papyrus that Sylvia had pulled out of her hair and tossed onto the floor when he'd had that chat with her in Betty's upstairs hallway. He had only mentioned this meeting to Betty — what she had called his undream.

"You're right, too," said Sylvan. "I *should* have known that."

The nightingale gave a quick nod and dropped the papyrus. It then launched itself off the branch — a bit clumsily — and soared back over the roof of the pub.

"She wants us to have this." Linnet picked it up and held it out straight. "It's got some squiggles or runes on it."

"Let me see." Sylvan examined the papyrus, knowing that he'd be able to decipher it if it were Egyptian or ancient Greek or even Celtic. He shook his head. "Gibberish. Doesn't mean a thing."

If I MAY be permitted to chip in my two cents' worth, I would advise trying the scytale.

"The what?" said Olivier.

Linnet's walking stick is actually a scytale, my dear boy. In other words a ciphering device. If I had been allowed out a bit more myself, I would have informed you of this earlier. You simply wind the papyrus around the stick and voilà!

"That's brilliant, Murray!" Linnet did exactly that. As she wrapped the strip lengthwise around the radius of the stick, the squiggles and marks connected up and a message appeared.

It read: **YOU KNOW THE SCORE.**

You see, children! Whoever wrote this also has a scytale, one with the same circumference, otherwise it wouldn't work.

"So what?" grumped Sylvan, galled at not having known this, either. "What's the message supposed to mean? Sounds more like something you'd get from a fortune cookie."

No one had an answer to this, not even Murray (who felt he usually knew the score), and Olivier was still trying to work out another puzzle. "You said 'she,' Linnet. So that was a female bird, right?"

"That's right."

"And nightingales sing at night, obviously. Nightsingers, Sylvan said."

"Only the males do. Why?"

"*Only* the males? Okay, never mind, then. I had this crazy idea that — " He paused. "Say, what's that noise?"

The pub door squeaked open and Olivier glanced toward it, expecting to see Betty. But it wasn't her.

"Trouble," he groaned. "Run!"

The Control Freaks had arrived. The children jumped to their feet, but that was as far as they got. Men and women, six of each, neatly attired in grey business suits and with precisely combed hair, poured efficiently through the back door of the pub and surrounded them. There was no point in trying to escape, for not only were they outnumbered, but the Control Freaks were armed. Armed in an uncommon manner (strange in itself) with icicles, sharp as stilettos, which they gripped in their black-gloved hands.

"What do you want?" demanded Olivier. "We haven't done anything wrong."

"Your clothes are not clean." Eerily, they all spoke at once. "You must come with us."

"You're kidding."

"Don't dawdle." One of the Freaks pointed his icicle at Olivier's head. "Tuck in your shirt. Stand up straight. Clean out your ears. Wipe that smile off your face."

Go take a flying leap, Olivier felt like saying, but instead answered, "Okay, okay, I get it. Let me tie my shoelace first. I hope that's allowed." As he bent down, he gave Linnet a look.

Without missing a beat, she pointed at one of the female Control Freaks and said, "You've got a speck of dirt on your sleeve. It's gross." The whole team snapped their heads to gawp, astonished, at the offending speck. "I do *not*," the woman blanched, hastily brushing her sleeve. "Don't be insolent." She now narrowed her eyes at Linnet. "When was the last time you washed your hair?"

Linnet crossed her arms and raised her chin in defiance. "I don't believe in it. It's not healthy."

This provoked a group gasp and a couple of moans.

"So where are you taking us?" said Sylvan, stepping in front of Olivier, who was slipping something into his pocket. This something wasn't Murray. Sylvan himself had pocketed Murray before the Control Freaks had a chance to notice him.

Once again they spoke in unison. "Facilitator Headquarters. Come, enough nonsense. Keep in line."

"All right, let's go," Olivier stood up. "We have to see this Sleek geek, anyway."

"Mind your language," the Freaks warned. *"Don't* play with your words."

Seventeen

Facilitator Headquarters was situated on the corner of "No Way" Way and "Nothing Doing" Drive, at the base of the mountain and directly below the Temple of Zephyrus, which was about halfway up. Even though it would have been a treacherous climb, and the Temple itself was crumbling and derelict with several tumbled columns and a gloomy, haunted aspect, they would much rather have struggled up the mountain to see it than be marched smartly into The Facilitator's lair. His headquarters were as mind-numbing as they had expected — a sterile, functional building that reeked of room spray.

As the Control Freaks herded them down a central hallway, Olivier noted the thin, sick-green carpeting, the budget-motel art on the walls and the potted, plastic ferns that were placed at regular intervals — depressing. The doors they passed were closed and bore plaques on them that designated particular departments: The Office of

Kitsch and Culture; Middle Management Resources; The Council for Clichés and Platitudes; and the office they had originally set out to find, The Department of Air Control Systems, Tourism and Flag-Waving.

At the end of the hall was a door with a plaque on it that read: **THE FACILITATOR.**

Actually, it had once read, **THE GREAT FACILITATOR,** but the "Great" had an 'X' scratched through it.

"Modest of him," muttered Sylvan.

As soon as they arrived at this door, it jerked open, and the person who opened it was none other than Professor Blank. He smiled faintly at them ... and then he winced. Evidently it hurt him to smile. Olivier suspected that this was generally the case, but Blank also appeared to have been in a nasty accident. A bandage was wrapped around his head, his nose was much flatter than before, his eyebrows were askew, his beard tied in a knot, and his one ear seemed to be somewhat loose. It was Olivier's turn to smile — it didn't do to cross his step-step-stepgramma.

Blank dismissed the Control Freaks with the order, "A not-yet-adult who lives in the Drone Apartment Block is having a birthday party. Get some wet blankets out of storage and deal with it."

The Freaks nodded simultaneously and, still gripping their sharp but apparently non-melting icicles, marched off to spoil the party.

"No one's allowed to have too much fun, Master Olivier," said Blank. "How gratifying to see you here. Your friends, as well." He glanced at the scytale, which Linnet was still using for support, but he neither claimed it as his own, nor tried to confiscate it. "Do come in. The Facilitator is moderately interested in meeting you. Follow me."

Professor Blank led them through a small waiting room and around an orange tweedy partition, into a sparsely decorated office. A child's desk and chair sat in one corner, and in the opposite one was a flag on a standard. This flag featured a turnip on a smudgy grey background and was possibly the least thrilling flag Olivier had ever seen.

A black metal desk occupied the centre of the room, and leaning up against it was Sleek, a man of medium height, medium weight and medium complexion. He *did* have some irregular features: a mole sat off-centre on his long chin, his nose was on the sharp and pointy side, his eyes were small and green. It was difficult to tell if his mouth was standard issue since it was presently stretched in a ghastly, administrator's grin. (Olivier realized that this was the very same grinning face he had seen on the postage stamp affixed to Heath's letter.) Sleek also had an acreage of forehead. His dusty-pink hair (pink!) was receding rapidly, by the looks of it, as if it couldn't wait to clear off and be gone.

"Children, *children*," he said, clapping his hands together. "Don't despair, you'll be adults soon."

"No, we won't," said Olivier.

Sleek ignored this. "No more adventures, but jobs, jobs, jobs, sleep, sleep, sleep, day in and day out. Adventures are excessively bad for you, all that running around, never getting enough quiet time, enough broccoli, enough dullness. Why, I doubt if you're scarcely sane, let alone sanitary.

Furthermore and in addition, I oculate that your growth has been severely stunted. Tell me, eh, what's the weather like down there, ha ha ha, do mice gnaw on your little ankles?"

"Oculate?" said Sylvan. "That's not a verb."

Sleek ignored this, too. "You don't want to end up like our Mr. Zero here, do you?"

"It's Blank," said Professor Blank, who had seated himself at the child's desk and was working on a sheaf of papers with an overlarge pencil.

"Yes, yes, *Blank*, of course. With a name like an empty slot on an application form, I simply want to fill you in, ha ha ha. You see, children, the Professor here is so useful that he has received a *special* dispensation from me, because this isn't Tiny Town, now is it? We *all* have to grow up." Sleek moved away from his desk and began to walk up and down, addressing the ceiling, the wall, the floor. "Oh, I feel for you. Believe me, I am cognizant of your sorry situation. But no pain, no gain, eh, that's the bottom line, whichever way you cut it. You know what, *I* am going to help you. Why? Because you're worth it."

"Ha ha ha," said Linnet.

This he also ignored, for he'd already launched into a spiel about his generosity, his accomplishments, his height, his *blah blah blahness*. For someone elected on a platform of modesty and moderation, they couldn't help but notice that he himself didn't appear to exercise much of either.

While he was blathering on, Olivier inched closer to his desk. Unlike Professor Blank's desk, which was piled high with papers, Sleek's was bare, except for a notepad and a fountain pen that lay across it. The Sibyl, Olivier thought. The pen had a nib made of bone and a barrel of scarred black leather, with the figure of a silver serpent winding around it and a spike-studded cap. Weirder still, the writing on the notepad more resembled dried blood than red ink. From what he could tell in having to read it upside down, it was a grim to-do list:

> *We will Burn Forests to Ash*
> *We will Grind Boulders to Sand*
> *We will Level Mountains to Plains*
> *We will Destroy—*

Sleek suddenly noticed what he was up to and Olivier stepped back quickly before he could read any more, but he got the picture. The Facilitator clearly had a partner in crime.

Sleek continued speaking while he moved behind his desk and opened a drawer. He took out a pen case that resembled a small sarcophagus and placed the Sibyl inside. After laying her reverently on the purple silk lining, he put the case back in the drawer, into which he also swept the notepad. Closing the drawer softly, he lifted his gaze to them, " … as the philosopher Mediocrates once said, 'Who do you think you are, pinhead?' Point well taken, eh. Ha ha ha. You see, the trouble with you three is that you *think* you're special, but you're not in the least. You're as ordinary as ordinary can be. No more wind powers, little girl? Nothing but a lame duck? Awww, *boo hoo*, get used to it."

"How do you know that?" said Linnet.

"Alvis, I bet," said Sylvan. "Where is that sneak, anyway?"

"As for *you*, smarty-pants." Sleek wagged a finger at Sylvan. "You know what I *think*? I *think* your brain could use a good washing. Clean out the old noggin, eh. It can and will be arranged."

"And YOU." His green eyes seemed to grow even greener as he fixed his gaze on Olivier. "You poor unloved boy. Abandoned at your grandparents' place because your parents are sick of you. They're so happy you're gone. To be quite honest, they never found you sufficiently interesting. Now they can do things they've always wanted to do. Children *are* such a nuisance, they take up so much time, they're always whining, and wanting dessert, and … *other* things." He waved his hand airily.

"Don't be ridiculous," said Olivier. "You don't know anything about my parents."

"I know quite a bit, frankly. And I can prove it." Once again Sleek opened his desk drawer and this time took out a packet of letters that were tied together with a black ribbon. He held these out, close enough for Olivier to see that they were addressed to him at Cat's Eye Corner. The handwriting on the envelope was unmistakably his mother's. These were letters he had never seen — in fact, he had received no mail at all since his arrival. Sylvia claimed to have eaten one, but he'd thought she was joking. "Your step-step-stepgramma, as you so childishly call her, *charming* woman, you know I think she's got a *crush* on our Mr. Miniature here," he smiled slyly at Professor Blank, who continued to work steadily, unperturbed.

"Yes, yes, and to protect you she's been hiding these vile missives, or should I call them missiles, so full of hate and deception are they."

"I don't believe you." Which was true, but he had a sick feeling in his stomach, anyway. "Let me see them."

He reached out for them, but Sleek jerked his hand up and held the letters over Olivier's head. "Jump, boy, jump. Ha ha ha. Not so fast, eh. You know, I *might* consider trading them if you happen to have something I'd like. *Do* you have something I might like? Some small, solid, insignificant little object? I'm not a materialist, as you can see. We don't believe in that sort of thing here in Nohow Town. Things, things, things. Have you ever noticed how *cluttered* the world is? In my view, we'd all be much better off if most things were *ground* into powder and buried. *That's* what I would call keeping one's house in order. But, let's see, where were we, oh *right*, we were going to make a deal." He waggled the letters.

Olivier glared at him. Then, with a pained but determined look on his face, he reached into his pocket and pulled out the stone.

"Don't!" said Linnet.

Holding it in his palm, he offered the stone to Sleek.

"Olivier, it's a trick!" Sylvan tried to stop him.

The Facilitator snatched the stone up instantly. "Aha! An infantile token. Utterly and totally useless, but I'll take it. And I am *so* sorry, I regret to say that I am going to have to keep these." He slid the letters into his suitcoat pocket. "See how naive you are? It *was* a trick! You didn't really think I'd hand them over, did you? Once you've been processed and fully normalized, you won't harbour such absurd expectations anymore."

"You creep," said Linnet.

"Temper, temper." Sleek tossed the stone into the air and caught it. "The fact of the matter is you are all slated to be searched, anyway. Personal trinkets and mementoes are *not allowed*. Searched, suited — grey business suits for all! — and normalized. Guess what, you're going to *finishing* school, and very shortly, too. Why, *shortly* is the operative word, isn't it, Mr. Dandiprat?" He snapped his fingers at Professor Blank. "Take them away."

Professor Blank rose from his chair and walked toward them. "Follow me," he said evenly.

"Oh, and kiddies," said Sleek, gazing with triumph at the stone, "I wouldn't be counting on any *abnormal* individuals you may have met in our environs to come to your aid. They, too, have been dealt with."

———

"We should have made a break for it." Linnet was surveying their prison cell, a glaringly bright and stark, white-walled room, with a single wooden bench against one wall, one barred window high up on the outside wall and a smaller barred one in the door.

"Too many Control Freaks around," said Olivier. "Besides, we have work to do here, as soon as we get shot of this room. You heard what Sleek said. Our friends are prisoners, too."

"Unless they've already been 'processed.'" Linnet shivered.

"That business with the stone *was* a trick, right?" asked Sylvan.

"Yup." Olivier smiled, and patted his pants pocket. "You guys were great, very convincing. I picked up another stone while I was pretending to tie my shoe and put it in my other pocket so I wouldn't mix them up. That's the one I gave him."

"I knew you were up to something," said Linnet. "So was he. Those letters were forgeries. Did he think we were too dumb to figure that out?"

"That goth pen of his could have written them, no sweat," agreed Sylvan.

"Possibly," Olivier frowned. "They also could be real letters from my parents that Sylvia has been keeping from me for some reason. I know Alvis swiped some stuff while he was wandering around the house. If he made it this far, he might have given them to Sleek." This *was* worrying. He knew his parents' feelings for him hadn't changed — if there was one thing he absolutely knew for sure, it was that. But he wondered if he'd been lulled into thinking that Sylvia was trustworthy. Was *she* the one who had knocked Linnet down in the forest? Olivier had seen her only moments before in the hall of Betty's house.

"What I can't figure out is why Sleek didn't try to get his hands on Murray or the invisible ink," said Sylvan. "He must know about them, and like you said, Linnet, he's a greedhead, despite what he says about not wanting things."

"And why didn't he or Blank grab the scytale?" said Olivier.

"We *are* going to be searched, everything taken away."

Linnet gazed anxiously around the cell again. "Blast it, there's nowhere to hide anything."

"Let's ask Murray what he thinks." Olivier got out the notebook.

"Right, almost forgot I had him. Hope he's not upset again." Sylvan retrieved Murray from his pocket and handed him to Olivier.

This time Murray skipped the fussing and got right down to business.

Questions, my friends? You've come to the right source. Who needs a trashy old Sibyl for answers. It's as plain as paper that Blank has kept the knowledge of my existence to himself. He's up to something, which is perhaps also why he didn't indicate that the scytale is his. If it is his, there has to be another somewhere. In any event, I know I'd be hatching a few schemes of my own if my boss dumped on me all the time. Speaking of which, I trust that none of you took what Sleek said to heart?

"About not being special?" said Olivier. "Who cares. I don't even think that way, none of us does. Not even Sylvan, who's got more grey matter than he knows what to do with."

"Get lost," laughed Sylvan, pleased nonetheless.

"Exactly," said Linnet. "I mean, my wind powers are part of who I am, no big deal. Who I *was*, I mean. I'm getting used to it. It's not so bad."

"You're the one who's special, Murray," said Olivier.

My boy, how unavoidably true! It is a burden, and one that you youngsters fortunately don't have to share.

"So, Murray, we're relying on you. What should we do? How do we get out of here?" asked Olivier. "If what

you say is true, and Blank is the only one who knows
about you, he could show up at any moment and take you
away. Sleek wouldn't be any the wiser."

Hmmmmn.

"Maybe he's envious of Sleek's pen and wants a more
brilliant one for himself," said Sylvan.

Yes, yes, that does make sense. I AM highly desirable.

"He's some sort of inventor, too." Olivier was recalling Blank's hat and how "clever" he said he was. "More
likely he'd want to take Murray apart to find out how he
works."

*Dear, oh dear! Cursive! Think, think, think. Why don't you
see what that pesky bird wants, the one that's tapping at the
window, and I'll report back in a momentito.*

"Murray's right!" Linnet was craning her neck up at
the window. "It's that same bird, it's our nightingale, and
she's got something in her beak. Something shiny."

"It's not what I think it is, is it?" said Olivier, setting
Murray and the notepad down on the floor. "Sylvan, let's
push the bench over. Linnet hop on. Do you think you can
reach the window?"

"And break it with the scytale? I can sure as heck try."

The nightingale was clinging to the ledge, her keen
eyes watching the proceedings inside.

When Linnet climbed up on the bench, she flew off
and circled in the air, letting Linnet pound as forcefully
as she could on the glass. A couple of blows and it cracked,
and with the next hit she poked a hole clear through,
raising a hand to protect her face from flying splinters.
"Did it!"

The bird landed back on the ledge, bobbed her head and dropped the thing she'd been holding in her beak through the hole in the window. Linnet reached past the bars and caught it before it fell to the floor. When she held it up, Olivier saw that it wasn't at all what he had thought. "What is it? I was hoping for a key."

"A pitch pipe," said Sylvan. "Depends what kind of key you're after."

"*Music* isn't going to open the door, is it?" Olivier was puzzled *and* disappointed.

"Doesn't matter." Linnet jumped off the bench and hastily pocketed the pitch pipe. "Blank's here." She lowered her voice, "If he's alone, we might have a chance. Three against one."

Professor Blank was peering in, his face framed in the small barred window, while his key *scraped* and *twisted* in the lock.

Olivier snatched Murray up and turned his back to the door. He could tell that Murray was agitated and bursting to say something ... he *had* come up with a plan. Olivier knew he'd be in big trouble if he ignored his pal yet again. He only hoped that if he let Murray have his say that it would be a short one ... and for once, it *was*.

Meeoww, Murray wrote.

"*What?*" whispered Olivier.

MEEOWW! Say it! Shout it! Come on!!

"Ohh-kay."

Then Olivier thought, *of course, that's it*. "MEEOWW," he shouted out as Blank stepped into the room. "MEEOW, MEEOWW, MEEEOWWW!"

Both Linnet and Sylvan looked at him as if he were nuts. But Olivier kept on *meeeeowwwing* and *meeuuwing* and *nrrrrrowwwing* and waving his hands, encouraging them to join in. When they saw the effect this seemed to be having on Blank, who had begun to stagger around holding his hands up to his ears, they got the idea and started up, too. Soon they were all caterwauling with flair and conviction, making as much creative racket as a trio of amateur felines at a Cat's Eye Corner poetry slam. Three against one, although it sounded like a *lot* more. They kept it up as they crept past Blank and out the door. By then the Professor was practically *catatonic*.

Eighteen

Two administrative assistants stepped out of the office that housed The Department of Air Control Systems, Tourism and Flag-Waving and headed down the hall on their lunch break.

"How about a cheese sandwich?" one said.

"We had that yesterday," the other answered.

"And the day before."

"And the day before that."

"Not that I mind."

"No, no, not at all. I like a cheese sandwich."

"Every day."

"Yes, every day."

"We could request a pickle on the side."

"*Could* we? Oh my …"

The children were pressed against the wall, doing their best wallpaper imitation as the clerks wandered off, absorbed in their exchange. Olivier moved along the wall and reached for the doorknob, which turned easily in his hand — they'd left the office unlocked. He opened the door a crack to see if anyone remained inside.

"All clear," he said, slipping in, with Linnet and Sylvan following behind.

What they discovered within was a regular sort of office with the usual equipment — desks, in-out trays, pencil sharpeners, neat stacks of paper, treadmills — along with jars lined up on the reception counter that contained clusters of turnip flags, much smaller versions of the one Olivier had seen in Sleek's own office. On the wall nearest the counter there was a calendar marking the compulsory flag-waving days, along with numerous tourist posters advertising the stunning attractions of the district: Yawning Man Canyon, The Taxidermy Petting Zoo, Nohow Town's Annual Yodelling Festival, The Macaroni Art Gallery and Toothpick Museum.

Against the farthest wall of the office, however, was something far more interesting — a bank of security monitors, six in all.

"Aha! Now we're getting warm," said Olivier. "I knew we'd find something useful in here."

"You think?" said Sylvan, as they hastened over to look at them. He flicked a switch below one of the monitors.

A picture immediately leapt into view. Olivier gasped. So did Sylvan and Linnet. No one had been expecting to see what they did: on the screen a severed head was bouncing frantically around, buoyed by a fountain of air that was shooting up below it. The head had a tidily trimmed moustache, a fluttering ponytail and a soul patch beneath its lower lip. It may have lacked a body, but was very much alive — its eyes were blinking rapidly and its mouth was moving equally fast.

"Max!" said Olivier.

"*That's* Max?" said Linnet. "Wow. He's ... *wow*."

"I guess now we know what happened to him. More or less." Sylvan was searching for the volume control. "This must be it." He gave the dial a twist, and Max's voice blared out. Sylvan cut the sound to a barely audible level — no telling how long they had before Blank recovered and sent out the Freaks.

"Head tax!" Max was saying. "Whoever heard of such a thing? The man's bonkers, he's loony — he's off *his* head. How am I supposed to *pay*? My pockets and I have parted ways! Losing your body is nothing but a fad diet? *He's* got his head in the sand, or *should* have. He's gaga, haywire, a head case. He belongs in one, no mistake. Needs his noggin examined, needs a headshrinker, he does. Just you wait, I'm going to give him a piece of my mind ... and it won't be pretty, no sir. Head tax! I ask you ... "

Max was going on and on in this way, his words travelling in a closed circuit and his head following suit (or it might have liked to follow one), bobbing and spinning around, trapped as it was on the relentlessly surging spout of air.

"It's a wind doing that," Linnet said grimly. "A cruel one. One of Sleek's servants."

"Maybe it doesn't have a choice," said Olivier. "This *is* the air control department. Where is it happening, though? That's what we've got to find out." He moved down the bank of monitors, flicking on the switches. "This might give us some idea." One screen displayed an empty room, empty of people that is, for otherwise it was piled high with snowballs, buckets of what looked like hail and stacks of icicles as long and sharp as lances — it was like a winter arsenal that some kids' gang had stored up. Another screen showed a cavernous, cobwebby room, with columns running down both sides, and a statue at the far end — too far away to see clearly.

"That room's in the temple," said Linnet. "I'm positive. It's exactly how my dad described it."

"It's the naos," said Sylvan. "The inner temple."

"Okay, right, the temple, that's where Heath said Sleek might be keeping prisoners. So that's where we ..." Olivier was looking back and forth between two of the other screens. "Cripes, it *is* Heath, he's trapped, too, and ... there's Alvis! I thought he was on Sleek's side."

They saw that Heath was imprisoned in a stark white cell, much as they had been, but he had fallen to the floor and was caught immobile in a half-sitting position, as if he'd frozen while trying to stand back up. He was buried up to his waist in a snowdrift, his handsome features stiff and pale, one arm held before him in a protective gesture, an apparently futile attempt to shield himself from an attack. And the attacker? A fierce, wintry wind that was blasting and whistling around him, and burying him deeper and deeper in snow.

"How did they capture him?" said Olivier, his voice full of anguish. "I guess an arctic wind like that would stop anyone in his tracks."

"Yeah, who can fight the weather? Not even a giant," said Sylvan sadly.

"*We can*, that's who," answered Linnet, clenching her jaw.

The other screen showed a teary, grimacing Alvis. A relentless, bullying wind had him pinned against a wall as it blew and blew and periodically smacked him with fat drops of rain. His satchel was gone, likewise his potato peel coat and his Brussels sprout pants. He was down to a dirty undershirt, smiley-face boxer shorts and his blue shoes — at least they were holding fast.

"A wind like that can drive a person crazy," said Linnet.

"Crazier, in Alvis' case," said Olivier, but his heart wasn't in it. No matter what Alvis had done, he didn't deserve this humiliating punishment.

"Thank goodness Betty's safe," said Sylvan.

"I'm not so sure about that." Olivier pointed to the final screen. It showed a bird, *their* bird — the nightingale — flying around outside the temple, dodging and diving as a gang of Control Freaks hurled snowballs at her. These weren't ordinary snowballs, either — as soon they hit something, they burst into flames. One of these fiery missiles winged the nightingale and they watched in horror as she went down, tumbling to the ground.

"Have you checked in here for them?" someone shouted in the hallway.

"Uh-oh," said Sylvan. "Hit the floor."

"No, the broom closet," said Olivier. "Quick."

Olivier knew that the door nearest the bank of screens led to the broom closet because it said so:

BROOM CLOSET
Authorized Personnel Only
KEEP OUT!
Get it? That means YOU!!

"Geez," whispered Linnet, once they were inside the closet, cozying up to the mops and brooms, buckets and sponges. "They sure take their cleaning seriously here."

"Shhhh," cautioned Sylvan.

As the office door banged open, they heard footsteps and the voices of several Control Freaks.

"No one here."

"Where are Mr. Thompson and Mr. Thompson?"

"Lunch."

"Yes, lunch, there's an idea. I could use a cheese sandwich."

"They left the monitors on."

"We'll have to report that to The Facilitator."

"Yes."

"Let's go. No non-adults in this office."

"Have you ever tried a cheese sandwich with a pickle on the side?"

"I wouldn't dare."

"How about the broom closet? We should have a look in there."

"But it says 'Keep Out.'"

"'Authorized Personnel Only.' That's not us."

"Yes, it does say that. We'd better not, then."

"Rules are rules."

"You know what happens when you break them."

This was stated in a low, frightened tone.

"I have an idea, let's check out the cafeteria. Non-adults are always hungry."

"Yes, that's true."

"Yes."

"Yes!"

"Huh. Real, bona fide yes-men," said Sylvan, once they were gone. "We lucked out."

"Pathetic," agreed Linnet. "If I never broke any rules, I'd never have half the fun I do. Okay, so, to the Temple. We have to find the nightingale and see how badly she's hurt. Then get inside somehow and find the others. I'm pretty sure I can climb up there. My ankle's a lot better." Linnet was trying very hard to convince herself of this.

"I wonder …" Olivier began to struggle to the back of the closet, pushing broom handles aside and stepping over rag bags and a toppled vacuum cleaner. It was a jungle of cleaning tools and products.

"What *are* you doing?" said Linnet.

They listened to him rattling and scrabbling and knocking things over, and then heard the unmistakable sound of a door opening. A door on the other side of the broom closet!

"Come on," Olivier called. "You've got to see this."

When Sylvan and Linnet fought their way through to this other door and stepped through it, they found themselves in a room like a mine shaft. It smelled earthy and dank, and was only faintly lit by a single lantern sitting on a ledge of rock. The only other thing in the room was a black metal staircase that ascended upward into the darkness.

"Explains the 'Authorized Personnel' business," said Olivier. "I thought there was something fishy going on."

"We've got to be underneath the mountain," said Sylvan.

"It's going to be a long climb. Linnet, do you think you can make it?" Olivier noticed that she had dragged one of the rag bags out of the closet with her. Now it was his turn to ask, "Um, what are you doing?"

"There's an animal trapped in here, a mouse, I don't know. I could feel it struggling to get out when I brushed against the bag." Linnet set down the scytale, then unknotted the cord that cinched the rag bag tight and loosened it. As soon as there was only the smallest of openings, the trapped creature was out of the bag and flying wildly around the room, zigzagging around the staircase, almost knocking the lantern over. "It's a bat!"

"No, it's not. It's the *carpet*," groaned Olivier. "How did it get in there?"

"Somebody obviously tried to get rid of it," said Sylvan, ducking as it shot straight at his head. "But they should have shredded it first. What a pest."

"Hey, you." Linnet reached up to grab the tiny carpet as it skimmed past her own head. "Whoaaa!" She snagged it, and then to everyone's amazement it lifted her right off her feet. It shot up higher into the air, then higher, and took her with it. It kept going up and up until both she and the carpet disappeared into the darkness above. "Helllllppppp ... "

"Linnet, *hang on,* don't let go," Olivier shouted. He snatched up the scytale then bolted up the stairs, Sylvan right on his heels.

They charged up the staircase, the sound of their footsteps ringing loudly on the metal treads. Then, oddly, the staircase itself began to move, twisting itself slowly into a spiral, first one way, then the other, then back again.

"What sort of idiot would build a staircase like *this*?" Sylvan panted.

"Sleek, who else." Olivier stopped to steady himself — with zooming around and around, he was getting dizzy. He grabbed the handrail, and the moment he did so they heard a juddering, creaking noise. The treads on the staircase then started to move upward and at the same time lit up with twinkling, multicoloured lights. The stairs seemed to have turned into a fairground ride — all that was missing was the jangly music.

"Holy, Olivier, what did you do?"

"Nothing. Unless I hit some switch by mistake."

"Or unless the someone who knows how this thing works got on down below."

"Better keep moving on our own steam. Let's go."

The boys raced up and up, keeping a firm grip on the railing as they ran. The stairs not only continued to corkscrew, twisting one way, then the other, but had also started to shimmy and sway. They could easily have been shaken off. If that weren't bad enough, the treads then reversed direction and began moving downward. Luckily, they were near the top when this happened and managed to struggle to the landing.

"I've *got* to see how this crazy thing works." Sylvan bent down to examine a mechanism that was set in the base of the stairs.

"*Later*, Syl." Olivier was trying to catch his breath and get his bearings at the same time. They were at a side entrance of the inner temple, about to step into the naos, as Sylvan had called it, the room that they had seen on the security monitor. It was a magnificent room, or rather once was magnificent. The temple had been ransacked: marble statues lay broken on the terrazzo floor, fixtures had been stripped, paint was splattered on the columns, and in the mural that ran along the walls, the faces of wind gods — shown streaking around in the air dumping urns of rain on the unsuspecting or blasting ships at sea — had been scratched out. Only the ceiling, painted a deep midnight blue and decorated with golden stars, had been left untouched.

"This won't take long. Here, give me the scytale. I know the score, all right," announced Sylvan.

When Olivier handed it to him (he knew better than to argue), Sylvan jammed it into the works, saying, "There, it's stuck in descending mode. That should keep them busy. Freaks, or Blank, or whoever it is."

"No sign of Linnet. Where could that *pesky* carpet be, we've got to find her."

"Her, and everyone else," said Sylvan. "We'll have to split up."

"I suppose." Olivier wasn't all that keen about this plan, but he knew it was the wisest thing to do. If one of them got caught, another would still be at large and have a chance to rescue the others. Besides, he wouldn't be sneaking around in this vast, scary place all on his own. He touched his shirt pocket — Murray was with him.

"I'll go left, you right," said Sylvan. "I have a hunch about something. I want to check it out."

"Watch out for those security cameras, eh." Olivier was staring up at the camera that was positioned to take in the naos. It had been screwed directly onto the face of one of the gods in the wall mural. The figure was depicted in flight, his long hair and cloak flowing behind him, and he was holding a conch shell very much like the one that had turned up on Sylvia's sale table.

"Someone's idea of a joke." Sylvan stared up at the camera, disgusted.

"But the last laugh will be ours, right?"

"That's the plan."

The boys gave each other a nod, and parted, Sylvan heading swiftly toward the front of the temple, and Olivier sliding like a shadow along the wall toward the back.

Nineteen

Olivier moved furtively along the wall, keeping out of the range of the security camera.

As he neared the large statue situated at the farthest end of the naos, the one they had not been able to view clearly on the monitor screen, he now saw that some attempt had been made to repair it. The original head was gone, and in its place a plaster head representing Sleek had been awkwardly stuck on. Likewise, the original object held in the statue's upraised hand was missing — along with most of its fingers — and in its place a larger-than-life pen had been attached. Carved out of black granite, it was the Sibyl held aloft like a torch or a valorous weapon.

"Murray," Olivier whispered. "What do you think of that?"

Great pride precedeth a fall, my boy, was what Murray might have said, but Olivier was in too much of a hurry for them to exchange their opinions in the usual way.

He passed through an arched portal in the back wall and entered what Sylvan later told him was called the opisthodomos. At least it would have been called that in a Greek temple. Here it had been transformed into a brightly lit area that more resembled a hospital corridor. A dozen closed doors stretched out in either direction, several with signs on them. Slipping past them, he read, Tornado in Progress (an ominous roar was audible behind this door), and BEWARE of FROSTBITERS! ("ouch! eee! ahhh! stop that!"), and **Quiet PLEASE, Rainmaker at Work** (and not having much success by the sounds of it), or **WARNING: FLASH FLOODS** (a toilet flushing), and (rattling, clacking noises) **ALL HAIL!**

He tiptoed over to this last sign and peeked in through the narrow glass window in the door. Inside, he saw a team of men and women wearing lab coats and handling an instrument that bore an oddly close resemblance to the eyeball-whapper and dimple-maker that Olivier had discovered in the basement of Cat's Eye Corner. Using a range of fixtures on these tools, the technicians were making hail, laboriously filling up tray after tray with icy pellets of various sizes, some tiny as pills, some as big as softballs. The faces of the workers were numb with tedium and their stiff, bluish fingers were plainly numb with cold. *No one works here willingly, that's for sure*, Olivier thought, as he moved away from the glass and crept further down the corridor.

Surreptitiously, he checked each room as he passed, seeing yet more people employed in making what only Nature herself should have a hand in. Even worse, these workers were perverting her designs. They were inserting explosive devices in snowballs, forging icicles as sharp as switchblades, experimenting with a fog that hurt the eyes. He watched this fog being sprayed into the faces of caged dogs, who were whining and cowering and then trying to rub their weeping eyes with their paws. Shocked and furious, Olivier almost kicked the door down. But he restrained himself and rushed ahead — he needed reinforcements. He needed to find his friends.

He passed two rooms that were empty, except for some discarded candy wrappers drifting around inside. *Trapped winds, or idle ones*, he thought. Then in the next one, he spotted Max.

The Horseless Headman was still being buffeted and twirled around by a tormenting wind, but he had stopped speaking and his eyes were closed. Asleep? Faint hope that, for the wind abruptly bumped him against the wall a couple of times like a loose buoy against a dock, and Max didn't waken, didn't respond in any way. Olivier grabbed the door handle — locked. He pounded on the door, but still no response. He ran to the next door … and there was Heath, now buried up to his chin as the snow skirled around his head and the wind roared in his ears. Even if Olivier shouted at the top of his voice, he would not have been able to make himself heard. In the next room, he saw Alvis, motionless in a corner, curled into a tight ball, head tucked between his bony knees.

Olivier ran to the last room, which had a soft glowing light pouring through the door's window. Desperately, he looked in — he *had* to find help — and saw Linnet!

She was standing before a glass case and staring at it, entranced. It was the kind of case you might see in a museum containing an Egyptian mummy, its eternal travel-wear dirty and fraying, its body, shrunken and dried and secretly being devoured by insects. *This* case, which was emitting that strange light, didn't contain a mummy, but a perfectly preserved young man, possibly a teenager. He had long golden hair and a rosy complexion — not a zit in sight — and there were flowers strewn all around him. He was wearing a belted white tunic and lace-up sandals ... and that's when Olivier did a double-take. He saw that there were small, white wings, folded stiffly on the young man's ankles.

"Zephyrus?" he said. *No*, he shook his head. *It can't be.*

Linnet must have somehow unlocked this door herself, for it opened readily. He hurried in and stood beside her.

Without removing her eyes from the young man, she said, "*He's* not an old duffer."

"True. He looks like a movie star. Only smarter." (Olivier had very decided opinions about this sort of thing.) He placed his hand on the glass case, which was surprisingly cold to the touch, more like a sheet of ice. "But, come on, Linnet, you can admire him later, whoever he is, we've got to — "

"He's alive."

"Really? Well, our friends aren't going to be, if we don't move it."

"How right you are," came an all-too-familiar voice from behind them. The voice was struggling to be sinister, but the speaker was clearly winded. "They won't last much longer."

"Sleek." Olivier turned to face him. "Have a good climb?"

"Indeed." Sleek brandished the scytale at him. "Children do love breaking things. Guess what, so do I! I knew I'd find you here mooning over this corpse."

"He's not dead." Linnet hadn't bothered to turn around, but continued her surveillance.

"Obviously you have an overactive imagination, girlie. Never fear, we'll soon have that processed out of you. A useless faculty, you won't miss it. Without one you won't have to worry about what's going to be done to you next, eh. Ha ha. As for *him*," he pointed the scytale at the case, "I'm almost ready for my Black Market yard sale. He'll fetch a pretty penny, I'll venture."

"I thought you weren't a materialist," said Olivier.

"One has to get by."

"Sleek is a greedyguts, all right. One of the worst I've ever seen. He takes the cake *and* everything else he can get his hands on." It was Sylvan who spoke. "See!" He walked into the room holding out his stolen flute and his Japanese fountain pen. She *was* a beauty. Murray in particular appeared to have taken note. Olivier felt a stab of pain around his heart area, as though his pen friend had become electrified.

"He's got this enormous storeroom packed with stuff," Sylvan continued. "Even those bikes we saw set out for garbage collection, this is where they ended up. You're ripping everyone off. Besides changing the weather — I saw all the gizmos and panels you've been using in that control tower up behind the tympanum."

"My, what a snoop you are. Curiosity killed the CAT, you know."

"Don't *say* that, please." Professor Blank had appeared in the doorway, gasping for breath.

"If it isn't my right-hand man. A short right hand, mind you, and only half a man, really. Carnifex? Hah! Talk about false advertising. Why, Blank's nothing but a *pussycat*."

The Professor's knees began to tremble, and his one loose ear wobbled dangerously.

"Yet you wouldn't have done any of this without him," said Sylvan. "He invented all that weather control machinery. It's brilliant."

"Aww, you're letting the *cat* out of the bag," Sleek purred.

Blank whimpered.

"Why, though?" asked Olivier, truly perplexed. "What's the point? Why mess around with the weather?"

"The Facilitator hates the wind," wheezed Blank.

"Agreed. It is detestable. It messes up my hair."

"You don't have hair," Olivier said. "Not much, anyway."

Sleek ignored this. "Wind is nasty, it blows dust in my eyes. It makes me sneeze. It hurts my ears, which are extremely sensitive. And *where* is it when you want it, eh, eh? Ever try to fly a kite? The wind *never* cooperates! I'm only going to allow it to blow for one hour every thirteen and a half days, and everyone will have to stay inside when it does. That will be the law.

"The point of it all, you ask? My, but you are a dim bulb, aren't you? He who controls the weather, controls the world. Just *think* what I can do!" He chuckled to himself. "Which reminds me, I almost forgot. I have something for you." He reached into his suitcoat pocket and pulled out, not the package of letters, which was what Olivier was expecting to see, but a handful of fine powder. "Here is your precious *stone*," he said. "Or what's left of it." He held out his palm and then blew the powdery, ground-up rock into Olivier's face.

Or he tried to. Olivier was too quick for him and jumped neatly aside. Then reaching into his own pocket, he said, "Wrong, *here* is my precious stone." He retrieved the stone that he had carried with him all this way, and held it firmly in the crook of his finger. Finally Olivier understood what he was supposed to do with it. Betty had been right — he did know when the time came. And that time was *now*!

"Nail him, Olivier," Sylvan shouted.

Sleek *did* deserve a rock between the eyes, but that's not what Olivier did with the stone. Instead, he threw it with all the force he could muster at the icy prison in which the young man was encased. With a noise that rang throughout the room like a lightning strike, the case cracked, then shattered into a zillion icy shreds that fell tinkling to the floor.

Sleek hissed at the Professor. "You said it was indestructible!"

"The Sibyl's prophesy," groaned Blank. "Only the stone …"

"Fix it! Right now, get on it! Don't just stand there moaning and snivelling. *You*," he glared at Olivier. "You'll pay for this, believe me. That *thing* will rot without the refrigerated case. Eww, already it stinks."

The stale and faintly acrid air was in fact much improved as a fragrance of wild roses and summer rain filled the room. The strange light that had been emanating from the case began to swirl around and flicker on the walls.

"Dry up, Sleek," said Sylvan. "The Professor can't do anything. I wrecked all your fancy machinery. Used a leg broken off one of the marble statues. Did a thorough job, too."

"You WHAT? Blank, DO something, take them away. Filthy, revolting, destructive children. Incinerate them. WHERE are the guards?!"

"Busy," Sylvan smiled. "Very busy. Thanks to Betty."

"SHUT UP! WHO?"

"Ohhhh," Linnet said. "The wings."

"Our nightingale!" exclaimed Sylvan.

Olivier, too, thought Linnet meant the nightingale. To his immense delight, she had swept into the room, but one wing was smoking, still smouldering from being hit by that incendiary snowball. "We need water, or no, something to smother it with." He started to unbutton his shirt.

"UGH!" bellowed Sleek. "You're right for once, kid. Kill that vile creature!!"

"I meant the fire," responded Olivier sharply.

The nightingale gave an indignant squeak. She dove down and jabbed Sleek's bald spot with her beak, then flitted back out the door.

"OUCH! OW! WHAAAAAAA!!" Sleek blubbered.

A second later, Betty stepped into the room, saying, "Greetings, everyone. Just thought I'd drop in and see how you were getting along." She slapped out a flame that had sprung up on her shawl.

"Betty!" The boys both cheered.

"Who are YOU?" Sleek was rubbing the top of his head and making a very sour face.

Betty fixed him with a forbidding look. "I'm that 'scrawny old bird,' as you so gallantly put it, whose school you closed down."

"Well, you are scrawny."

"And you, sir, are *boring*. So shut your trap."

"How DARE you! I'm a very IMPORTANT person, I OWN everything here, I CONTROL everything, I even KNOW the future."

"Not any more, you don't." Betty reached into her shawl and pulled out a used hanky. "Drat, that's not it." She tossed the hanky at Sleek and rummaged around some more. "Aha! Here it is. I must say, you have the dreariest office I have ever seen, and that *flag*. Turnips have their place, but honestly." She held up the Sibyl. "In my opinion, I suspect she's been leading you on, selling you a load of goods. Or bads, rather. She can be a terrible old thing, you know, treacherous. More full of guile — and gall — than ink."

"Give that back," Sleek ordered. "You stole it, you witch!"

"Watch who you're calling a witch, sonny." Betty was not amused. "You stole the Sibyl from a friend of mine, and now I'm sending her back." She snapped her fingers. "Special delivery." She snapped them again. "Express post ... airmail ... come *on*." She put her fingers to her lips and let rip an ear-piercing whistle.

Suddenly the little carpet shot into the room, circled around Olivier a couple of times, and came to rest, hovering in front of Betty.

"It's that joke coaster!" said Sleek. "Miserable piece of junk. Kept spilling my drinks on me. I told you to get rid of it, *didn't* I?" He glared at Blank, who himself was staring goggle-eyed at the young man. (A session with the eye-whapper might have been called for here.)

"Good for you." Betty was addressing the carpet. "I underestimated you when I saw you at the yard sale. Let's see what else you can do." She placed the Sibyl down on the middle of the carpet, saying, "Don't be rambunctious. Off you go, skedaddle, you know the way, *shooo*. Watch out for Lake Fingers, don't fly too low."

With the spiky, leather-clad pen digging in, the carpet didn't need further encouragement.

It zoomed out the door and was gone, taking the Sibyl with it and leaving Sleek behind to face the music.

"Not fair! You've no right! That pen was MINE, MINE, MINE!!" Sleek was stamping his feet and on the verge of throwing a tantrum.

"Don't test my patience," Betty warned him. He was still clutching the scytale and was about to club her with it, when she snatched it out of his hand.

"Let's proceed, shall we." She turned to Olivier and Sylvan, who had been happily watching this latest development.

"Boys, you know the score, remember."

"We do?" said Olivier.

"You do," she said. "I'm ready, and I believe Murray is, too. Linnet, dear, can you give us a nice windy note on that pitch pipe when I give you the signal?"

"Sure thing." Without taking her eyes off the young man, Linnet retrieved the pipe from her pocket.

"Do you mean a *musical* score?" asked Sylvan.

"Correct." Betty waved the scytale around like a conductor's baton, and for good measure gave Sleek a crack on the knuckles when he tried to grab it back.

"Yes, I *think* I get it," Olivier said. He was improvising, but felt that he was on the right track. He dug in his pants pocket for the invisible ink. Then he got Murray out and let him swill some, but not too much. He knew it was powerful stuff.

Murray himself then took the lead. With Olivier supporting him, he began to write in the air above them. He penned a whole astonishing stream of dancing, silvery musical notes that shimmered in the air for only a few seconds before vanishing. The strange light that had been filling the room seemed to allow for their visibility. Long enough, anyway, for Sylvan to read them. Betty gave Linnet the signal, tapping her lightly on the shoulder with the scytale, and Linnet blew a high, mysterious-sounding note on the pitch pipe. Sylvan put the flute to his lips, and following the score that Murray was composing, he began to play.

To Olivier's ear, what Sylvan was playing sounded a bit like the composition he'd been working on when Olivier had unearthed him from the rubble in his kitchen. Although this music was richer, livelier and even more astonishingly beautiful. (Even more beautiful than Mozart's *Grand Partita for Winds*, Sylvan said later.) The music was so arresting that even Sleek and Professor Blank were transfixed by it.

Murray wasn't holding back, either. He was scoring these delicate, evanescent notes in an irrepressible creative flurry. He'd been seized with inspiration, and no wonder — the Japanese pen was perched, attentive, in Sylvan's own shirt pocket like Juliet in her balcony. Murray was in a deeply romantic mood, and practically busting his barrel to make a favourable impression ... *if music be the food of love, WRITE ON!*

"The wings," Linnet said again.

This time Olivier understood what she meant, for the wings on the young man's ankles had begun to move in time to the music. His eyes fluttered open. He raised his hand and rubbed his forehead, frowning slightly.

"Ye gods," his voice cracked. "That was some party. I told Boreas not to invite that cyclops. The guy was crashing around half-blind, trashing the place. And his idea of party food! I don't even want to think about it."

Zephyrus yawned, stretched, took a deep breath of air and sat up. He looked at Linnet and smiled. When he exhaled, her long hair swirled around her head and her sky-blue silk shirt rustled and billowed.

"Hello, little cousin," he said.

Twenty

Olivier thought it was the best party he'd ever been to. For one thing, there were lots of dogs. Zephyrus, or Zeph as he asked to be called ("It's more modern."), had released all the dogs from their cages and then had blown gently in each of their faces, clearing the fog and confusion and pain from their eyes. Now they were running all over the place, joyously barking, wolfing down desserts (Zeph had a caterer blown in), and some were even dancing on their hind legs and doing other doggy tricks.

There was a gentle breeze circulating around the room, offering canapés and drinks, and flowers were floating through the air — you had to be careful not to eat one of those instead of a canapé, unless of course it was an edible flower. Although he was not *usually* aggressive, Heath had punched Sleek's plaster head off the statue in the naos, and Max was presently perched there, singing his heart out — or maybe he was trying to sing it *in*.

Max was a bit peaky looking, and Heath still had frost clinging to the back of his jacket, but both had recovered from their ordeal. Heath had been lured into a trap, he confided to Olivier, embarrassed at having been fooled so easily. After checking with his underground sources, he'd discovered that Max had been caught in a headwind and carried to the temple. The treacherous Sleek had then invited Heath there to negotiate his release. The moment Heath had arrived, he'd been blasted with a quick-freeze of arctic air.

"No doubt Sleek was planning on selling me, too," the giant had said.

After rescuing Heath and Max, Zeph had sent all the *bad* weather scurrying away in shame. Although, as Olivier had surmised, it wasn't really their fault. Professor Blank's controlling machinery was certainly very clever and Sleek had employed the inventions ruthlessly. Both men had caused so much unhappiness that Zeph decided to hold another housewarming party to cheer everyone up. "The last one had happened ages ago, anyway," he'd said. "I downed so much fermented ambrosia at the time, I can hardly remember it." Only months ago, Sleek had discovered him still sleeping it off under one of the stone tables and had taken full advantage of the situation.

"The temple's already a mess," Zeph reasoned. "Besides, these townspeople, *by Zeus*, they need to loosen up and have some fun."

After destroying Sleek's wintry arsenal and calming the disturbed winds, Zeph relieved the imprisoned weather technicians of their hateful duties, and with an inspiring breath cleared the dead air out of their heads.

"Conditioning is fine for the hair, but not for the mind," Betty had observed, approvingly, at the same time releasing the Control Freaks from the spell she had cast over them. She denied having done any such thing, but it was an excellent and generous spell nonetheless. Instead of following orders like robots, the Control Freaks had been possessed of a sudden, irresistible desire to tell silly jokes. No matter how corny — the cornier the better — they laughed at these uncontrollably, holding their sides, guffawing and snorting, wiping tears from their eyes. This was followed by play fights with the icicle daggers, whereby they smashed them all to pieces. Sleek and his restrictive rules were entirely forgotten, and by the time Betty broke the spell, the former Freaks were more than ready to party.

Zeph invited everyone. "You can't miss it! It's going to be a real blowout!"

And it was that. Olivier was having a riot just watching everyone else have a riot.

Sylvan had discovered a whole cache of stolen musical instruments, all winds: flutes, whistles, recorders, clarinets, kazoos, saxophones, mouth organs, bagpipes and a foghorn. He put together a wind ensemble, and not some genteel affair, either — it rocked. His group stood on a raised dais at one end of the naos and blasted out catchy, raucous dance tunes. The temple was crowded with people (and non-people) jiving and jumping up and down and running zigzag every which way. Zeph and Linnet were doing a dance together called the Twister, spinning around and around so fast that they finally had to stop before they actually did dance up a storm. Zeph then grabbed his conch, which Sylvan had also found, and, leaping onto the dais, performed a foot-stomping, hair-raising shell solo.

"All *right*!" Olivier shouted. He began to clap enthusiastically, but stopped when he discovered that he'd squashed a free-floating canapé. Smucked brie on a triangle of toast — he happily ate it, licking the runny cheese off his palm. He waved at Heath, who was on the other side of the room devouring a yard-long veggie hotdog and dribbling ketchup on his tie. Heath waved back and pointed at Alvis, who was still wearing his smiley-face boxers and being pursued around the room by Linnet's whiffs. Everyone had forgiven him for his spying activities when he explained that he'd only been spying for Queen Bacteria. She'd been worried sick (not a pleasant sight) about Sleek, who had threatened to plow The Heap into landfill. The deal was, if Alvis brought her the dirt on Sleek, something they could use to stop him, she had promised to let Alvis out of his engagement to her niece, Thrud.

"I can understand why you'd want *that*," Linnet had said earlier, patting him on the head.

"Aw, you're way nicer than Thrud. You *could* learn to be miserable. For a while there I figured you had the hang of it. But I guess you like that blustering bag of hot air more than me."

"Sure, I like him, he's my cousin. Well, you know, two or three hundred times removed."

"She's feeling *divine*," Sylvan had teased. "La-di-dah."

Linnet had only laughed at this.

"So, Alvis, let me get this straight." Olivier had said. "You tried to steal Murray, and then did steal my stone, so you'd have something to barter with?"

"Yeah, that's it. Thought I could get on Sleek's side, then snoop around. Double agent, eh. But that rat-fink pen of his snitched on me. Told him I was going to give him the wrong stone. I picked it up on the beach after those light-fingered fingers picked my pocket and took the real one. I *had* to stop there on that beach, I mean, did you see those swell boats? Total wrecks!"

"Hold on," Linnet had said. "Olivier, why didn't the Sibyl tell Sleek that *you* gave him the wrong stone, too? She must have known."

"Dunno. Maybe *she* was a double agent."

Olivier looked over at Sleek and Professor Blank, the only ones at the party who were not having a riot. Blank because he didn't know how, and Sleek because he'd been turned into a piece of cheese. A very big piece, a cheese statue — a bland and tasteless mozzarella with mould already growing out of his nose — and it was Blank's job at present to see that no one helped himself to a chunk of him, even though he wasn't all that tempting.

Olivier chuckled to himself, recalling how Alvis had made a beeline straight for Sleek after Zeph had freed him from that windy torture chamber. Sleek had been stomping around and yelling out orders that everyone was ignoring. He was furious at the way things were turning out, and when Alvis ran up to him to give him a swift kick in the shins, Sleek stomped on one of the little guy's blue shoes.

"OKAY, that does it, THAT DOES IT," Alvis had

shrieked. "You better smile, buddy, you better SAY CHEESE, because *presto chango* I'm turning you into … *oh*. Oh wow, I DID it! It worked … I …"

True, Betty had been standing near Alvis at the time, and twiddling her fingers in a curious way, when all at once Sleek had been transformed into a chunk of cheese. Processed cheese, suitably enough. No one wanted to mention this coincidence to Alvis because they'd never seen him so happy. He was so pleased with himself that the huge grin on his face actually matched the ones on his smiley-face boxers. They hated to spoil the effect.

"What are you going to do with our Cheese Man?" Olivier now asked Betty, who had wandered over to him, eating what looked like a grub on a cracker. "And the Professor?"

"Heath has offered to counsel Blank, perhaps help find him a position. There's always room at universities for people like him. The Professor's a smart cookie, you know, all those ingenious inventions of his. He *was* trying to get out from under Sleek's thumb. I suspect that wicked business card of his was only the Sibyl having a bit of fun."

"You know, when we were imprisoned and we gave him the CAT treatment, I wonder if he'd actually come to help us?"

"Perhaps so. Perhaps … well, who knows. Blank is a hard one to read." Betty devoured her cracker, then made an odd chirping sound. "My, do excuse me, dear. Ate that too quickly."

"Uh-huh," Olivier smiled. "Betty, there's something I've been wondering about. Do only male nightingales sing at night?"

"Ornithology!? Not my area of expertise. Let's just say that I'm not without admirers." She patted her hair modestly.

As she was not about to be more forthcoming on the subject, Olivier asked, "Sleek? What about him?"

"We'll get him sorted out right enough. Can't be a Big Cheese forever, and there's plenty of cleaning and tidying to do here at the temple, since he's so keen on that sort of thing."

"I'd sure like to have those letters of mine. Except ..."

"They've been turned into cheese slices, yes. Hmm. I'll see what I can do, not that I'm capable of much, mind you. I believe that only the top letter was actually from your parents, dear. The rest were blank envelopes."

"Thanks, Betty, I'd really appreciate it ... and thanks for bringing my old clothes along." Olivier felt terrific in his freshly laundered and stretched jeans and shirt — Betty had even sewn on the missing buttons. He had passed along his ratty old clothes to Zeph, who'd been eyeing them enviously. "*Man*, I'm tired of wearing this minidress," he'd said of his tunic. Apparently Sharon didn't need them anymore. Betty had explained that after a term of indecision spent at the Academy, she had switched professions and was now a court jester!

"How is our Romeo doing?" Betty asked.

"I'm not so sure."

Olivier and Betty glanced over at a private side table where Murray and Ishi were sharing a tall cool glass of inkberry juice.

Oh, lad, lad, Murray had gushed when they'd managed a quiet moment to chat, *I'm a goner! It's love at first write.*

Ishi, on the other hand ... or, *in* the other hand, なんと滴り！Sylvan's, had not been quite so taken. , she'd written, which roughly translates as, "Eeek. What a drip!"

"She's shy," Betty offered, unconvincingly.

"Shy, eh? She wrote reams of stuff that Sylvan *said* he couldn't translate."

"Playing hard to get, very hard to get," laughed Betty.

"Like Linnet," groused Alvis. He had scooted over to hide behind them, trying to avoid the whiffs that kept chasing him away from her.

"Alvis, have you ever given Putrid any thought? I understand that she fancies you," confided Betty. "Now that Thrud's out of the picture ... and Putrid's not quite so fresh, she's a most ... suitable choice, I'd say. I've sent a report to the Queen on your behalf, by the way. A glowing report, or maybe *reeking* best describes it."

"Yeah? Putrid, eh. Yeah, she *stinks*. She's always had a soft spot for me. A soft *rotten* spot. Putrid, eh. Say, anybody have the time? I've got, uhh, stuff to do back at The Heap." Alvis dug around in his satchel, which Sylvan had *also* found, and pulled out a pocket watch, the old-fashioned kind in a hunting case with a hinged cover.

"Hey, that belongs to my gramps," said Olivier, indignantly, before Alvis had a chance to check the time.

"No kidding? If you're going to be a crybaby about it, here." With a smirk, he tossed the watch to Olivier. "Let's go then, let's move it, eh. Grab that lovelorn inkhorn of yours and let's blow this hotdog stand."

Olivier slid the watch into his pocket. "You go ahead. It's a long walk back." If they had to return the way they'd come, Olivier sure didn't want to be stuck with Alvis again. Although now that he thought of it … his gaze swept around the temple, the party was in full swing and he hated to leave, but … it *was* time to go. He admitted as much to Betty once Alvis had run off again in search of a few snacks for the road. "I want to find out what's going on with my parents. Sylvia might know. In fact, I think she might have a message for me."

"Ah, of course, dear. You'll want to find out about that, and a speedy return would be most preferable. Let's talk to Linnet, shall we. I believe her powers are stronger now than they were before she lost them, and even her ankle is completely healed. Did you see that dance she and Zeph were doing, goodness!"

"No problemo," said Linnet, when they approached her. "I'm ready to go, too. Zeph said he'd drop in later and see my boat, so I want to get it fixed up, and I want to help Sylvan with his place. Besides, Fathom will be getting anxious about us."

"Great," said Olivier. "How are we going?"

"Jet stream," answered Linnet, whooshing her hands back and forth. "First class. Hang onto your hat!"

"I don't have a … hey!"

Before Olivier could protest, he was lifted up into the air and plunked down in an invisible seat — at least there was plenty of leg room. An attentive breeze slotted a champagne glass full of sparkling ginger ale in one hand

and a chocolate truffle in the other. It then stole Murray away from his new flame (much to her relief), and slid him into his usual spot in Olivier's shirt pocket.

(Parting is such sweet sorrow!)

(Not from you, it isn't!)

Sylvan and Ishi were the next to be carried on board and seated beside Olivier. Then Linnet herself ascended a flight of invisible stairs — her whiffs curling like airy slippers around her feet — and took the pilot's position up ahead. Alvis was nabbed with his face half-buried in a bowl of pasta salad and tossed into the cargo hold, noodles flapping onto his chin and his mouth too full for him to complain.

"Last call for Cat's Eye Corner!" Zeph announced, giving a blast on his conch shell.

As they rose higher into the air, all the partygoers gathered below them, waving and cheering. Max floated over to Olivier, and bobbing slightly, said, "Cheerio, young fellow. It's been a lark, hasn't it? A real *coup*! Be sure to keep your head screwed on tight."

"I will, Max. You're the tops. You too, Heath."

Standing tall, Heath was practically level with them. He shook hands with Olivier. "It's been an honour. You'll go far, son," he said. He bowed to Linnet and gave her fingers a gentlemanly kiss, and after shaking Sylvan's hand, said, "I'll send you those research papers I mentioned."

"Wonderful," said Sylvan. "That'll give *my* head a workout."

"Okay, fasten your seatbelts. We're out of here," said Linnet.

"What seatbelts?"

"Goodbye!"

"Goodbye!"

With a final strident blast from Zeph's conch, they were away, weaving through the inner temple, swerving around the broken porch columns, and out, sailing over Nohow Town.

"They'll have to change its name," Sylvan shouted.

"Yeah, to Some*kinda* Town," Olivier called back. "Say … over there! It's Betty! I mean, it's our bird again."

The nightingale had indeed appeared, and was flying along beside them. She was having a fantastic time doing flips and dips and twirls. Then, as they approached the Nameless Forest, she sang out to them merrily and plummeted into the woods below. Observing her descent, Olivier was greatly relieved to see that there were no more forest fires burning. Zeph had told him that the blue hands from the lake had doused the fires by cuffing great splashes of water into the trees.

Olivier settled back to enjoy the ride (except for Alvis startling everyone by blowing up the empty paper bags he'd saved from the lunch at Linnet's and suddenly popping them). He knew it wasn't the same as riding on a magic carpet, but he wasn't about to complain. It *was* first class! And since it was a warm jet stream, they didn't freeze, either, as they rose into the upper atmosphere and began zipping through huge puffy clouds. *Who needs in-flight movies*, he thought. *This is incredible*.

It was fast, too. In no time, Linnet had them descending again, gliding down over The Heap.

"Jump, Alvis," she called back.

"Jump!?"

"Yeah. See that old mushy mattress on top of that big pile of junk? Aim for that."

"No way!"

"Go on, Alvis, you can do it," Sylvan encouraged.

"Get lost!"

"See, there's a girl waving at you."

"Huh? Hey, yeah, if it isn't Putrid. Huzzah huzzah, she's a sight, eh?"

"I'll say," agreed Olivier.

"Um, okay, here I go. I'm brave, really really brave, eh. Ohhhh help. *Arrrrrrgh.*"

"He did it!"

"Hooray!"

"Good … no, bad for you, Alvis."

"Have a crummy lousy miserable day!" they all called down to him.

"You too, guys!" he called back. "Suck eggs!"

They laughed and waved as Linnet guided them back up and away.

When they neared Cat's Eye Corner, Olivier asked, "You're not going to make me jump, are you Linnet?"

"What? A VIP like you, Olivier?"

"I'm no VIP, but …" he patted his shirtfront pocket. "Murray is. A *Very* Important Pen."

He addressed this comment mainly to Sylvan's shirtfront pocket, where Ishi was, in the hopes that it might advance Murray's prospects. "Why, compared to him, all other pens are as dull as lead pencils."

"Too true," said Linnet. "Not everyone gets to ride in a private jet stream. He's a renowned writer, after all."

"A benevolent dictator," added Sylvan. "No, make that dictatee. A prince of pens."

"Better land him safely, then," said Linnet. "Almost there. Will the roof do, Olivier?"

"That would be perfect. I've never been on the roof."

Cat's Eye Corner loomed into view. It was twilight, night almost fallen, and there were bats swooping around the cupola at the top of the old house and a few lights winking on below as if in welcome. Linnet swooped in on a warm gust of air that sent a cluster of dried leaves on the roof swirling and tumbling away. While she idled, Olivier hopped out of the stream, his legs a little wobbly, and turned to his friends.

"This is it, I guess," he said.

"Come see us soon," said Linnet. "Don't make us wait too long."

"Yeah, Olivier. I have some really neat ideas for my new place; you can help me rebuild it."

"I'd love to. I'll be there once ..." His broad smile faded. "If I can find the way, you know how it is, and ... I don't know, I have a feeling that something's up."

"Besides us?" said Linnet. Then more carefully, "What do you mean?"

Olivier shrugged. "I'm sure it's nothing. I'd better go in and find out, though. See you *soon* then."

"It's a date!"

"Don't forget!"

Linnet raised her arms in a gesture that was partly a

farewell wave to Olivier and partly a signal to the wind, and they were away, cruising toward the Dark Woods … and *gone*. As Olivier stood on the roof of Cat's Eye Corner watching them go, he realized how happy he was to be back, and how full of misgiving.

Twenty-One

Olivier turned quickly to see who was tapping on the window of the cupola. One of its eight windows — it was octagonal in shape. Despite this, the cupola was dark inside and all he could make out was a figure silhouetted behind the glass. This person raised the window and called to him. It was Sylvia.

"Olivier," she said. "Do come in. Have you been on the roof long?"

"Not very." He climbed in through the window, as there was no door to go through.

"I suppose that wind blew you up?"

"Sort of."

"You'll never guess, but it blew all my yard sale earnings away."

"Really? That's terrible." His own ten dollar bill was safely tucked in his pocket, and as freshly laundered as his jeans. It was so crisp, he even suspected that Betty had ironed it.

To her dismay, she had also restored his water-damaged notebook to its previous condition and in doing so had wiped it clean of all his conversations with Murray. Olivier had assured her that the notebook had been over-full anyway, what with Murray yakking endlessly about Ishi, and she'd saved him the trouble and expense of buying a new one.

"I was overcharging for everything in any event," Sylvia said lightly. "Time for a chat? Good." She turned on a lamp that sat on a table between two wicker chairs. It was the orange lamp left over from the yard sale, even more bashed up than before. "Some items simply refused to blow away," she sighed, taking a seat. "But then, a few nifty things were blown my way. Like this." Sylvia held up a shopping bag full of candy: gumdrops, licorice whips, rockets, peanut brittle, cinnamon hearts, chocolate bars, Turkish delight, jelly beans, and jawbreakers. "Someone's Halloween treats, I assume."

"A little early for that, isn't it?"

"Ah, but it's never too early for Halloween. Help yourself."

"Thanks." Olivier reached in for a piece of peanut brittle the size of a dinner plate, then looked around. Typically for this house, there were interesting objects tucked in the corners, and the cupola had plenty of corners. There was a telescope, a wooden box with a padlock on it, a shellacked iguana, an eggbeater, a Venus flytrap, and a stack of very old books bound in red satin with a human skull resting on top! Impressive. He also spotted the scytale — or a scytale — leaning up against one of the window ledges.

"Where did you get that?" he asked, nodding at it.

"That? Why, I can't honestly recall, Olivier. My memory's not what it used to be. Most regrettable."

"Yes, it is," said Olivier, narrowing his eyes. "I don't suppose you remember knocking Linnet down in the woods, either?"

"Linnet? Do I know a Linnet? I do sometimes bump into acquaintances when I'm strolling in the woods. But I don't recall … "

"After we met in the hallway of Halfway There?" he prompted.

"My dear, you've been dreaming."

"I've hardly had a chance to sleep!" Dodgy as usual, he thought.

"Nor will you," she smiled.

"Why not?"

"You'll be far too busy, won't you? Did you know that the Tower of Winds is structured like this very cupola, and on each of its sides a frieze features one of the eight wind gods."

"Eight? Is Zephyrus one of them?"

"That's one, yes, clever boy. Soon you'll get to see them all! How thrilling."

Olivier still hadn't taken a bite of the peanut brittle and it was beginning to stick to his fingers. He was reluctant to ask, but did. "Where is this tower?"

"Not far below the Acropolis. And the Parthenon. I don't imagine it will be too hard to find."

"But those buildings are in Greece, aren't they?"

"Spot on, dear."

"I'm not going to Greece."

"*Au contraire*, but you are. Family trip. I've been meaning to tell you, but sometimes you're so hard to locate. Your mother apparently found a stack of cash abandoned on your front doormat that no one has claimed … so she gets to keep it. Isn't *that* lucky?!"

"My mother *found* some money? On the doormat?" Olivier stared hard at his step-step-stepgramma. "You're not trying to get rid of me, are you?"

"By no means!" She placed a long bony hand on her chest, her purple fingernail polish glistening in the lamplight. "Why would I want to do that?" She then pulled opened a little drawer in the table and reached in for a letter, the very letter that he had last seen in Sleek's own hand, the one from his mother that had been bundled with the blank envelopes. "Here, this should explain everything. Unfortunately, it was misdirected and only arrived today. It certainly looks as though it's been through the wars."

Olivier had to grin when he saw that his mother's letter was covered with greasy, cheesy stains and fingerprints. "How do you know about the trip, then?"

"Your parents have been calling and calling, as usual. They do worry about you, it's ridiculous. *I* wouldn't if you were *mine*."

With the slab of peanut brittle balanced on his lap, Olivier slowly opened the letter and read it. **Darling**, it began, and ended with so many kisses xxxxxxxxxxxxxx that it looked like it was stitched together. The letter shouldn't have made him feel sick, but it did. He was happy that his parents still loved him, of course, but he didn't want to go anywhere, not even to Greece, and that's what the letter was all about. It brimmed with excitement, as it was to be an extensive trip and his parents hadn't been anywhere special in such a long time (unlike Olivier). At the beginning of the summer he would have been only too eager to go, but not now, not with his friends expecting him and with so much of Cat's Eye Corner left to explore. *You'll go far*, Heath had said, but surely he didn't mean to Greece!

"Olivier, dear, as a going-away present I've decided to give you the Persian carpet, after all."

"The carpet, it's here? It didn't blow away in the wind?"

"It did, yes, but then strangely it blew back. I'm afraid it met with a *little* accident, though. Wool, it does shrink. At least it's portable now. That pen of yours might like to have it."

"I'm not so sure he'd want it, but, um, that's very thoughtful of you." (Yeah, right!) A thought then struck him. "Murr — I mean my pen, that is … it, he can come with me, can't he?"

"Naturally. I'll be wanting a postcard or two from you, won't I? … *Curses*, that reminds me." Sylvia reached into the drawer once again, and this time retrieved her own pen … a pen that happened to be covered in black leather and decorated with a silver serpent and sharp spikes. "If you'll excuse me, Olivier, I have a few poison pen letters to write. Most urgent, you understand."

Olivier gaped at them, *both* of them — Sylvia and the Sibyl — then got up from the chair, gripping his untasted peanut brittle, and sliding his mother's letter into his pocket.

No point in asking her to explain. He knew it wouldn't get him anywhere — it never did. "Guess I'll go find Gramps and say goodbye," he said slowly. His heart felt like a stone lodged in his chest.

"Yes, do. He's repairing the back door downstairs. Those pirates were the loveliest fellows, but we don't want any more getting into the house at present. They wore us out with all their singing and yo-ho-hoing and dancing of jigs. Our aging timbers have been shivered quite enough. Oh, and Olivier?"

"Yes, step-step-stepgramma?" He was standing by the stairs that would take him down down down to the first floor of the house.

"You don't have to go on this trip, you know."

"But my parents will be really disappointed if I don't. Right?"

"I'm afraid so," she said, with a quick Sphinx-like smile.

On the way down the stairs Olivier passed several of the Poets — Byron, Gwendolyn, Theodore, Seamus — who were lounging around, thinking their inscrutable thoughts, as poets *and* cats are wont to do. He stopped to greet them and scratch a few heads. Even Eliot, the most dignified one of the bunch, tolerated this familiar address. The only active cat he encountered — mousing instead of musing — was Emily, her paw evidently healed … as was Sylvia's hand, now that he came to think of it. Emily was jumping high into the air as she ran, trying to snag a mouse that was clinging for dear life to the pint-sized flying carpet. The carpet and its passenger tore past his nose, then peeled off down a hallway with Emily in hot pursuit. Olivier might have found this funny if he weren't feeling so low. Homesick for Cat's Eye Corner and he hadn't even left yet.

"Crazy carpet," he muttered to himself, continuing down the stairs. "Who'd want it."

He found Gramps by the storm door, fixing it with a lock. He was humming a tune from the *Pirates of Penzance* and wearing a black patch over one eye.

"Hey, Gramps. You okay?"

"Yaar, right as rain, Ollie." He pulled off the patch. "Giving my eye a rest. Had a twinkle in it, darn scratchy things, worse than slivers. But I want to see you with both my eyes … home safe and sound. How about a hug? Then how about sharing some of that peanut brittle?"

Olivier gave his grandfather a big warm wonderful hug, which helped him feel better, and then he snapped the peanut brittle into two chunks, and they set to work on those, munching and crunching like industrious beavers, which also helped.

"So, pirates, eh, Gramps? You've got a peanut stuck to your face."

"Ah." He peeled the peanut off his cheek and popped it in his mouth. "Yep, pirates, trolls, ugly stepsisters, mathematicians, you name it. By cracky, it was open house here for awhile. They all got called back to work, though. Said things were all shipshape and straightened out. Sylvie wants to make sure this door stays closed. I swear there used to be a doorstop here, little fella, pointy ears, blue shoes, like one of them garden gnomes.

Darned if I know where it's gotten to."

"Hmm." Olivier crunched the last bite of candy thoughtfully. "Lots of coming and going around here. Even me, looks like."

"So I heard, son." He didn't sound thrilled at the prospect, either.

"Gramps, you mentioning that doorstop reminded me of something. I have your watch."

"No kidding? That's funny, 'cause I have my watch, too."

"You mean, this isn't yours?" Olivier dug in his pocket and held up the watch he'd gotten from Alvis.

"Looks the same, but here Ollie, let me see it."

When Olivier handed him the watch, Gramps examined it closely, back and front, then flipped open the cover. "Hmph, how about that. It's a gum-holder."

"A what?"

As Gramps held it out, Olivier could see that instead of a timepiece inside the open case, there was a piece of gum, or more accurately, a pre-chewed, dried-up, blue wad of gum that resembled a tiny brain.

"Ick," said Olivier.

"I'll be savin' that for later," Gramps said, snapping the lid shut again.

"*Much* later."

"Like that trip your folks are so set on. I don't see what the big rush is, do you? Lots of summer left here, lots to see in this corner of the world. Lots of rooms and rooms ... say, why don't we send the kitchen instead of you? It likes to travel, and it could bring us back some souvenir souvlaki."

"There's an idea," Olivier laughed. "But Gramps, you know, you're right … maybe I can talk them into going *next* year. Why not? Mum's a real softie, well, they both are."

"Worth a try. They'd do anything for you, Ollie. They want you to be happy. That's the main thing, far as I can see."

"Yeah! What would work best, do you think? A call or a letter?"

"By jiminy, I bet you could write a plenty persuasive letter with that pen of yours."

"I'll do it! See you later, Gramps. Did I miss dinner?"

"Yep."

"Great. Maybe this *is* my lucky day."

Olivier hurtled back up the stairs and into his room, where he snatched a clean sheet of writing paper out of his suitcase (it so happened that they were *all* clean, as he hadn't gotten around to any letters as yet). He carried Sylvia's book, *Enquire Within Upon Everything*, over to his bed and sat down with it on his lap, intending to use it as a kind of portable writing desk. It had grown very heavy, he noticed, as if it were turning into stone. He lifted Murray out of his pocket and positioned him at the top of the paper where the date should go on the letter. Olivier wanted it to be perfect — a combo business and friendly letter that was full of charm, affection, convincing arguments, some philosophy and a sprinkling of jokes to lighten the tone. Not to mention artful penmanship.

Murray didn't do a thing, so Olivier gave him a gentle shake to get the old ink flowing.

When it did, it was rather clear, but not as clear as the invisible ink.

My boy, my boy, I am SO choked up.

"I know, Murray. It's hard to even think about leaving. But listen, we won't have to go if we play our cards right."

Oh that. The trip? I wasn't referring to THAT. No, no, I'm just so touched. All those TRUE things you children were saying about me! A prince and all that. A renowned writer! Finally, my worth has been recognized! Would you like my autograph?

"Uhh, yeah, I have the paper right here. And guess what, you'll be even *more* renowned, with me anyway, when you get this letter written."

Very well, then. Fine, a letter, did you say? Tell me, do you still have that ten bucks? What we could use is some scented ink, something manly ...

"Manly? You mean like sweat?"

Noooo, good grief. I was thinking more along the lines of delphinium, in a steel blue shade. And we need better stationery, too. Clairfontaine, perhaps.

"If we get to stay, sure, whatever you want. Otherwise, I'll have to take spending money on the trip, you see ... so how about it?" Olivier waited, giving Murray time to ponder this and gather his thoughts. The book on his lap grew even heavier, and he saw that it *had* turned into stone. Hardcovers are nice to have, he thought, but this was a bit much, wasn't it? He lifted up the sheet of paper to look underneath. The book's title was now written in fossils. So here was yet another reason he couldn't leave. This strange occurrence had to portend *something*, but exactly *what* he couldn't imagine. Not yet.

Olivier replaced the sheet, and even though the writing surface had grown somewhat bumpy, Murray was ready to begin.

My dearest and most precious Ishi, my little plum blossom, my —

"Murray! You can write to Ishi later. This letter is supposed to be to my parents, remember. We have to convince them that we *need* to stay."

Of course we're staying! Don't be absurd. I can't leave Ishi, what are you thinking, I won't even consider it. She would be utterly devastated if I were to go. Heartbroken!

"Um, yeah, I'm sure. So ... the letter?"

Yes, yes. Fine. Shall we use the invisible ink? Good stuff, that.

"Somehow I don't think that would be very effective. Although, gosh Murray, I just realized — I don't have it. I left your inkwell in those other jeans, the ones I gave to Zeph. Boy, that was dumb. Good thing Betty asked to tidy up my money and notebook, or I wouldn't have those, either. Huh, so much for what we were going to buy at the yard sale! Your inkwell's gone and my carpet's turned into a mouse taxi."

Bah, who needs that junk? Let's get to work on this missive, lad. It will be SO brilliant that even though I'm no Sibyl I can safely predict the results. Before we write it, however, there is one thing that I DO want. You and Sylvan were talking about it earlier.

"We were? What's that?"

Why, the last laugh, Olivier. I've ALWAYS wanted one of those.

"Murray, my friend, it's *yours*." Olivier smiled happily, tapped him on the cap, and shifting under the weight of his book, readied his pen pal at the starting line once again.

Marvellous, my dear boy, simply marvellous. All wwwarighty, get rrrready, here it goes, blast off ... HA HA HA!!!

Author's Note

Murray gets to have the last laugh (the *pen* ultimate one), but it's the poets, furry and otherwise, who should perhaps have the last word. Although not a poet myself, the poetry of others often provides a kind of talismanic presence for me when writing. Thus Emily Dickinson's "How happy is the little Stone" helped both Olivier and the writer make their way through this particular adventure. Also, I suspect that Nohow Town was founded upon the lilting verbal grounds of e.e. cumming's "anyone lived in a pretty how town." Just try to get *that* poem out of your head once it's settled in. And while I'm at it, I'd like to make mention of Wallace Steven's "The Emperor of Ice Cream,"great bad-guy inspiration for *The Silver Door*, and lurking more shyly in the leafy heart of *Cat's Eye Corner* — an elusive allusion — is the marvelous "Wodwo" by Ted Hughes.

I'd like to add a word, too, about Lewis Carroll's riddle — "Why is a raven like a writing-desk?" — that appears in *Alice in Wonderland*. The riddle initially didn't have an answer, but enough readers must have puzzled over it, because the author later provided one. According to a footnote in my Norton Critical Edition of *Alice*, Carroll writes that a raven "can produce a few notes, although they are very flat, and it is never put the wrong end front." As a child, I didn't have this edition, so puzzled over the riddle a fair bit myself. What I liked mainly was the *sound* of the question, and what I figured out eventually, years later, was that the answer had something to do with writing itself and how words make connections and forge bonds between the dissimilar. It's a metaphor in other words, which I suppose is the secret business of riddles. (When is a window like a star? When it's a skylight.) So you could say that I rediscover the answer to Lewis Carroll's riddle every time I put pen — and not just *any* pen — to paper.

About the Author

TERRY GRIGGS writes for adult and children. Her adult fiction includes the short story collection *Quickening*, which was shortlisted for a Governor General's Award, and two novels, *The Lusty Man* and *Rogues' Wedding*, shortlisted for the Rogers' Writer's Trust Fiction Award. *Invisible Ink* is the third book in Terry's **Cat's Eye Corner** series, which also includes *Cat's Eye Corner* and *The Silver Door*. Terry was awarded the 2003 Marian Engel Award which honours a distinguished body of work by a female writer. She lives with her family in Stratford, Ontario.

HAVE YOU READ THE FIRST TWO BOOKS
IN THE Cat's Eye Corner SERIES?

CAT'S EYE CORNER

Olivier joins his grandfather and his step-step-stepgramma Sylvia de Whosit of Whatsit at the fabulous Cat's Eye Corner. There he meets a new pen-pal, Murray Sheaffer, the So-So Gang, the teenage oracles Holy Moley and Holy Hannah, a fire-breathing dog and a girl named Linnet who controls the wind.

THE SILVER DOOR

Olivier is given an unusual book by his step-step-stepgramma — *Enquire Within Upon Everything* — and the strangest things emerge from its pages. Meet a reluctant ghost named Peely Wally, a thief named the Emperor of Ice Cream, a tiny "Ink" monkey, and — back for more adventures — Olivier's pal, the "talking" pen Murray Sheaffer.

*By printing this book on paper made from
40% post-consumer recycled fibre rather than
virgin tree fibre, Raincoast Books has made
the following ecological savings:*

- 61 trees
- 5,849 kilograms of greenhouse gases (equivalent to driving an average North American car for one year)
- 49 million BTUs or energy equivalent to half the annual power consumption of one North American home
- 35,840 litres of water (just less than one Olympic sized pool)
- 2,190 kilograms of solid waste (equivalent to one garbage truck load or half a female elephant)

RAINCOAST BOOKS
www.raincoast.com

ANCIENT FOREST
FRIENDLY